Listen for Water

MARIE BESWICK ARTHUR

Fernando,

Thank you for
bringing so much joy
and kindness into
my life —

May all our mountains
be as beautiful
as those in Michoacán.

love
Marie
Beswick
Arthur

Published by Ingenium Books Publishing Inc.
Toronto, Ontario, Canada M6P 1Z2
www.ingeniumbooks.com

ISBNs

eBook: 978-1-989059-94-4

Paperback: 978-1-989059-93-7

Cover Design by Jessica Bell Designs via Ingenium Books.

Praise for Listen for Water

A superbly written story by an exceptional Canadian author, *Listen For Water* is an atmospheric journey of survival, forgiveness and redemption. Prepare to laugh, to cry, and to never forget this incredible mother and daughter.

— JOYLENE NOWELL BUTLER, MÉTIS AUTHOR
OF *MÂTOWAUK, WOMAN WHO CRIES*

This story is a delightful read about redemption and relationships set in a hilariously larger-than-life scenario. Marie touches on some pain points in a dysfunctional mother-daughter relationship, but interjects humor at precisely the right moments. I found that I was actually laughing out loud several times while reading this book. I also found myself cheering for the characters to make the right decisions. While the context has the potential to be dark, the story pivots to one of hope over and over again. Amazing work!

— C.A. GIBBS, AUTHOR OF *THE PICTURE WALL: ONE WOMAN'S STORY OF BEING (HIS) (HER) THEIR MOTHER*

An immensely enjoyable read! A mesmerizing and truly refreshing twist to a young girls understanding of the world and a testament that miracles do happen. A remarkable off road journey which unfolds a daughters love for her mother. A magical story of two hearts and their journey from abandonment to healing. A masterful illustration of our potential for human growth and how much we need each other. Child development against the all too familiar backdrop of family dysfunction; with an inspiring heartfelt outcome.

— CHERYL TURNER, MSW, RSW

A survival story in more ways than one, *Listen for Water* is a fascinating study of a mother/daughter relationship as it changes, reverses, and grows. Ray's use of a self-help survival book in a real survival situation adds humour and strengthens our appreciation of the love between the two formerly at-odds protagonists. An impressive first novel by a talented author.

— CORA TAYLOR, AWARD-WINNING AUTHOR
OF *JULIE* AND *SUMMER OF THE MAD MONK*

Melodic, poetic, majestic. *Listen For Water* reaches through the forest of life to capture the drumbeat of a damaged teenage girl, an unwelcome adventure in a u-Haul trailer, an addict mother, and a survival manual. Marie Beswick Arthur's brave words take us on untraveled roads that sing of survival, a reckoning, and a transformation.

— KATHY KLAUS, AUTHOR OF *WILD RIDE*

I love the descriptive nature of this book and the depth to which Marie Beswick Arthur goes into the thoughts of Dakota is amazing. Turning a simple story into an adventure through the thoughts of a young girl reminds me of *Rumble Fish* by S.E. Hinton. Everyone no matter what age should enjoy reading this book.

— TODD GRAY, AUTHOR OF *THE 49TH PROTOCOL*

Contents

for all those who were parentified
and to the loves of my life
may you forge the future
through your honourable and exquisite patterns

and for Laura

Prologue

THE DREAM

T here is a certainty that moving away from the drumbeat will be fatal. The steady rhythm hammers like a drum major in a marching band. I watch a slo-mo video of a tadpole in a pool of cloudy water. The form curls in a position that resembles a letter C, though I—the observer in the dream—know that the fish-baby has no knowledge of the alphabet.

Boom-ba. Boom-ba.

The form communicates to the dreamer-me that "we" are supposed to be in this tepid pool. An epiphany jolts the sleeping-me into realization: I am the dreamer, the observer, and the tadpole that looks like a letter C.

It is then that I dive in, because in dreams anything is possible.

It's dark. Distant echoes challenge my decoding skills. The only clear sound is the ever-present beat. A strong current of significance emphasizes survival.

Boom-ba. Boom-ba.

In the dream I hear C's thoughts. She think-speaks to me: "*I know I'm connected to another world. Tell me about it. If I knew what an aquarium was, I could be in one. See me flip my little arm-fins and breathe easily, without breathing the way you breathe, dreamer girl? I'll breathe your way after. After what? I don't know any what after."*

I want to float the idea of the concept of life over Fishbaby, but profound powerlessness overwhelms her as she reacts to the chemical cocktail of whatever the Mothership has chewed, sipped, inhaled, spoken, heard, sensed, and thought. It is impossible for me to reach into the depth of the dream so that I can hold the tadpole-C in my arms, bring her into my heart, and soothe her. She is untouchable.

Fishbaby tells me: "*This floating time is preparation for something important: a birth into a world known as Earth, or a return to an unborn realm where one might temporarily shelve sacred blueprints, as science meets angel in a living test tube—take a shared number and hang out in the ether, waiting to sign a contract for human assignment and designation. Souls on hold. A natural order moving along a conveyor belt to becoming human or adding energy to the collective of the factory. A woman called RAYLENE will decide, has every right to decide, and I am okay with that because right now I could not survive in any earthly form outside this pool. And, if I do not have a human birth day, I will still contribute to the universe whole, for I am pure energy, as is everything.*"

I'm impressed with how smart this un-child is. I deliberate whether I magicked my pro-choice views into Fishbaby's mind, or if Fishbaby can think such complex thoughts. Within the dream, I am an observer gone crazy, riding a horse on a carousel that is spinning too fast. I cannot separate the dreamer-me from the dream-featured creature-me.

Boom-ba. Boom-ba.

A crush of emotion is delivered to Fishbaby through a lapping tide against her reptilian skin. It suggests a notion: human. Information relayed through a wireless connection delivers a message she does not want to take: the Mothership is ambivalent about the situation—not knowing how to handle her own life, let alone Fishbaby's.

More awareness comes to Fishbaby in spirals of genealogical knowledge. She turns her tadpole-like head toward me and conveys, *"What the heck does ambivalent mean?"* Since I can't speak to her in oral language, I don't know how to tell her that it means "unable to decide what kind of action to take." Instead, I look through her transparent parts and register she's ping-ponging the Mothership's WTF's back to the surface as fast as they are being served to her tadpole flippers.

In a conundrum of not being able to define ambivalent for her, I check for an exit marked *wake*, but drift deeper into the developing brain of the wondering and growing Fishbaby.

Boom-ba. Boom-ba.

The dreamer-me sees Fishbaby's imagination as an ever-changing spectrum of colour stretching to understand the secrets of the universe. I reach out to trace an outline of what I know of life, so I can draw some of the mysteries on a blackboard for her but, when my finger touches a stick of chalk that has appeared, the chalk turns to powder, my illustration crumbling before it can take shape.

There should be some things the little creature-me ought to be experiencing, but there are barriers in the surrounding sea. Opaque jellyfish cast a misty view of what lies beyond. The threat of sting-able tentacles preventing access and inciting fears.

Flashes of explanation zap in currents around Fishbaby. The Mothership is finding it hard to connect with the growing life inside her. The Mothership is doing the best she can with the skills she has. The Mothership, herself, bears the burden of ten-thousand unfulfilled promises made to her in her own before-babyhood.

Boom-ba. Boom-ba.

Other tides bring chemical messages of things to come. Some stress the cells in Fishbaby's body, and parts of her brain come under siege. Fragments of everything the carrier consumes pass through an unforgiving filter. Sometimes her insulated world speeds up, sometimes there is a threat that her lifeline will be choked off. Other times compounds flow through, offering hope and consolation, like advertisements for exotic lands, or simply a comforting message as satisfying as a decent grilled-cheese sandwich.

"It's okay, dreamer girl, don't worry about me. I float through each day, a thick cable attached to the middle of the roundest part of me—I'm an astronaut; a roped mountain climber; a masked, tethered hawk— independence is limited in that touch is possible, some other senses are unavailable. It's okay, dreamer girl, don't worry about me. I am equipped with a primitive imagination, and liquid promise ebbs and flows in waves that bubble and foam against me. Gurgle-giggle-giggle."

Trillions of neuro-sensors spark and tingle in Fishbaby's developing body. It is daunting. How can this Fishbaby-me, in my dream, have no language, no proper way to survive outside, because organs are still developing, yet have an active foundation of thought? I conclude it is time travel, melded with the chemical science of dreams.

Boom-ba. Boom-ba.

Everything is energy: molecules, thoughts, even dreams. I witness the unborn me emitting a kind of joy to the Mothership. The dreaming me totally gets that the baby is begging her host to be kind and gentle with herself.

"Out there will be a world of words. Gone will be the muffled sounds that bubble and gurgle to my hearing heart. Who will help Dakota Starr line up all the feelings, emotion by emotion, in the outside world?"

Hey! Dakota Starr? That's me, I think in my dream. Though I can tell that Fishbaby doesn't know how I will cope, I think it's cool she knows what our name will be.

The recurring dream process is like a time-locked vault; there is no way in until the next REM session. Before turning away from the dream, I steal a final impression. She has arms and legs. For now,

Fishbaby knows only touch a stubby toe, suck a mini-thumb, somersault, listen to the drum.

I hear it too. The drumbeat. There will be knotted sheets when I wake.

And there were.

One

The budgie barked. Ray and I thought it was a dog until we fell off the earth.

I woke to crashing dishes. Ray was eating again. I'd told her a hundred times: this stuff's ceramic, not *Corelle*, but she pitched plates into the sink as if tossing rings onto the necks of bottles at a fairground.

In the silence that followed, I picked up a distant howl from outside, then untangled from my sheets. A steady beat played in my head, overspill from the drum dream, and a word that was so faintly written behind my eyes that I wasn't sure it was one: fishbaby. But that was always the case. The beat, the word, and no other memory other than there had been a dream.

The thin, Shrek-themed comforter made a cape housecoat with enough left to pad the window frame so I could lean comfortably while looking down on the world one floor below.

I'd been fourteen—Ray, thirty-two—when we'd moved in the year before. A twelve-block social experiment sandwiched between inner-city and suburbs; intentionally planned by sociologists and contemporary designers to house the down-and-out in subsidized style.

Our turquoise front-doored apartment topped a slick insurance agency with a purple door that side-by-sided ours. The purple opened to commerce and fashionable furniture. Ours exposed a narrow set of stairs that led up to church-donation, mismatched minimalist.

The tip of my nose squished against the glass, the windowpane a giant slide containing a cross-section of our lives. Our street separated the experiment of us from the real world. A green boulevard rolled out on the other side of the road, then a row of single-family homes on wide lots, beyond which sprawled acres of affluence. An I'M SOLD! sign decorated the lawn of the bungalow closest to us.

The 8:30 buzzer sounded at the local elementary school, even though it was Saturday. Ray slammed the fridge door. The eviction notices we'd received—we'd had at least four—seemed to have engaged some primal appetite.

As well-meaning as help-the-marginalized plans can be, our sponsorship had disappeared months ago with a change in civic leadership. Advocacy groups were enraged at the rent increases delivered to the poor. While not-for-profit organizations rallied on our behalf, we missed two months. Each time a rent reminder arrived I'd hint to Ray that she try to find a teeny-tiny part-time job. The suggestion hadn't even scared her off the couch.

The experiment had failed. Given the proximity to downtown businesses, our shiny clean designer-hood had become desirable. Revenue undermined the original concept and the demand for apartment space increased. People wanted to be where we lived.

Though we were not someones, we were somewhere the someones wanted to be. But it sucked that those someones would take our space now that we couldn't afford it.

The blanket slipped to the ground. I threw on my jeans and a white t-shirt with a Carter's Drugstore logo on the right sleeve.

"Well, if it isn't the Lovely Princess Granola." Ray greeted me while she lobbed a chicken bone into the sink.

She wore a grey oversize sweatshirt—circa 1970s Goodwill; no pants; and mismatched ankle socks that might have been white at one time. "You're up already? Got a job interview?" I asked. Sarcasm was my middle name.

"It's the strangest thing, Koda, I've been watching *Breaking Bad* since four-thirty this morning and only just realized they've been playing the same two episodes on repeat."

She ate from a boxed chicken dinner; must have gone out when I was sleeping. How she'd paid for the food was a mystery because, a few days before, she'd lost her purse and wallet somewhere between the sketchy locations of None-of-your-business and Nowhere.

"Did you find your purse?"

"Someone's probably picked it up and traded it for smokes," Ray said.

"How long will it take to get new ID?" I wasn't specific: how long she'd take to initiate the process, or the length of time the authorities would take to issue replacements.

"I can't remember how long it took last time," said Ray. "But one thing's for sure, I must be getting bad karma for something 'cause this is the rankest KFC ever."

"Not your weekend is it?"

Ray didn't recognize rhetorical. "No Koda, it's not. Lost purse I can deal with, but bad KFC is heart wrenching." She sucked dark meat off another bone and her elbow bumped the misaligned lid of the cat cookie jar. Dammit, she'd raided it and taken the laundry money—fast food instead of clean clothes. I'd topped it up Wednesday with a few bucks Morgan Insurance gives me to water their plants and listen for intruders.

Another bone in the sink, and she remembered something from her route to KFC.

"Carter's got a special on ass-wipe," Ray said. "They're setting up a display outside the store. Maybe they're gonna have testers, you know, like a poopsie challenge."

"You're gonna clog the drain again with those bones." I opened the fridge door and prayed there'd be something left to eat in there.

She thudded out of the kitchen. Her footsteps encouraged the drum from my dream. The dream I could never remember except that it had a drum—and a fishbaby. The drumbeat that sometimes broke into lunchbreak, emerged when I was writing a test, or leaked out in a foot-tap when there was no music playing. I blocked it by thinking about my favourite dream with the golden retriever puppy that grows into a dog and, because I'm dreaming, the dog goes through all the stages of dog growing-up time while I stay the same age and wear the same clothes; like it works with the characters' in cartoons like Scooby-Doo.

In that dream, Ranger my dream dog and I always run across a field of knee-high daises. Sometimes in that dream I rise over the white flowers and get an aerial view of a perfect life.

In the year at the apartment over the insurance company there were times when the drumbeat's rhythm leaked out into my waking world and I'd believe it to be something in the heating vents, or maybe a machine in the office downstairs. I'd searched for the source a few times, but I knew it was self-created—an inside job. Like puffs of air escaping through a weak membrane, it invaded my conscious life when I opened my locker or rode the bus. I worried it would turn into something else, like when people talk to windup toy animals in public plazas. I got a break from it at Popeye's Dance Studio because there was actual drumming there.

Popeye's is not its real name. Its officially the Western Canadian Non-Denominational Multicultural Centre. The kids who dance there call it Popeye's Dance Studio. Those who play pool there call it Popeye's Pool Hall. And the people in the community kitchen—low-income moms making a lot of meals from a shared supply of groceries —call it Popeye's Spinach. They even painted the kitchen door green. Popeye's a comic character sailor from a gazillion years ago who got his strength from eating spinach.

Collectively, it is a ginormous warehouse that used to be an official gym for bodybuilders and boxers. The original Popeye's sign on the outside stayed. When the gym closed, around the time I was born, a bunch of community people got together with the Indigenous community and made it a motivational mall of sorts. Drop-in and participate in something that you like. Come in for a hug and a chat, we'll listen to you. Attend AA or NA. Visit the monthly job bank, or the semi-annual career fair. Use the computers in the lab. Obtain your GED, we'll help you with college applications and funding. Get serious and sign-up as a member—it's free, and there's a newsletter.

I'd been going there for dance since kindergarten.

The thought of dance brought back the drum, which reminded me of the dream. But all I knew about the dream was it contained a lot of need-to-know information, yet it never left me with any recall. It began with a sense of stillness, a freeze-frame right before a major storm, that nanosecond before the first raindrop, when the earth says, "Okay, bring it on." This calmness led me to some kind of sanctuary, an entrance to a cave. There, my waking memory was checked, like at a fancy restaurant when diners give their coats to an attendant who lives in a little dark room outside the dining area. It was always there when I'd notice the freaking drum.

Then I'd wake and think, *crap, I dreamed it.* Every time, I would struggle to capture it before my eyes were completely open and, when it didn't materialize, I'd head to the kitchen. A spoon of granola into red-bowl, then a splodge of peach yogurt—when we had it—never the other way around.

"Dakota Starr?" Ray saying my full name startled me.

She chewed the end of a pencil while leaning on the kitchen

counter pass-through. Her music books littered the surface alongside an *Elton Rocks* mug she'd stocked with stolen pens. The mention of the idol's name always led to Ray's speculation of how she and the legend could be related—their physical likeness, something about distant family in Middlesex. Oh, and the talent.

"It's a new one. Buildin' My Baby A Mansion In Nashville. Get it? The goal and song are the same. It's like we're looking for a home, and writing the song not only tells that, it's the way we get the home. It's like when the song sells and becomes a big hit, we'd be able to buy a home."

"Ray. I get it, okay?" But I knew Ray would never sell a song. She'd be content to continue to collect "Support For Independence" which is basically not quite enough money, given to people by the government, for rent and food. Most people still call it welfare.

SFI is believed to define and inspire. The government supports you to find a way to be independent, and when you are, you won't need this monthly cheque.

Ess-eff-eye has many creative incarnations, always inspiring some smart arse to create their own words from the three letters.

Ray did not treat SFI as a temporary measure. In Ray's mind the government employed her, sending monthly instalments for wasting her life. Totally different than Green Jean, who, if she'd have accepted financial assistance, might have lived longer.

I left Ray humming with the fridge. One of us needed to help the two of us. Ten minutes later I'd caught a bus. Fifteen more and the bus passed the condemned twelve-suiter where, over the years, we'd lived in several apartments. Four blocks past and I got off at Popeye's and crossed to the Dairy Queen. The Now Hiring sign fluttered as I opened the door.

"Job?" The question came from a Shawn Mendes lookalike wearing a Dan nametag. An application appeared faster than I could say soft serve.

"You're at Sir John, eh?" He'd made a joke with the "A" and a Canadian "eh," and guessed correctly, attaching me to the closest school: Sir John A. MacDonald. The original Big Mac. First Prime Minister of Canada.

"Uh-huh," I answered.

That was the only interview question.

Dan projected that by summer break, in two weeks, I'd know the ropes. Same day training entailed wiping, sweeping, and mopping, interspersed with listening to a girl named Donna explain everything about everything at super-high speed. Each time she imparted valuable information I managed to forget what she'd said previously. *The ice cream machine must be wiped with hot water. The milkshake maker must always be plugged into a separate wall socket than the toaster oven.*

Obsessed with Dan's front tuft of hair that resembled the trademark curly cone top, I formed a mental image of an ice cream scoop carving out a hole in my brain to free up space for valuable DQ policy, even though DQ doesn't serve the hard variety. Later, while cleaning tables, I did mental math over and over: thirteen dollars an hour multiplied by three hours equaled thirty-nine bucks. Four after-school shifts would make over a hundred dollars. A summer week with more hours would eventually lead to Goodbye Ray. I'd save some money and prepare myself for a different kind of independence. Sure, this September I'd still have three years of high school, but the income would be the start of freedom.

Two

B y the end of the week all the DQ new job butterflies were gone. At dance, Martha said I looked taller. Working student status topped up my confidence and demanded more organization as I juggled dance and moved homework to a later spot. On Friday night, total fatigue greeted me when the turquoise door swung open and my foot met the first of nineteen steps.

Ray was sprawled on the couch.

I slipped into the kitchen.

"Ray, the dishes are still in the sink."

"There's something wrong with the TV." She might have been saying it all afternoon.

I peeked over the pass-through and read the bubble over her head: *Did Dakota come in? Did I hear water? Maybe there's a leak and the kitchen is flooding. Oh well, I'll close my eyes and it'll all go away.*

"I thought you were going to wash the dishes."

"We've only got two channels, Koda, and they're real snowy."

When I slapped off the faucet, she increased the volume of whine. "That's because the cable's been cut off," I called.

While the soapy action broke down day-old spaghetti sauce, I leaned on the pass-through, setting off a dust explosion from a stack of music magazines. Her ancient pay-and-talk plan cellphone, which she'd never paid, so never talked, slid from underneath.

She looked toward the kitchen.

Next thing, creaky springs under upholstery signaled she'd gotten off the couch. Bingo. Forced off the sofa by curiosity. She would come and find out if I was there. A countdown from three gave me time to think about how great it would be if, when she came in, she'd start the dishes. But when she didn't materialize, and the familiar music of the video game began to wind up, I realized she'd only gone as far as the television stand. Made the best of a bad situation. Nintendo to the rescue.

Resourceful Ray.

Whether she thought the "something wrong with the TV" conversation was imaginary or not, it no longer mattered. She was now in Mario territory: a land where golden apples are ripe for the picking, and no one pays rent. A place void of mothers and daughters.

I swiped the counter while the dishes soaked. This time she hadn't even bothered to put the lid back on the ceramic cat. Maybe she'd done laundry. Maybe she'd gone to the store for real food. I opened the fridge. "Where's the milk?" I shouted above a repetitive pattern of beeps and zig-zaggy tones. I recited the "Old Mother Hubbard" nursery rhyme, slammed a cupboard door, and made my way to the sofa.

Satisfied with an upside down sideways view of me, she managed one syllable.

"Hey."

"There was milk money in Chippy Cat. Enough for peanut butter. And jam. And the white stuff we put the PB and J on?" Knowing we had nothing made me hungrier, even though I'd had a free cheeseburger on my break. "Ray, where's the peanut butter, jam, and bread?"

She remained reclined and couched, alive only between fingertip and wrist.

"Sheesus Ray." I pictured going to the foodbank, again.

She squirmed like a dying fish that had found a pocket of oxygen-rich water. Her thumbs worked a pattern of success without having to look at the screen.

I'd heard about people who played video games blindfolded and wondered if it paid.

She paused a little fat man on a green hill. A purple balloon monster, about to burst over his head, froze too. Ray released the controller, reached behind a rough fabric pillow, and pulled out a brown paper lunch bag, definitely not large enough for peanut butter, milk, or bread. A bundle of straw tubes poked out the top—Pixie Stix —which I knew were filled with coloured, sour sugar. Closer observation revealed a Caramilk and an Aero.

"I didn't get smokes." Her attempt at redemption didn't sit well. She hadn't even risen.

"Oh, aren't you a good girl. What about the groceries?"

"I didn't get cigarettes."

"How much you spend on candy? Where's the change?"

Ray shook the bag—a few coins, maybe.

"You spent it all? Again?"

"I didn't buy cigarettes. Isn't that good, Koda?"

"You don't smoke, Ray."

She sat up. I braced for the grand entrance of "the parent."

"That's Mother to you, Dakota."

This was a Ray rerun. Spending money on stupid things and then offering me some. My hands were too wet to reach into the bag. Ray narrowed my choice by helping herself to the caramel-filled chocolate bar—couldn't even wait until I'd dried my hands.

She is not Mom, I told myself. She has never been Mom. I am Mom. She is selfish Ray. I snatched the Aero.

She burrowed further into the sofa. I couldn't tell where the worn floral upholstery started and her clothing began.

"Did you cut your hair?" I asked.

Caramel drizzled from the corner of her mouth.

"Are you wearing a muumuu?" I looked toward the door.

She sucked melted chocolate off her finger. "You're not going out again, are you?" She applied her whiny, don't leave me tone. Her assertive parent had briefly shown its shadow, then retreated, a sure sign of another six weeks of ridiculousness. I was positive she would've liked to pile on a little more attitude, but it was getting dark. Not so much as a "where do you think you're going, young lady?" She didn't like to be alone at night—scared of the dark.

"Foodbank." I turned my back to her.

She didn't offer to go, ask if I wanted company, or think to question where I'd been after school until eight. "Can you make sure to not get the crunchy peanut butter? And see if they have some fish. I really fancy some Brunswick thingies."

"Some what?"

"Those little lined up fishies in a pop-top can."

"Ray, that packaging freaks me out."

"I fancy some."

"Fancy? Were you watching British television before the cable quit?"

"I just remembered. They're called sardines."

"Two words: mass grave," I said.

"I want some."

"Well you shouldn't have bought candy then, should you?" I searched for my knapsack and discovered I hadn't taken it off.

"And Koda, see if they have something better than dried milk."

I banged the door behind me and wished for the driest of dry, really dry, dry milk. I hated it more than she did, but still wished for it. Besides, powdered was lighter for carrying home.

She didn't even get that the foodbank shouldn't be open. If she read or listened to the news, she'd know the charity changed their hours to help the court system. This summer, people who had made poor life choices and had to serve court mandated community service could have a place to fulfill their contribution.

Even though I took care of things, and I handled Ray, she was still officially in the driver's seat.

I often wished Green Jean had been my mother and, rather than the small room overlooking Safeway's dumpsters, she'd had a small house in the country. There would have been basil and rosemary in our garden. And a small satellite dish on our rooftop to stream Gaia or Curiosity TV.

Jean was a widow-lady with red hair and emerald eyes. I didn't know her when she was married, but her husband was Levi Jean. By marriage, she'd ended up with the same first and second name: Jean. Everyone called him Blue Jean, so she'd called herself Green Jean.

Green Jean used to say, "Lord loves ya, Dakoda girl," which I always believed meant she loved me.

But Green Jean wasn't my mother. And Green Jean had died violently. And I lived with Ray. And only occasionally, if it had been possible for someone to peek through our window, would they have been able to identify the parent.

The same route that took me to school, dance, and—over the last week—work, went to points beyond, like the building where volunteers packed the bare necessities of life into cardboard boxes for people like Ray and me.

A bonus "hello" from the driver I recognized improved my mood. A geezer sitting near the front offered a genuine smile, not a pervert one. There were decent people in the world. Even in my world. A seat without a butt imprint presented itself. Planted in its freshness, I wished for a phone so I could listen to music, stared out the window, and wished for a lot more things.

The transit driver braked hard and came to an unscheduled stop. Four girls in matching orange hoodies, who'd frantically waved him down, climbed aboard. One of them thanked him. I swallowed the lump in my throat and turned away from the logos on their sweat-shirts—imagined thousands of unmarked graves with five-year-old versions of them trembling and weeping in spirit-bone form. All of them victims of a system called residential schools, all of them having their hair bluntly bowl-bobbed, and being forbidden to speak their language, by power hungry, total mental cases whose behaviour no real God would or could ever command.

Out my window, the neon-lime biceps on Popeye's brick wall flashed. Below it, a graffiti artist had redesigned a gang's tag into a series of brown, black, and dark green triangular trees. If it hadn't been June it could have been mistaken for a Christmas tree lot. Still, when I squinted, the effect was almost sink-into-able in an "I'd like to hike in that forest" kind of way.

The bus boarders shuffled by and "heyed" me. I "hey there-ed" them back; knew one from a dance recital. The energy between them was the BFF kind. I wondered where my friends were, then remem-bered I didn't have a personal life. I had Ray.

And I had a job. And I had dance.

Jean had taken me to dance when I was five years old. From the first class, I'd clung to every step as if it was my lost soul. Jean had tried to get Ray to go to some things there; Ray wouldn't have any of it.

"A natural, Dakoda-girl," Jean had said to me after every recital—she always pronounced the "t" as a "d" and I loved her for that.

Three

I bit into my chocolate bar and hoped Ray was puking from her Caramilk. Then I got carried away with the thoughts of the upcoming recital and forgot, for a minute, I was going to the foodbank.

It began with ballet and tap, but at eight my heart fell for hip hop. Not long after, improvisational dance twirled new life into the corridors of Popeye's. An older instructor, Martha, blissfully flowed multi-layered skirts of jewel tones past the administration office, and tipped a flamboyant hat to the stiffer board members. Natural Reflection Global Steps was her own invention for which there were two other teachers: one in Toronto and one in Edmonton.

Popeye's other dance instructors objected to Martha's teaching style, and the materials she used, and said she flagrantly disregarded all form. They put an age requirement on enrollment: twelve. All that did was make kids want her class even more.

It was sad that Martha was ostracized, because Popeye's was supposed to be this huge friendship place. She didn't seem to mind, her popularity grew, many students quick-stepping away from traditional classes, and an equally large group—including me—longing to be old enough.

The more the other instructors tried to hold on to their students, the greater the draw to Martha's NRG.

Martha persevered and gained a reputation. It didn't take long for word to get out that she embraced 'all forms' because she seminar-ed the heck out of every student, in extra sessions, covering the entire history of dance.

Month after month, with my nose to the vented windowed viewing area made for parents who wanted to watch their kids, my heart ached to be one of her students. She beat a stick against an overturned pail. *Be the grass. Be the bear. Be the heartbreak. Be menstruation.* The recordings she brought in were whale calls, ocean waves, and storms.

More than a year went by. I hadn't realized Jean had been watching me watch the class, but she had. Next, she was petitioning for my inclusion in Martha's classes earlier than the age parameters the board of directors had been bullied into establishing by the body of traditional teachers.

"After all, Popeye's motto is Everybody Belongs," Green Jean had written in a letter she showed me.

When she'd read it aloud, a guy came up to her and said, "You's as strong as the real Popeye." Then he sang: *"I'm Popeye the sailor man. Popeye the sailor man. I'm strong to the finich, 'cause I eats me spinach. I'm Popeye the sailor man."*

Jean and Martha and the guy had broken into laughter, three of them sharing some memory about a cartoon character. They reminisced about Popeye's girlfriend: Olive Oyl. Then the laughing guy went away singing more verses about fighting, and Jean went into the executive director's office and emerged triumphant. I was ten.

Martha took us beyond the stage, showing videos of iconic choreographers and pioneers in dance. She raved about legends Agnes de

Mille, Katherine Mary Dunham, Bob Fosse, and praised the contemporary artists, Paula Abdul and Alvin Ailey. By way of demonstration and video, she exposed us to national dances from all over the world and, if she could have, she would have taken us there in person. Her explanations of Indigenous influence included a yearly field trip to a Powwow, which someone from the Spinach Kitchen said was on Martha's own dime.

Timeless, vibrant, inclusive—Martha was human expression in big screen surround-sound.

Martha and I loved Green Jean. Six months after Jean was buried, we stole away to the cemetery and danced for her. When Martha's own mentor, Betty Isenhour, passed too early in life, Martha took a few weeks off and went to the funeral in North Carolina. On her return, she wore more colourful layers and added more feathers to her hats, then kicked everything into a higher gear, training some of her older students to be teachers, setting them up time slots and spaces at Popeye's and a couple of other locations in the city.

Even though she was on the news, and featured in a Toronto magazine, she remained at Popeye's, pushing the envelope, encouraging each of us to put our own stamp on Natural Reflection Global Steps—to dance as if there was no tomorrow—as if our lives depended on it.

My heart warmed as I pretended to see through the brick walls to the studio. A little excitement stirred. Almost a decade of dance, every performance with a borrowed costume, was about to change. Right while I rode city transit to the foodbank, a dress that I'd been told represented the seasons of life, dripping with strings of glass-like beads, was zipping down the Queen E Highway in a courier's van.

The dress was on its way to me because, apparently, we are all connected. Separated by six degrees. That's what Martha says. Last month, Martha told me she'd been asked to share her list of registered pupils with an official government social worker. Because it was all done privately, Martha hadn't known it was me who was being looked for.

But it *was* me. A report called a Lifebook had surfaced in an office clean out. The worker who had found the report had decided it was my property, and that it should be sent to me if I could be located.

"Written when you were three. The department understood you would be adopted, so it was prepared for you. You weren't adopted though. But the book exists, and it's your property." That's what a social worker named Joanne said to me on the phone when I went to the admin office at Popeye's to take her call.

It got a little crazier after that. This social worker turned out to be someone who knew Martha through NRGS dance in Edmonton. Two days after the phone call, when I gave Morgan Insurance's address to Joanne—I didn't want Ray getting it—Joanne broke some rules and phoned Martha because she'd had an idea about a dress which was totally unrelated to the Lifebook.

"You see, Joanne the social worker had a granddaughter," Martha said. "She was in NRGS in Edmonton. And there was this dress—handcrafted by Joanne's eighty-five-year-old mother. But there was some ecstasy. And there was some meth." When Martha told me this she'd started to cry.

Turned out that there was also a highway. And an eighteen-wheeler.

"It's never been worn. It'll be perfect for body narrative—the story you're working on. It's got three-hundred-and-sixty-five strands of beads sewn onto it. It's meant to sing. Can you imagine that? It has a voice. It was inspired by the Jingle Dress of First People—remember at the Powwow? She only asks that you send photos," said Martha. "Photos of you in the dress. I'll take them if you like. It'll help the family with closure."

Lucky me. A dead girl's dress.

Nature Reflections Global Steps is physically taxing. The

costumes can be heavy. Sometimes they incorporate representations of issues people deal with—one time a college age girl danced with a giant piece of concrete chained around her ankle. A girl who used to cut her arms—but stopped after she started Martha's classes—hauled in an electric range on a dolly then, for the performance, danced on the stove's top.

My dance for the season finale was a personalization of an homage to life—I called it Reverence—focusing more on the story and steps than the costume I'd need to cobble together from what I'd find on Martha's wardrobe racks. But now a dress was on its way to me, for me. It would be good to get used to one costume instead of several someone else's I'd worn in the past.

As excited as I was to receive the dress, I hadn't forgotten the Lifebook. I had no idea I'd spent time away from Ray that had been legal, and almost permanent. As far as I knew, when I was a baby, I'd mostly been with Ray and, after I started school, there were a few unofficial times when Ray took off and Green Jean stayed over.

A Lifebook was on its way to me, packed alongside a dead girl's handcrafted, beaded dress. And all I had to do was provide a few photographs in exchange.

Four

∼⌒∽

The girls in the orange hoodies tumbled out the back door of the bus. As we pulled away, and the engine drowned out their laughter, it occurred to me their happiness was the same colour as their hoodies. Creamsicles. Bright like the summer sun. With Green Jean gone, the only bright thing in my life, other than dance, was red bowl.

Did Lifebooks have a colour? Were there any illustrations? What about photos? Were Lifebooks, written for children who were removed from their parents, just black print on white paper?

Was separation a deep bluey purple on account of it being like a bruise?

Separation from Ray had never featured in any of my thinking until the call from Joanne the social worker. Then I began thinking about how I didn't know squat about what happened in the blur of my early years. Maybe there was an injury inside me caused by the taking me away from her. Maybe it was layered with scar tissue of a dozen years or so. Or was there an injury caused by them giving me back to her?

If there could be such a hurt from disruption, then there'd be a lot of kids that had it. Flooded by visions of multitudes of children—a line of victims from the dawn of time, separated from family because of war causalities, genocide, famine, and colonization, residential schools, and plain old generational dysfunction—my thoughts threatened to knock me off the bench seat. I imagined the breaking of thousands of hearts in a generational train of sorrow.

The bus ride and our proximity to my stop helped me self-diagnose—maybe Dakota Starr was only slightly broken. A little crack in my core.

If I had not been returned to Ray's care, would I now live in another city? If so, I would never have met Green Jean, and I wouldn't be taking classes with Martha. Would I have known that girl who walked onto the highway? Would I have been her?

In an acceptance of "whatever happened had happened," I knew that expression through dance took some of the brokenness away.

And then I noticed the thoughtful driver had stopped right at the food bank instead of at the end of its block. I rushed to join the other four who were getting off.

Five us went into the old Safeway and, for me, this is how it went: robot mode, head down, show ID, lower head further, bundle donated goods into knapsack, unfold a canvas bag to carry the rest, say hi to the same bus driver on his reverse loop.

Most of the way home was spent deciding if the bus engine was droning or groaning, and being grateful it blocked out the drum. Closer to the apartment, the driver put on Vivaldi's Four Seasons. I reached for the bell, overcoming temptation to stay on a few extra stops—despite the weight of the groceries.

A wave of relief came over me when we stopped for a pedestrian with a walker, the delay offering a bit of respite from going home.

Five

A week later, five shifts under my belt, the sixth a few hours away, I reclined on the stoop we shared with Morgan Insurance. A sealed box containing the dress and Lifebook beside me, delivered to Morgan's ten minutes earlier.

Muffled conversation about payroll worked its way under the purple door. Such words were now part of my vocab: timesheet, shift, pay-period.

Warming my butt on the concrete was combined with spying on the family in the house with the I'M SOLD! sign across the street. The movers had loaded an entire truck and had started stuffing a U-Haul kind of trailer that was hitched to the larger unit.

When my dutiful caregiver internal clock registered Ray's hunger, I went upstairs and made us each a peanut butter and jam sandwich. It was a deposit in the bank of karma to boost a fantasy that she'd eventually do something for me. Plus, it was important to make her feel indebted because she hadn't thanked me for more sardines I'd picked up and she'd long finished.

Room service came with a price for the sofa-sprawling Ray. I balanced the plate on her chest. "Work for it baby," I whispered.

The signs for imminent landlord intervention sat on the shelf by the front door: unopened bills and eviction notices; the cable was still out. She'd worn the same oversize t-shirt and baggy sweatpants for three days, slept in them too. I pictured returning to a padlocked door after my shift, Ray cross-legged beside a few black garbage bags of our stuff.

I replaced the science text in my backpack with a clean pair of underwear, added my hoodie, and tossed in the almost full jar of peanut butter. My wallet, a gift from Green Jean, held a bit of change, student ID, social insurance card, and proof that Ray and I were genetically linked. My work schedule remained folded around a wad of DQ napkins. They peeked out of a zippered pocket that contained an emergency ten-dollar bill.

With Ray nearing the breaking point, the half-roll of single-ply toilet paper wedged behind the twisty pipes under the bathroom sink was a must pack.

Toilet paper is always a valuable commodity, but this roll had something secreted inside it. As a little kid, I thought Ray was talking about a friend when she mentioned Emma—the princess kind, because Ray said such nice things about her. It didn't take long to learn that Emma is the pretty name for morphine. This particular roll had four Emma's stuffed between its centre sheets and the cardboard tube.

She hadn't chemically medicated in years, but Ray's "old friend" remained. It was my way of monitoring her state.

Ray knew they were there.

I knew Ray knew they were there.

She didn't know I knew she knew they were there.

Backpack over my shoulder, I clutched my own sandwich and ordered a prone Ray to eat. Another caregiving job well done, thank you very much Dakota.

The plate teetered on her chest when she breathed. I liked

knowing she couldn't move without having to focus how to coordinate getting up with keeping the plate level, while not letting go of the controls.

And then I remembered I'd left the package from Edmonton outside on the step. "EAT," I demanded, raced out the door, and bolted down the stairs, though by the magic of a speedy imagination I still had time to think it might be stolen. I even lived through a scenario of shame—showing up at Popeye's without the dress and trying to explain how I'd lost it. Another vignette followed: not going to dance at all, only to find out thirty years later that the dress had been returned to Popeye's the day it went missing, so Martha would have known all along I lost it. Sometimes I wished for a less active mind.

The package waited like a dog that never needs a leash. Like Ranger. My dream dog.

I was going to take it upstairs, then remembered Ray's presence on the sofa. This package was private. I pictured Ray's locked brows, the plate wobbling on her chest. I could have been meaner and served hot soup. What would a few dropped crumbs mean to Ray? I repositioned myself and purred like a cat in the sun having had more fun than torturing a cornered mouse.

Morgan Insurance's railing made a firm backrest and the box a perfect footstool. I set up observation. The faded mural emblazoned on the side of the truck and trailer combo read: Full House Moving. A spread of cards, like you'd hold in your hand if you were playing poker, presented five smiling faces—one on each card: two identical redhead males and three identical baldies. What were the odds of a set of triplets and twins coming together and forming a moving company?

When the sun caught the painted faces in a mirrored glint, the faces were duplicates: Quintuplets? Give me a break—five born-at-the-same-time siblings survive and then start a haulage business? Doubtful, universe. Doubtful.

The back door on the larger unit had been rolled shut for a while. Only the ramp to the hitched trailer was open to the street. Two moving guys filling it box by box.

A family sedan with two occupants pulled up in front of the moving truck/trailer combo. The driver beeped the horn. The guy I called Dad of the house escorted the woman I called Grandma of the house to the waiting car.

I'd seen the wiry granny before. She lived with the Mom and Dad and their two children. Lately she appeared bundled in shawls so only her face showed: a bitter one—mouth like a thin scar sutured shut. Maybe a scrapper in her day.

The Dad of the house, who was older than Ray, and who I'd decided was Grandma's son, had his hand near her elbow as she clutched a long, thin, gray, meowing cat to her chest. She shook the son-man off. The feline's body dangled so low that its back legs came level with the old lady's knees. When the granny reached the side-walk, the cat tried to make a run for it, but the tiny woman was stronger than she looked and muscled the pet into a headlock. Once she and kitty were inserted in the back seat of the car, the Grandma-picker-uppers drove away. It was then that the actions of those remaining—Mom, Dad, Child One, Child Two, and the two movers —shifted into high gear.

For sure the Dad would have said, "Meter's running." And in response, the Mom would roll out a cooler with potato salad and ham and cheese on crusty rolls. Everyone would be happy about their move because Grandma wasn't riding with them—maybe she wasn't moving with them at all—and they would never again have to cut up her food or watch her try to force crusty buns into that always-closed mouth.

It wasn't a surprise to me when the Mom danced out onto the driveway and stocked the family van with pillows and a bag of toys.

Inventorying their move, I was reminded that real families have a lot of stuff. Ours would fit in a couple of boxes; these people had more than a moving van's worth. Sure, there were two children, a Mom, Dad, and Grandma, but so much swag. More than a Full House move's worth—probably why they needed that extra trailer. I was dizzying myself over their family dynamics when I noticed how massive the moving truck was. Then I had a brilliant idea. Why hook up a little pull trailer to it? Because that was all Tiny Granny's stuff. She was going to be somewhere else. They were going to drop her belongings en route to wherever it was they were moving. Pleased with myself, I pulled on an imaginary air horn, looked in my rearview and couldn't even see the puny trailer.

During what seemed like the final act, one of the guys in coveralls brought out a cage with a bird inside it. They suspended the cage from a bar that framed the roof of the U-Haul-ish trailer. Not a nice place to put a pet—jammed inside an extra trailer with things people don't want to dispose of, yet can't throw away: vintage-granny-crocheted poodle toilet-paper covers; scratchy blankets; containers crammed with birthday after birthday of cheap and smelly bath crystals. Junk.

My senses must have been dulled because I didn't pick up Ray's odor until it floated above me—after she'd stepped off the sidewalk. The only place Ray ever went was to Jack's convenience store and KFC—neither required street crossing.

She walked a slow, determined pace across the grassy boulevard, her Nintendo console, games, and controller gathered haphazardly in her arms. The cords trailed on the ground, and I worried she might trip in a child-without-her-shoelaces-tied kind of way. She was all the way across the street before I noticed she'd hooked her pinky through Elton's handle and realized what she was going to do.

I seized the cardboard box and sped after her, hitting the middle of the road as she zombied up the ramp. Self-conscious of my presence in the middle of their move, but sorta convinced the mover guys might think I belonged because I was holding a box, I slinked closer.

Ray ducked under the dangling birdcage and negotiated her body around and into a wide chair that had winged sides and faced the narrowed part of the trailer, right where the hitch would be on the outside. Once she'd inserted herself, she simply disappeared, enveloped by the large blue and brown plaidness of it all.

I moved up the ramp, hiding my face with the box, then picked my way over drop-cloths. "Ray," I whisper-called while crouching behind a stack of bins bungeed to a rail. She did her best impression of ignore my you-can't-stay-in-here. The game components were balanced on her lap, her eyes fixed on the metal in front of her. I gave it a look in case she was looking at something, like when people see sacred images in clouds or oil slicks, but there was nothing. No Jesus. Not even St. Nintendo. Just a sort of nosecone of metal.

Family conversation neared the mouth of the trailer then veered off.

"Ray, we have to get out of here. We can go to Jack's for Pixie Stix. Or KFC. I'll hook up your Nintendo." The drumbeat began to spill out. I had to put down the box and vice my temples with the heels of my hands.

Ray tightened her grip on the console. I charaded springing forward—a sort of taking off action without taking off, hoping she would follow. Acting out the first few movements of leaving—over and over, to urge her to copy—didn't help. I mentally willed her to reconsider her decision, begged for any way to get her out without me having to rat on her.

Closer, I wedged myself in front of her feet, kneeling before her like she was the queen, and made a final attempt to convince.

"Mother, please. We need to get out of this trailer." She remained tight, still, and silent with ceramic Elton right by her side.

Foot scraping preceded dust, shaken from unused, quilted moving blankets. I fought with a sneeze. Part of me wanted to stand up and say something like, "Hey Mister, we're here." But I wasn't a rat. I willed the sneeze I'd suppressed. Not even a tickle.

Overcome with twisted loyalty, I listened while a few more boxes arrived, a child's voice in tow. "Pwease Daddy, take Binky outta dare."

"Bird'll be fine son."

"No Daddy. Gwamma no want Binky in the twailer."

Unless they stepped in and over the boxes, they would never see Ray. She was invisible, not to mention comfortable. I tucked myself down in a not-too-tight ball, thinking for sure they'd still see my back. I wanted to be discovered without me giving us up, even if it meant hanging our heads all the way back to the apartment we wouldn't have in a month, but the boy was too short, and the father preoccupied.

"This is a super-reinforced kryptonite trailer." The father told the whimpering child.

"Weally?" The little boy sniffed a long snotty inhale.

"Really. Try to roll your r's. Never mind. See these extra rails here? The guys there told me it's armour plated; used to transport valuables." A father's final authority on said budgie's security only rattled the bird more.

"Like tweasure?" asked the boy.

The man cursed the child's speech delay and urged him away, ignoring the budgie's wild staccato protests. Bird language for: *Stowaways. Chirp. Forward cabin. Chirp.* Or more likely directed at us in a statement of observation followed by a plea: *Idiots. Both of you. Idiots. Get out while you can. Take me with you. We can't ride in this death trap.*

"See you at Gwamas in Bancouber, Binky." The child's voice

squeaked on the heels of a heavy-footed moving guy who called out a medic's "Clear," as if he was about to use some heart zapping paddles.

He hoisted the ramp and it became a bolted door, sealing us in.

In a response to eviction notices, Ray had initiated adventure.

A split second of dark erased the world, then powerful sunbeams broke through the vertical spaces each side of the ramp-door and illuminated a strip where, when closed, the ramp's edge met the roof. A little more light filtered in from a spot around a vent on the roof.

For five seconds it was totally silent. Even the drumbeat had stopped. Then:

"*Woof, woof.*"

"Oh my God, there's a dog buried under this crap," I said.

"Assholes," said Ray.

"*Woof, Woof.*"

"It's near the bird," said Ray, though she didn't bother getting up.

I moved to try to find the pooch without squishing it underfoot.

"*Woof, woof,*" said Binky.

Gobsmacked, I looked over and caught enough of Ray's expression to know we were both thinking the same thing. We stared in the direction of the caged budgie. He barked again.

"Unbelievable," said Ray.

"Yes, you are," I said quietly to the metal walls and the bolted door.

Oh, the signs had been there. She'd been ready to move on for a while, and the nature of our relationship was that, while I always had too much responsibility, ultimately, once Ray made a decision, there was no going back. Gratitude swept through me for the backpack and its contents, including the toilet roll and my secret ten dollars zippered inside an internal pocket. Prepared, carrying loo-roll the way experienced globetrotters to third world countries do.

Six

A horn sounded, a "let's get this show on the road." The backpack slipped from my shoulders in acknowledgement of fate. My eyes adjusted to a new reality.

We were a strange trio, Ray, me, and the barking budgie. Though I knew we were headed to Vancouver, I wasn't sure Ray'd heard the boy's mispronunciation. As for Binky, he'd have heard his human family talk about moving to the coast, and who am I to say he didn't understand in some birdbrain-like way? But I can speak for his fear and panic. He'd had a mass-molting. So small a blue pudgy-creature, yet so much fluff—a pillow exploded.

As he barked, I took myself into the industrial stretch on the far side of our block to the Doberman that lived behind the chain link of Inner-City Auto Body. Binky the budgie, sentenced to life behind bars, must have been ignored to the point of mimicking the sound of the body shop's guard dog. Maybe the imitation had helped him fend off Tiny Grandma's cat.

My mind went into overdrive. Damn Ray. I loved that apartment. Oh my god, my shift started at three. If I couldn't get out of this thing in the next couple of hours, I'd lose my job. Of course, I couldn't get out of this thing; it was moving. She'd done it again: screwed me over. Denied me my first paycheque.

The whole confusing mother-daughter bond flooded over me. After all, I could have called out to the movers or to the Dad.

Able to multitask, even during a meltdown, I remained a human GPS. A right turn from Lake Street, left at the next intersection, and five traffic light stops put us at South Point Mall. The intercom from the car dealership across from the shopping centre confirmed it—Jack to the showroom, please. Jack to the showroom.

Based on the itinerary of a junior high school trip to the mountains I'd not been able to take but had memorized anyway, I estimated we'd be through the Purcell Mountains via the Kicking Horse Pass by nightfall. If the guys took turns and didn't pull over to sleep, we'd be on the west coast this time tomorrow.

"Where we going?" Ray sounded stoned. The numbing agent of the last few years rattling in her lap alongside the plastic sheathed discs needed to run the machine of obsession.

"Vancouver." My reply rode bumpy sound waves while my eyes used the zigzagged flashes of light to showcase her forever-in-recovery flatlined brow and hollow eyes.

The little boy's innocent voice returned and touched my heart. He probably had no clue his new city was two days away or what might be left of the bird when it arrived at Granny's.

I secretly pledged to save Binky.

A thread of hope appeared from surviving previous Ray-crazies and I inserted a rationalization: DQ would be totally understanding about my mother's condition and mail my first check. Dan would probably even write a letter of recommendation to a franchise DQ on the west coast. But surely, we wouldn't stay there. Maybe Popeye's administration would loan us the bus money to get back. Back to what? Homelessness? Maybe I'd call Martha, escape from Ray, make my way back, set up secret digs in the wardrobe room, filch scraps from the community kitchen. Leave Ray. Maybe I'd get a second job as a coat check girl and live in a closet.

With closed eyes, the first step in summoning my ideal mother kicked in. She looked a bit like Ray, but was older and wore the expression of someone more stable—a younger Jean, minus the nervous breakdown she'd suffered after she'd received her doctorate. My ideal mother didn't ask brainless questions, like Ray did, nor did the ideal mother ride her children's asses about how much time they spent watching television, like other mothers that were not Ray might. Instead, my perfect mother provided books, board games, and craft supplies. She supported music lessons, endorsed public television, and baked hand-sized oatmeal cookies with fair-trade-chocolate chunks. Her scent was citrusy from actually doing dishes. Even after working part time at a not-for-profit job, she was tuned into the family pulse, promoting independence while being available with unlimited teddy-bear hugs.

All I wanted was to be loved by someone who smelled like lemons, not tolerated by a joystick-wielding alien sitting in an ancient armchair hurtling down the highway in an airless bucket of tin.

After a long silence I got over the frustration of who made her Queen of the Plaid Throne and scrambled around, making a little nest with an ancient fake fur coat that had been tossed onto the floor of the trailer. It poke-scratched me with something like the staple of a dry-cleaning tag, but I wasn't deterred—knew a deal when I felt it. Though the lining was stale smelling it was soft, silky, and luxurious.

Chair envy was replaced by a surge of greedy happiness for having claimed Coat. Now that it was mine it took on a personality and became the protagonist of my story. Chair, by virtue of being hers, became the antagonist.

Coat was better than Chair in the way paper trumped rock. It could be worn, slept on or under, tented, or balled up. And because it was fake it didn't have to be imagined as a dead animal. Coat had more stories than Chair. Spoke of better times. Like Christmas parties or winter festivals. Some carolling wearer had been gleeful, glamorous, and warm. Coat's pockets had been shared with hands of grandchildren when mittens had been forgotten and the wearer walked those children to school. Even if Coat had belonged to the cat-grandmother who never smiled, it was mine now.

Cat Granny must have known better times. What did better times look like to Ray? I knew her child side, but not her dreams. Her capabilities were always sub-par, accompanied by a cloud of lethargy. Her history was unknown to me. I was in a confined space with a stranger, and that fact heebee-geebee-ed me so much that I crushed my face against Coat's silky lining and escaped to fantastic imaginings. But sadly, my mind refused to stay in fantasy.

It's natural to wonder about family history when a back-story has never been given. Ray kept her childhood in a vault. The only fragments she'd made available were what happened after she became pregnant.

She'd mentioned a guy who was not my birthfather. That she'd talked about him a few times told me Ray'd liked him a lot. Jean said she'd heard he kept Ray clean during pregnancy. Though she was stable in his care, there was no fairy tale ending—she was not touched by angels and inspired to name her daughter from the majesty of a sunset in North or South Dakota. No, Ray named me after the guy's Dodge crew cab.

Seven

Pickup trucks remind me that I don't have a real father. And because I am named after a truck that did not belong to my father, I am embraced by fatherlessness every time someone calls out my name.

Birth father is the nicer sounding cousin of Sperm Donor. Not in the context of a clinical procedure, but a casual way: "She didn't know him, he was just the sperm donor." Sure, the pregnant woman would have to have known the biological father in one way but, when that colloquial is used, it means she wasn't in a relationship. Another phrase is one-night stand.

To me, the word *dad* has always been synonymous with a living person in your life, or the memory of someone strong that you had access to before he tragically and heroically died. Dad is a word that begins with a capital letter, and on Father's Day, all three: D. A. D. He's a guy who reads newspapers, subscribes to blogs for woke men, grills hamburgers, plays Frisbee golf with his peeps, and takes the dog for a walk when everyone else is too busy.

Children all over the world each cover a soup can in white glue and elbow macaroni, then spray silver, for a Dad.

The word conjures an image: height, weight, hair, eye colour, and personality. But "his" only presence in my life was a cellular contribution—before I was the tiniest form of anything Dakota-like when, for a moment in time, Ray's x contemplated joining with the x's and y's of his chemical alphabet.

I'm one of the lucky ones. In social worker speak: no cognitive damage. Hurray to Dakota-truck guy for looking after Ray. No mind-altering substances, other than junk food, that could have fried my fetal brain. It was written on a pre-kindergarten check-up that I was not impulsive or aggressive, and that I did not show any signs of learning challenges. Beyond that, I've speculated the combination of chocolate and licorice permeated the placenta and altered some of my brain cells, allowing me to learn quickly, read early, and grow up fast.

I fell asleep thinking about what the world would look like if people didn't put budgies in moving trailers.

I woke to slumbering diesels in surround-sound. An asphalt mattress, maybe an acre of it, where dreams of "the family back home" mixed with "freedom of the open road." Ray snorted herself awake. I imagined the budgie tucking his head under his wing, feeling our love, finally free from the malicious intent of Cat Granny's cat, and the dad of the house who didn't give a damn. Outside, deep drones backed by the faster hum of highway traffic sneaked through the cracks in our armour.

"Truck stop." Ray announced it in the manner of a nearly retired train conductor.

To take my mind off being hungry for meatloaf one of the driver-guys might order, I made up a mind-story about Dakota-truck guy returning after many years. The scenario: he would have seen Ray enter the trailer, followed us, then, while the driver guys were having a dinner, come to let the ramp down so we could slip out and into his newer model pickup, with the full-size back seat and real back doors. We'd all live happily ever after.

"I have to pee." I hadn't meant to speak it, but doing so increased the urgency. Our space became brighter; the penetration of headlights from more Kenworths and Peterbilts streaming through three sides of the ramp-door. Ray turned her head toward the corner.

"No way," I said, looking in the direction of a bag of cat litter.

She rose from Chair, shuffled to the bag, tore the top and squatted, like a mother animal demonstrating for one of her cubs. I buried my head in Coat.

When I sensed she was finished, I reached out with some DQ napkins. She accepted without even thanking me, then directed me with her index finger to the bag-toilet. Midstream, trucks pulled away and we lost our spotlight, leaving me to deal with personal hygiene blindly. The stench of fresh urine was only partially absorbed by the litter.

Hunger was replaced by nausea. We settled into our spots again, like we did this all the time.

Thwunk! Rattle.

The trailer bounced, as if someone had jumped on the towing connections. Chains jingle-jangled the way heavy links would—nothing Christmassy sounding. And then we were struck—that is, the trailer hitch was hit—maybe by a tire iron. It wasn't a Full House friendly action. The *thwunk* sent a reverberation through the walls and into my body. I almost pounded against the wall in a flurry of Morse Code shorts and longs, but stopped upon imagining murderers hooking us up to some kind of traveling serial-killer show. Ray stayed in Chair.

More diesels thundered in. We didn't roll anywhere. I decided the bad guys had been interrupted during an attempted trailer-stealing, if that had been their intention. Then I considered they were malicious hitch-tamperers set on causing road accidents and loss of property. Convinced we'd been vandalized, I hoped it was Full House Movers' protocol to check the connections after a stop.

I settled back on Coat.

The bird howled a wolf's call. Even though he was close, his sound was distant. The way he'd heard it from far away was the way he mimicked it. It was eerie, as if he wasn't in the trailer with us.

If Ray had any theories, she didn't share them. I didn't share mine either, but a partial dismantle would make us beyond vulnerable. Hopefully, we'd been completely unhooked, and we'd come off right away.

With the hope of being left in the parking lot, I concentrated on how the door might be opened from the inside and, as I began figuring out a way to break out of a "standing" trailer, laughter came right up to the ramp-door. The moving guys called out something that rhymed with Binky—it was difficult to make out over the idling of engines and grinding of brakes. I made an executive decision, banging on the trailer's side—Ray didn't stop me, didn't join either. Hard fists against the frame. "We're in here!" I called out.

The guys' voices faded. Seconds later, the trailer lurched, and we were off, meaning "on." On the road again. The less fortunate bit at the back of a Full House move.

Being doomed stowaways moved being regular stowaways up a notch. I tensed for immediate peril, and when nothing happened, I got used to listening to the jolt-click-slide combination that registered with every incline and decline. A mechanical trio of malfunction I'd not heard prior to the vandalism.

Ear popping, caused by elevation changes, required frequent fake yawns, jaw snapping, and lobe pulling.

It suited me that Ray remained mostly silent, though a death-is-ahead confession of her wrongdoings against me would have been welcome. The only thing she did was hum. An ironic way to end her career, humming being kind of a weak version of singing. Though she called songwriting her profession, it was not. She had always penned poorly chosen words to suspiciously familiar melodies—most of which then trailed off into the first line of the melody of "Your Song." She used actual music dictation books, but the talent stopped directly after a stylistic treble clef.

False starts were normal for Ray. Always in and out of rough patches, there had been a steady stream of community helpers to assist her in life-skills. And from these professionals, the child—me—learned how to help mommy instead of chalking giant happy faces on the sidewalk.

Survival had prevailed over childish art. I could navigate my room in the dark from the time I could walk, not because I couldn't reach the light switch, but because light bulbs were a luxury. I was so used to moving that my version of playing house consisted of hauling a vintage suitcase containing a hairbrush and a tube of dry mascara from room to room. I could make a sandwich at three years old, boil the kettle for instant coffee at four, and make generic mac 'n' cheese by the time I started kindergarten.

The thing is, I'd always liked learning, even if it was beyond age appropriate. Some of that liking-to-learn might have started as a toddler, at story time at the library. Ray had a set of friends who hung near there, which worked for her social life. It was there I met Green Jean whose nose was always buried in oversized picture books of faraway places. We became friends—a preschooler and a former professor. Whenever Ray went AWOL, Jean would stay at our place.

Jean taught me so much that by grade one I could read, write, and do simple math, as well as fool school professionals that all was peachy-functional at home. First grade was where a public health nurse recognized me from years before—she immediately cupped her hand around the back of my head. I thought she was stroking me, like a dog lover would do, but she was checking me out—told me there used to be a flat spot there from being left lying in one place for too long; expressed she was pleased it was no longer there.

After that I ran some experiments with soft-skinned fruit and concluded it would take a lot of being left in one spot to dent or reshape the head.

Eight

We reached for each other as soon as the click did not
follow the jolt. C'mon sliiide, we willed out loud.

Another jolt.

Ray's addiction dropped to the floor, my body pitched over
her lap, my chest on her thighs, my knees on Coat.

"We're gonna die," Ray spoke in monotone. She draped her body
over my back and wrapped her arms around my right side.

I extracted her fingernails from my ribs. "Ray, you're already
killing me."

"Gonna die," she droned on, repeatedly, to the tune of something
eerily country-western-funereal.

I pushed harder into her lap while my eyes sank into the darkness
of the chair cushion where crumbs gather and people lose television
remotes. Face to face with Elton John, the force of Ray holding me
pushed the Rocket Man farther until the metal bar beneath the
cushion opened like a fish mouth and swallowed the mug into the
springs.

Ray stayed hunched over me, thrumming on my spine. Sliiide
dammit.

When I blindly reached for the knapsack, to secure it around my wrist, the significance of seatbelts entered my head. "Ray," I said, extracting myself from the twist we'd become, "we don't know how it will all go down. We need to be secure."

Strangely enough, she responded.

In the darkness, Ray delivered a play-by-play of her actions. She'd removed her sweatpants and tied herself into Chair, figuring Chair might bounce around but she'd stay affixed to it.

I had time to imagine her as a gigantic, plaid projectile targeting me.

Putting on Coat and feeling for a tie-down on the trailer's wall, I secured myself to the side railing by wrapping the strap around my torso then cinching the mechanism until the point of hardly being able to breathe. My hoodie became a turban-helmet. I wore it low, so it covered my eyes.

I measured my final words: "If I don't make it, Elton's inside the chair."

My ears registered a series of altitude pops—a sure sign we were at a summit. The entire unit shivered uncontrollably, and then bounced. Something underneath scraped, but I didn't know if it was the hitch end or the ramp end because of the extreme vibration.

I kept a story running in my head: if we stay sorta-hooked, that'll be good till the guys stop again. They might even sense they've got a problem.

Hope is a good thing. Momentum is a scientific thing. The latter began as one might imagine an elevator malfunction.

And then, in all the chaos around our anchored selves, one sound had disappeared. There was no engine. The moving van pulling us had literally left us chasing them in the dark.

But quick forward changed to slow forward and somehow converted to backward motion.

There was a constant sense of imbalance. The gel in my inner ear registered the directional change and sent out *Jell-O Jiggler* messages to my stomach.

"Woo-hoo," cheered the trailer's wheels, "the chaperone's gone. Let's get this party started."

The opening scene of *Hook* appeared before my eyes: the bit when Peter Pan's baby carriage careens down a hill.

It became as rough as Westerns featuring driver-less stagecoaches dragged by spooked horses. Our speed increased to the fairground level of "you have to be taller than this to ride."

Metal scraping against road, grinding, tearing, ripping, shredding. Name any terror onomatopoeia. I expected the floor to rip from underneath us. So loud were the combined sounds that they penetrated my ears through the sweat-suit material of my hoodie head protection. I vibrated inside Coat and remained anchored to the side-rail waiting for everything to split. Even if it had been silent, we could not have called out to each other because of the repetitive shaking of every organ in our bodies.

Thick dust streamed through spaces I hadn't known existed. Cat litter, seed, feathers, and bird poop joined the cloud of gravel dust choking me.

Boxes violently dislodged; my feet became trapped by a loose carton. Then our speed decreased, evidenced by more stretched sounds—but the quality of the ride remained fierce. Given the amount of chattering, I expected to spit teeth.

The strangest thing is that while it might have taken twenty seconds, the entire experience played out in ultra-slow motion; time for the brain to process every micro-second.

And when I couldn't be shaken any more, I begged some great creator by using my thinking inside my head voice: *Let me go now. I don't want to do this anymore.*

And then silence.

Is that all there was to leaving life? That I only had to ask with all my heart, and the "end" was delivered?

It was as if a vacuum had sucked out all the dirt. The scent of pine poured into the trailer. Heaven smelled like floor cleaner.

Swooooooooooosh. Our metal parachute plunged. A nothingness surrounded us. The drop from the road must have been steep. I knew we were airborne; gravity speaks to all body parts.

And then: contact. A soft scraping under, on top, all sides and ends of the trailer—like we were in some sadistic carwash with monster brushes.

We were in the trees. I anticipated a large branch skewering us. Dark on dark in my head, my crazy brain registered the words, Ray-kabob. I quickly dismissed the accompanying image.

We swooshed then slowed. Though I was forced against my restraints, there was time for my body to recover before being jerked around again. I waited to be hit by box or budgie cage, but we stayed pretty much solid as my stomach rolled and pitched as we plunged.

The "highway and gravel shoulder" phase had been relatively quick compared to the "sail off the edge and the plunge." There was time to categorize phase one while experiencing phase two. As we plummeted, I waited for us to flip. My brain anticipated increased blood flow from being upside down, but it didn't happen.

It seemed a random act of kindness from nature. Something incredible like the densely needled branches of huge trees parting enough to cushion our fall, offering safe passage to the ground, in stages.

In reality it probably wasn't that graceful, but it was miraculous. The trees helped slow and steer us through the air—breaking the fall —over and over.

Our landing was springy. I imagined the forest floor containing thousands of years of pine needles. Nothing grew under fir trees, not even in the city when people intentionally planted stuff. That kind of needle buildup was tantamount to a feather bed. The hitch must have become a combination of anchor and rudder, digging into hundreds of years of humus.

We were shaken and stirred. The only image I held as I lost consciousness was of Ray standing at my grave. She was asking herself how she would go on without me. Even my semi-conscious imaginings were laced with realism and sarcasm—the words "as if" bursting into the visualization. Still, within the mind-movie, her face came closer until there were only teardrops. My eyes zoomed in on them as if they were crystals or diamonds. It was all over, and the afterlife was just beyond the close-up glittering.

The imagined teardrops came into focus and became stars casting a soft light through a hole in the trailer's roof. My turban lay unwound at my feet. A bare-legged Ray tipped backward in Plaid Chair, which rested on its back feet. A moonbeam travelled through the jagged opening in the roof and set about illuminating her with a Tinkerbell spark over her heart. I watched her chest rise and fall. Suspended somewhere between heaven and hell, I was glad she was semi-alive with me. Because I would not be alone? So that I could cling to the hope someone could care for me? My brain-lens closed the shutter and registered that the picture, stars and all, would become one of those totally recallable frames of life. As I remained tethered to the inside support bar of the trailer, wrapped in arms of Coat, the stars went out.

Nine

My eyes opened with a commitment to consciousness. Chair was empty.

Powerful blue filled a jagged opening above me. I un-ratcheted myself from the railing and clambered on the arm of Chair, then pulled myself through the roof to see the biggest sky ever.

Other than the hole that made a handy exit, the trailer seemed okay. The unit was upright and reasonably level. My eyes followed a ladder molded into the outer shell, stretching from roof to base. Years before, at the Pick-Your-Part auto-wrecking yard, I'd seen a row of holiday trailers rendered irreparable, their sides ripped off by Southern Alberta's high winds; I decided this particular trailer must have been manufactured from kryptonite on some super planet.

I clung to the handrail and took in the view of everything around me. Ray was fully dressed, leaning on a stick, staring at a colourful beach-bag and a tree stump at her feet. I zoomed out, squaring an imaginary border around the two provinces of Alberta and British Columbia, to get some idea of how many million square miles surrounded the thumbtack that was us.

A human periscope, I scanned high and wide for the highway.

Where were the crashed-through spaces? Which trees had held out their branches, taking our weight for a few seconds, cushioning our fall? Where was our pine-needled path?

In the dizziness of turning, I remembered a news story I'd seen as a kid. A woman had dropped her baby from the Capilano suspension bridge in Vancouver. It was on the news for ages because of the controversy about whether it had been accidental. The shaky, amateur video from a tourist, when slowed, clearly showed how the branches of the trees had interrupted the total drop, one by one, breaking the one-year-old child's fall every three or four feet. The child landed unscathed.

I flicked a piece of cat litter off my cheek before rechecking Ray. She massaged her neck with one hand while she, too, took in our surroundings. An open dry-grassy plot, surrounded by mountains, enveloped by more mountains, layered by thick forest, next door to no one.

To maintain perspective, I made up a tree clock. Naming the largest and closest tree to the trailer as Three O'clock Tree put Ray at Six. I finished assigning numbers to the other trees. When I looked at Ray again, she was sitting on the stump, poking through the contents of the bag. All of a sudden, she straightened. "Koda, lookee here. A book. *Ten Days to Personal Freedom: Recovery and Survival for Life.*" She waved it about, like she'd struck gold.

She'd taken it literally. Like a self-help book was going to save us.

"Eureka," I said.

"I reek of what?" she asked.

The wave of arrogance, for being top dog in knowing more words than her, ranked me superior but created discomfort at the same time.

At first, she read silently—lips moving.

"Day One." She yelled the words like some people do when they speak to a person who is hearing impaired, as if increasing the volume bestowed the gift of hearing on the listener. When the echo of "Day

One" boomeranged back she startled, then looked around. She shouted it again, waiting for the word-ricochet.

She registered her echo and seemed satisfied we were alone, then continued: "Take inventory of your surroundings."

She trotted toward the trailer and stood beneath me. From my position on the roof I checked her head for lacerations, and read from high over her shoulder. Not that there was much to read. One bold statement followed by two blank pages.

Something had jarred her brain and restarted her motor. I checked out a blob of congealed blood on my jeans; a cut on my thigh I decided I'd hide. Given her energy, she might want to sew it together with something that was no doubt in the pile of crap we'd landed with.

"Oh, I get it," she said, flipping back and forth. "One for writing the inventory, and the next one blank. Uh-huh, uh-huh, so you don't peek ahead to the next day."

As usual, I let her have her fantasy, humming a few bars of, "Oh sure, Ray, we're really going to survive." The fact we hadn't died during the fall simply increased our chances of starving to death. That, or we'd kill each other.

She became a Dickens' character wandering the streets of Victorian London, using her stick like a walking cane. While I was melting into the steel roof, and thinking about making my jeans into cut-offs, she climbed the ladder and inserted herself into the trailer. Minutes later she emerged with a mechanical pencil and a heating-pad, totally absorbed in her own craziness.

To a stranger it would have appeared that she had done this before, landing in the wilderness and setting up house, a regular Mrs. Robinson from the marooned Swiss family of fairy tale times. Disney would have signed her on the spot.

By the time I'd started to tear my jeans into long shorts, she'd wrapped the heating-pad cord around the Six O'clock Tree and used a clippie thing—probably meant for attaching the pad to a blanket—to secure the book at Day One. It reminded me of a Home Sweet Home sign normal families put up.

She was pissing me off by calmly embracing the situation. But I let her have her fun; it couldn't last forever. I hoped to have a geographical solution before she left fantasyland.

She cleaned away some deadfall at the base of Six O'clock. Seriously, if a mountain goat had wandered by, she would have wrestled it to the ground, sheered it, spun the wool, and knit a sweater. Maybe all the years of being totally pathetic had somehow run out and the fall had dislodged something and shifted her to competency.

"I'm going to find the road," I said. "Make sure you chink the walls when you've got the cabin up."

Ten

We'd fallen off the earth and only the two of us knew we'd disappeared. No one knew where we were. We didn't even know where we were. That put me into a survival stupor of sorts.

The appeal to stay in camp and claim the spoils danced in and out of the trees like the Pied Piper. The trailer held more stuff than we'd ever had—our apartments were often rented furnished. It would have been like Christmas if not for being stranded in the middle of nowhere.

Endearing scenes of Laura Ingalls Wilder at her little house on the prairie flashed through my mind. I stopped counting the boxes at twenty-two. It was so "our luck" to be no place with tons of stuff. I stuck to what I'd told Ray—that I'd go find the road.

I set off, checking out the patches of earth which looked as if a humongous golf club had been used to take divots out of the forest floor. The gouges had to be where the hitch had dug into the earth. The depressions led to the edge of a stand of trees. The road had to be somewhere beyond and, obviously, up—we had, after all, fallen. I continued through the woods in a narrow, pine-needle-strewn line that followed a haphazard path.

I became so caught up in tracking our trailer-footprints that I stubbed my toe and bumped my head into a wall. The rocky outcrop rose right out of the ground in a vertical barrier. Up and up it went.

Flip flops proved ineffective for climbing. I managed to scramble about five feet. Even if I'd had mountaineering footwear, I couldn't have made it. The terrain needed those anchor-thingies hammered into the rock, and pulleys to navigate the face. And if I could have gotten up to the top, then what? It wouldn't be like following an outlet mall map to find an Old Navy. There'd be decisions to make as to which direction the road might be.

Somewhere above was the road to home. Between me and that road was the massive void we'd come through. I kicked at the mountain in frustration, dislodging a few stones. One hit me on the head. The sharp pain cancelled the throb in my toe.

Face it, Dakota, you are an urban survivor, I told myself. You've never even been to a girl-scout meeting. I turned and came face to face with two streaks of claw marks on a trunk. The shredded bark on the ground made me hightail it back to camp.

There'd be another way out. Had to be. I remained on the periphery and watched Ray. I had time to search for the drumbeat. Perhaps the altitude had thinned it to an inaudible frequency that say, only certain animals could hear.

"You're not doing it right," I said.

"Whaaat?" She elongated the word in her vintage meow-like-a-cat voice.

"The deadfall. You can't make a bench that way, if that's what you're trying to do."

"Might be. Might not be." She lapsed into four-year-old mode, which made me reasonably happy to rise above her in the conversation.

"*Whaaat* I mean is there'll be nothing to brace it." I couldn't help mimicking. "Be better off leaning them against the trailer, so they have support and we can have a backrest."

"You're right, but the trailer starts above ground," she said.

"You're right." I found myself playing the repeating game, but not playing the repeating game. My age was upside down and inside out. I needed time to get perspective. There would be another way out. I was sore, perhaps even feverish. Survival shock told me to shut up and concentrate on building a bench.

We discovered that vertically anchoring smaller pieces of deadfall between the ground and the triangular hitch frame made a stronger foundation for the seat. Why we began to construct something to sit on instead of figuring out what we were going to eat, or building a huge help sign, is beyond me. It was what we did.

"Don't use that one." She snatched her walking cane from in front of me.

"Okay. Okay," I said. Her possessive sting hung in the air. "Special is it?"

"Yeah. It's my special stick." She used it to wave away some bugs before propping it against Six O'clock Tree.

"It's like your staff." Outplaying her word "stick" with "staff" kept me intellectually ahead while trying to mend the error of mistaking it for construction material.

"And when I have broken the staff of your life, ten women shall bake your bread in one oven." Ray lifted it to the sky.

I shuddered.

"Leviticus 26:26," said Ray.

"Fine with me. Keep your silly stick." I continued to tremble, considered myself safer with the bear than the crazed. I moved off to find more tree trunks, leaving her to spend quality time with her wooden friend.

Eleven

"Outstanding." I congratulated us while checking out the sun's position. "And we did it on the north side for shade."

She raised her hand as if to smack me. I ducked, but halfway through bending realized she wanted a high five, so I readjusted and brought up my hand to complete my side of the celebratory clap. A twinge of happiness for teamwork and an attack of confusion overwhelmed me. Unsure how to react, my mouth opened, and words spilled out. "Whoa it's hot."

"A scorcher," said Ray.

"A scorcher? You sound like a cowboy grandpa."

"Sure as shootin' do." She tipped an invisible Stetson then stared at the bench. I tried the shady seat. She plopped down next to me and stayed in character. "Mighty fine. Mighty fine, yes indeedy."

I held back laughter, enjoying the bench too much to comment.

She stared at Six O'clock Tree. Day One clung to the heating pad clip in the breezeless day. "Well, ma'am, I reckon we gotta corral it all. You ready to mosey and take inventory?" she asked, as if we were about to brand cattle.

While the north side of the trailer was benched and shaded by large trees, the south side gave me reason to consider the melting temperature of metal. We moved to the ramp-door, taking time to examine a few dents. Ray started up again: "Well there missy, we gotta open it, and empty it so we can sleep in her, which means if we don't get it closed, which is likely what yer thinkin', then we leave ourselves open to—"

"Being eaten by grizzlies?" I finished for her.

"Grizzly. One, ma'am. Them bears they's loners. Less a'course we be dealin' with a sow, then she be totin' a couple a cubs. Dangerous mama then, don't-cha know it."

"That's reassuring." A smart-ass reply was necessary because I didn't want to recognize her knowing nature facts. I'm not sure which I feared more, a grizzly or scary cowgirl Ray.

We released several sets of solid metal rods, one of us to a side, working the puzzle of lifts, twists, and slides.

The bolt on my side slid across smoothly, but Ray had to hit the stubborn left-side bolt with a stumpy piece of wood. She smiled. "Houston, we're a go." Now she was a space cowgirl.

After we'd placed the weight of the ramp door on the ground, she tested it on a walk up, then looked up at the cloudless sky. "It'll be fine to spread it all out—it's not gonna rain." Her effortless switch from cowgirl to weathergirl did not bring any comment from me. There probably hadn't been a cloud in the sky for months. What little grass existed was so crunchy it might not have rained forever.

"Wait." She touched my arm, so I knew she was serious. "Before we empty it, I have to know it will go up and close. If it doesn't, we've got time to fix it before it goes dark."

"We're gonna die anyway," I said.

"We're all terminal," she replied.

I considered the genetic link of cynicism while we each claimed a side of the door-ramp and lifted it halfway.

"It'll go up," I said. "And we've got lots of time."

"You think?"

"It came down, so it'll go up." I waited on her decision—to unpack or to close it and open it again. We swatted at bugs that tried to take pieces of our skin away. Then a barking dog caught our attention.

"We're saved," I said. I looked around for friend of man's best friend. Then I remembered Binky: the budgie that barked. My secret vow to the little boy surfaced. A frantic search led to finding the cage on its side.

"You can watch us little sweetie," said a sickly sweet, maternal Ray as she reattached his cage to the metal beam.

His reply chirp seemed optimistic. Rescued from the clutches of his neglectful family and into the warm bosom of Mother Ray, his life had improved about three percent or a thousand, depending on those polled.

The bottom of his cage was wet. Bits of seed and newspaper had become stuck to his wings. He did not respond to my chirpy sounds that were supposed to encourage him to his perch; could probably tell my sentiment was laced with sibling jealousy. But he performed for Ray and climbed up his purple ladder to the perch beside his blue plastic likeness, a twin ornamental budgie.

Most of his seed was still inside a feeder that had a bit of a trap-door that only let so much out at a time. This was a good thing, Ray indicated with a smile and a pointy finger. She frowned at his empty water container, slid out the bottom tray of his cage, and squeezed water from the newspaper into his dish.

"Clever." I praised her, and then continued with an enthusiastic theme. "They'll come get us. They'll figure out where the trailer came off and come find it."

Her smile faded. "Sure, they'll report it missing, but not right away."

"How do you know?"

"They'd been boozin'. At the truck stop. Or maybe behind the truck stop."

And I knew that if anyone knew slurring, even through walls of steel, Ray would. Even through kryptonite.

"Besides, it's junk," she said. "The insurance company will write a cheque."

"We're not junk." I looked at her seriously.

Memory continually cycles. Something happens, like ensuring Binky had food, and that triggers something else. In my case, remembering the contents of the knapsack. We spent a satisfying time on the bench, dipping cardboard spatulas into the peanut butter jar. We became so involved in the meal we forgot about the bugs.

"You're sure the ramp will close okay?" She took a bite out of the cardboard, sucking up all the absorbed oil and flavour. And then we got to work.

Our system of categorizing boxes consisted of moving the ones with descriptive labels to one side, and going through the ones with sketchy abbreviations on them. After two weighty boxes of trashy paperbacks, we figured RN stood for Romance Novels. All future boxes with those letters—and there were an unhealthy too many— were put aside without checking inside.

As for the protocol of sorting: when we saw an immediate purpose for anything, we'd temporarily abandon the inventory and creatively apply the item—like when we discovered a shower curtain, we immediately repurposed it for the hole in the roof.

Eventually most of the boxes ended up stacked outside the trailer. I'd done the lifting and Ray'd used the blank sheet from the survival book to list all the contents, rather than writing some kind of emotions the book had directed for the first day of the program.

Though we had a bench, Ray thought if we brought out Chair, we could put it on the west side and have a sunset viewing area. Her point being that along with the child's highchair we'd uncovered, we could create a sun porch.

Each of our butts was skinny enough to fit in the child's seat, but with her prior claim to the plaid throne I knew I'd be baby. It was confirmed when she collapsed onto cushioned comfort. In Britain there's a huge telecommunication company called Sky TV. Mine and Ray's was a much larger sky. In the end, we'd created a version of retired couples' recliners in front of the largest screen ever, permanently tuned to all-nature programming.

Ray smiled approvingly at the arrangements, then rose to work again, zigzagging a heavy box of RN's as a coffee table between the chairs. "Our library," she boasted.

Inside the trailer, Ray made two narrow mattresses out of the quilted moving pad-blankets. The side-by-side beds, though narrow, worked for our body types. Mine was topped with Coat and hers with three embroidered tablecloths. Rolled dinosaur curtains became pillows for each of us.

Directly below the hole, between the head of the sleeping arrangement—which was at the tapered end, not the ramp-door end—she stacked two boxes of steamy paperbacks and reinforced the top with a child's blackboard. "Our staircase to heaven," she said. Then, as if I was thick, demonstrated repeatedly, stepping up, pulling herself up through the hole, then dropping back down.

"Works." I interrupted loudly to stop the remedial demo.

The sun had not quite set. A final burst of energy was applied to my suggestion that we number the boxes and write those numbers on the list of contents. She was nice about the idea, like she had been about Coat—more proof she'd sustained a brain injury. Dislodged cells had allowed electrons to fire, loosening her hardwiring to create a chemical line-up that equaled "improved." It was possible nature had provided a lobotomy.

We found more linens and books, and a fondue set without the pot—the stand, fuel, and forks. A fishing tackle box contained craft supplies, a slow cooker's ceramic roaster with an ill-fitting lid sans its electric cradle, matches, bubble bath, and candles. Felt pens, crayons, highlighters, Bic brand blue, red, black, and even green, had been randomly thrown amongst everything. Maybe the old cat lady had packed her own stuff; tossed in all the pens in a frenzied protest after a final diary entry that said she wasn't going to no old folks' home.

The box containing my dress and Lifebook showed up on my bed. Surprisingly, Ray hadn't asked about it or opened it.

Eclectic as our collection was, we admitted it was quite a haul. A windfall in a finders-keepers kind of way: useful only if we were found, essential for some form of survival.

We decided it had been a good day's work. Ray wanted to get the ramp up and secure. I agreed to close-up after one more job—I wanted to extend our coffee table a bit more by grabbing another box of RN's.

Which is when I discovered the box that would save our lives.

Twelve

~∂∞∂~

"**R**ay," I called as if she was far away. We listened to the box slosh as I rocked it.

"Sloshing means liquid," said Ray.

"Liquid has to mean food. We deserve that," I said.

The packing deception required an excavation. Layers revealed a diet book, rubber jump rope, a receipt for $375.00 from a company called Vi-Canada, and food glorious liquid food. Four shallow boxes held rows of pull-tab cans of meal replacements. Two flats of chocolate and two of strawberry. On the poorly-applied labels were basic stick-sketches, representing women of various ethnicities who were even thinner than me, above small print: Yummy Tummy Meal Replacement Incorporated.

A third package, inside the main box, was filled with the kind of meal replacements meant for the opposite of dieting. High-calorie protein shakes to boost the nutrition of immune-compromised senior citizens. I'd seen them stacked near the incontinence products at Carter's drugstore. I pictured the granny with the long thin cat and gave thanks for her nutritional deficiency and her preference for vanilla—unless this flavour had been rejected after one taste test.

I went with the Yummy Tummy drinks; chugged a strawberry, then savoured a container of chalky chocolate from the comfort of the west facing library room.

"I'm really glad people don't stick to their diets," said Ray.

"Those others must belong to Cat Granny," I said.

"Did you know people can't survive without liquid for more than three days?" Ray asked.

"So, what if we hadn't found these?" I held up my two empties.

"We'd have found something to drink. Animals must be finding something."

"What animals?" I pointed in multiple directions with the tin cans, conveniently forgetting the bear claw gouges on the tree at the bottom of the vertical mountain wall. "And thanks for not mentioning the seventy-two-hour thing until now."

"You're welcome."

She'd never understood sarcasm.

She licked her lips. "We should finish the inventory. There might be more... foodstuffs." I'd never heard her say that unusual word before, but I shrugged off my evaluation because I totally agreed: there could be more foodstuffs in wrongly labeled boxes.

We jiggled every romance novel box, but heard nothing sloshy. Then she had an idea: food didn't have to slosh to be food. At that point we tore into all the RN boxes and hit pay dirt with a case of pop-top canned cat food. Twenty-four Under The Sea meals with reduced "something we couldn't pronounce" to promote urinary function in mature felines. The same carton held a half-filled bag of cat kibble and a box of budgie seed.

Other than the occasional work of contemporary fiction, and an interesting set of science books which we stockpiled separately, the remaining romance novel boxes remained true to their anonymous, lustful packer.

We were happy exhausted, bug-bitten and muscle-sore, proud of our accomplishments, and thrilled with the finds.

And then, it was like the sun said, "Just a minute I'm popping out for—" and didn't have time to finish its sentence. Mountain shadow blended with a navy sky and we hadn't closed the ramp.

"GET THE OTHER SIDE." Ray decided, if she shouted what I was already doing, it would make the ramp go up faster. "Lift, pull, and buckle it." The order was panicked.

"It's not a belt," I said.

She moved her side of the ramp like it was a blanket, which made it bounce in my hands. I was as amazed by her strength as I was livid at her futile suggestion. Even if we could make it go up—and it didn't seem to want to go all the way—we'd have a hard time seeing the mechanism to bolt it.

As she became more anxious, she upped the volume of her demands to secure the trailer.

"Ray, put it down. Gently. Yes, that's it. You're doing great."

Her fear of the dark gave in to my soft commands and we lowered the ramp.

"But Koda, you said it would be okay," she whimpered.

A few stars appeared and my eyes became accustomed to the surroundings so that I could poke and smell my way to the bathroom box. A minute later the yellow-duck-candle secured inside an empty YT can eased her fear.

"There, Koda." She pointed to a piece of metal in need of a bit of bending. She sought out the clomping wood she'd used earlier. After two misses and one firm connecting blow the metal was out of the way.

"On three," I called out.

Whoosh. Instantly her side was higher than mine. I had to make my muscles catch up with my hands. "Who taught you to count? That wasn't even two."

"We should leave the ramp up," she said breathlessly. "Always use the top as our entrance. You never know when the hinge might go.

When we'd passed the candle down through the roof opening, we settled and then blew it out. "We can't waste anything," I said.

"We can learn about how much time there is before we lose the sun," she answered in her calm, I'm-safe-inside voice.

"We can learn to go to bed by moonlight," I romanticized.

"Or starlight." Ray's words drifted about.

I didn't want to spoil the mood by ranting about having learned to negotiate all my bedrooms, all through the years, without light bulbs. My arm snagged the sharp piece in Coat, but a pain in my thigh took priority. Then the rest of my body began to ache, a lot. I wondered if Ray hurt too. We might be suffering delayed whiplash from falling off the earth.

My feet bumped the unopened box containing my dress and Lifebook. I pre-dreamed about things we'd unpacked and repacked. A second shower curtain, magnetized fridge letters and numbers, china cups and saucers that Ray'd placed over a tablecloth on the box coffee table—she'd put her Elton mug alongside the china and filled it with the pens we kept finding. In the blur of my pre-dream it wasn't clear if they were real china cups.

I snuggled into my faux-fur bed-nest, drifting in and out.

"Whoa," sleep-talked Ray in a bit of a snore-snort.

"You okay?" I asked.

"I wasn't sleeping."

"Were too."

She turned over. I adjusted my own body. We'd never slept together before. It was strange and special at the same time. If we'd have been attacked by a bear, it wouldn't have been nice, but we hadn't been, so it was survival-nice. She sang spontaneous original lyrics to the tune of a nursery rhyme. Not "Mary Had a Little Lamb," not "Rock-a-bye Baby." Something in-between.

The moon and the stars they are our night light. No leck-tris-sit-tee near this place. The moon and the stars they are our right light. So far are we from the human race.

It turned low and hymnal; faded with her trademark salute to Elton, *It's a little bit funny, this feeling inside.* Weirdly comforting.

Thirteen

⁓⁂⁓

When the sun made it too hot to sleep in, I emerged through the shower curtain topper to: "Hey, sleepyhead."

Her mommyishness was chronic.

The lofty perch inspired me to flap my arms, which reminded me of Binky. I stuck my head inside the trailer and saw him sitting beside his little plastic twin. With the identical model beside him, and a mirror reflecting both of them, it looked like he had three bird buddies. I eased down to see if I could surprise him with my reflection, but shocked myself, seeing a portion of my face—totally sunburned.

I poked out again. Ray'd been busy. Opened boxes showcased more items which I guessed Ray was prioritizing. I hadn't told her about running into the vertical wall, or started any more conversations about finding a way out. Not that I was treating it as a vacation, but it was only our second day. The urgency to leave had eased since we'd found food. I wanted more time to think about what to do next.

Squinting hurt from taut skin. "You been up a while?"

"I been up a while, child." She did a reggae dance as she popped open a chocolate Yummy Tummy. She'd woven wooden beads into her hair. The braids were secured by several Barbie barrettes. She took a swig of the opened drink, then shook a tin of strawberry and pointed it at me. I slid down the ladder, ignoring my throbbing leg, flipped the tray over the back of the highchair, and parked myself in the seat.

"Check this over to see if I missed anything." Her head bobbled to the inventory list on the outdoor, cardboard-box coffee table.

I waited to see if she'd hand me the can she'd sipped from or toss me the new one, but her words distracted me. "Whoa, Koda, you're really red." She brushed back her bangs and resecured them in a barrette, then winced, revealing a white stripe where her hair had— the day before—protected her forehead. "Oh my God, we're both sunburned." She ouched as she started to bend her arms. "Sheesus Koda, my skin feels too tight for my skeleton."

There was only one thing for me to do: secure the full strawberry.

"What's this?" I asked, showing her the permanent-markered #1 on the side of the can.

"Yummy Tummy. YT."

"I know *whaaat* it is, Ray." I changed my voice so as to make her the stupid one.

"I mean this." I pointed to the black #1 on the side.

"That's your ration number. I've done the math. We can have a couple a day, for a month, plus Under The Sea. Then we can have the Granny drink after that."

"A couple each?"

"Yes, each." She frowned, which must have hurt. But it didn't prevent her from prolonging her disapproval of my dissing her math.

Surely, we wouldn't be here for a month. What made her think a month? Could we be here longer? I clambered back into the overheated trailer. The box labeled YT KODA had three layers of three rows by six cans for a total of fifty-four—not quite two a day for a month. The small box of budgie seed had been inserted to keep my rows tight and orderly. YT RAY appeared as a jumble of tins—impossible to count, but fewer than mine. I wanted to tell her the drinks made for the infirm and aged were more nutritious than the YT's, but was too messed up by her generosity.

When I next saw her, her face was completely white. She came at me with a jar of cream and I forgot about the whole we-should-drink-the-Cat-Granny-drink-first-because-it's-more-nutritious concept.

"Diaper cream?" I turned up my nose.

"Suit yourself." She made the sounds of relief while soothing her arms. I watched her skin absorb it, then surrendered to the salve.

"Props to you, Ray, on the cream idea." I'd decided to be nice after applying instant first-aid to my face, arms, and legs. She'd been smart to keep her sweatpants long, too, but I chose to save that compliment tidbit. It was my practice to bank her positives when they showed up, because they showed up so infrequently and were required for pep talks during her low times.

She collapsed in Chair and directed me from there, shaking her empty #4 can toward the book attached to the tree by the heating-pad and clip. I walked over and read aloud. "Day Two. Today list five things for which you are grateful."

I continued with silent reading. *The inventory and gratitude list are paramount in forming a knowledge base from which to move forward. Your life is about to change. You are about to learn the techniques of survival.* It was too creepy to read on. I returned and leaned on Chair's arm, evaluating Ray's little blocked printing on a page she had torn out of the survival book. Turned out there were other pages, blank ones, and some with questions and blank spaces, meant to be used, even removed, by tearing each along a perforated line. The deal was to fill them out and place them into a pocket inside the cover of the book. Ray had the Day One's inventory in front of her, and a sheet for Day Two's work which was adamant that the participant create a gratitude list.

She'd grabbed a paperback novel to lean on. The headshot of a nun was featured in an oval frame superimposed on a raunchy cover —a sort of separate entity from the rest of the illustration—a castle background overlaid by an anatomically enhanced couple who held each other in what might be described as enraptured embrace. Large breasts and massive biceps took up a quarter of the page.

The nun in the oval appeared to have been staring directly into a camera's lens. She wore a wimple—the traditional headgear of a habit —and maintained a neutral expression to suggest nonjudgement. It was the kind of combination cover where the nun in the oval would appear on many books within a series.

"It's a Sister Gabriella novella," said Ray. "I've seen her on TV. She's a miracle worker for sure." Ray held the mechanical pencil and revealed a blank page ready for Day Two's work.

"You know it's fiction, right?" I asked.

A flattened cardboard box invited me to sit on it as if it was a floor cushion. I sipped my YT and returned her stare. Poised with pen and book, she was ready to write, and I knew what she wanted me to do. I knew I wanted to make her speak first, so I applied a steady gaze, keeping it slightly below glare with an if-I-do-this-long-enough-you'll-talk scale.

"Five things, Koda." She held the pencil, ready to take dictation.

"I'd have to look through all this crap to find five," I said casually, while recording my made-her-talk-first victory.

"I don't think they mean that, Koda."

"I know." A short reply because I was inviting everything chemical-strawberry to dance with my taste buds.

"C'mon, fess up, five things you're grateful for."

"Fess?" I rolled my eyes, but Tinkerbell made an appearance overtop of Ray, highlighting her hair. It made her look pretty. She may have taken physical inventory on day one, but now she was taking day two as the survival guide intended—emotionally.

"C'mon." She smiled. And for a few seconds, with the two effects, hair and smile, as well as the extra YT in my box, I liked her a little bit more.

But I wasn't going down that road; my gratitude was not going to be touchy feely as the book intended. Avoiding the obvious: air, water, shelter—and the obscure: sperm donor, egg donor—I recited flatly, "Highchair, extra-special plaid chair, YT, shower curtain, and that fake fur coat."

I spoke of Coat and Chair in a lower-case way, and made Chair better than Coat so she'd think she was better off with Chair, and not try to claim Coat out of jealousy.

"Dakota Starr Harrison, those are inventory items. The exercise requires, erm, bigger..."

I knew she meant profound but wasn't inclined to give her a vocabulary lesson since she'd used my full name.

"I don't have five non-inventory things," I replied, mildly impressed at her use of the phrase "exercise requires."

"You must."

"I don't. And I'd rather pick from what we have."

Her head turned in a spinny-huff. She'd attempted to make me choose items from life, specifically with her on it.

The heat must have been getting to me because I gave in easily. "Books," I said, gesturing toward the real literature stored a safe distance from the RN's. Our library included a unique set of scientific history books in a format I'd never seen at the library; scientists in alphabetical order and the stuff they were famous for. "Not necessarily these books. Just books. Five books."

An eagle soared so high she could only be identified by her call.

We both watched the dot of her until the blue sky had completely absorbed her wings.

I knew Ray was waiting for me to ask her what she was grateful for. I savoured my drink, then conceded and put the question to her in the same words the book had used.

"Okay, Ray. List five things for which you are grateful."

"From life or inventory?" she asked.

"Inventory." I didn't want intimacy, to not hear my name.

"Aha, only from our inventory. Playing it safe eh? Let's see. YT, trailer, Plaid Chair, candle, fondue, matches."

"You don't get six. It says five."

"Too bad. You didn't choose from life, so I get one more from the inventory. Besides the last two can be joined to one. Fondue-matches."

"Touché."

"Huh?"

"You win." I clarified it for her.

"Touché means you win? In what language?"

"Swahili." I was deadpan.

"Oh. Thanks. I appreciate when you tell me things I don't know."

"I'm touched." I decided to say the meaning without clarification. That way it was on record—I'd told her what it meant, just not directly.

A clean letter-size sheet of paper appeared in my head. Magic typewriting began to appear one letter after the other. Below a centred header titled Gratitude List. 1. A functioning brain. 2. The ability to reason.

"Whaaatcha doooin', Koda?"

"Thinking."

"About whaaat?"

"Nothing."

"You can't think of nothing, Koda."

"You do it all the time," I said.

I watched the pen slide around in her diaper-creamed, greasy grip. "I'm doing Day Two for real," she said. "I intend to graduate." Her eyes returned to the paper, tongue out between her lips, a clear sign of her multitasking.

When she finished, she came toward me and wafted the paper. "I have nothing to hide," she said.

From up close, grey cat hairs stuck to her moisturized skin. Score one for Coat, I thought. It's not infested with cat cooties like Chair.

I'd never paid attention to her printing until she'd done the inventory—never read any of her songs, only saw her fake music notation.

Her printing was neater than mine. Tiny, consistent, blocked upper case. I liked that I liked it. I was learning about her, even though tomorrow we might be dead from an animal attack, or in a while from dehydration, starvation, or fried by the heat of the sun.

"Ray, the trailer's gonna be an oven. We should make some place to sleep outdoors, in case we can't sleep inside. Maybe some kind of tent on the north side by the bench."

"It cools at night. It'll be fine inside."

"I know, but in case we can't get in it, like if the sides are frying-pan hot and the inside hellish."

"I can't sleep outside unless there's a campfire and there's no way I'd ever light one here. One spark and the whole valley'd go up like…" She ran out of description.

"You mean what's not already on fire," I said, admitting we were in a tinderbox. The sky might be blue, but the band of haze in the distance could not be ignored. We may not have watched the news much, but we'd lived in the west long enough to know about forest fire season.

"Koda, I'm not sleeping outside."

The rest of the day was spent completing a detailed inventory. There were a lot of curtains. Some had been repurposed as paint drop-cloths, others were covered in residue: soap or a patina of age, we never could tell. A few were from a period of time when purple and rust were trendy. A pair of pleated drapes held interest for us in being some kind of mustard mixed with green. We decided to call the unrecognizable colour gaudy puke. There were baby, toddler, and kid themes on various valances.

"What a waste. How many window coverings should a family own?" I said.

The problem with having no inner dialogue is that thoughts spill out the mouth as quickly as they develop in the head, sort of like hitting print to connect to an unreliable printer, during a paper shortage, before you've spell-checked. Ray incorrectly identified my out-loud thinking as a conversational opportunity, and as an excuse to slide out of her chair and recline on the flattened empty box on the dry ground.

"So much stuff," she said. She held the lower part of her walking stick tightly. It rose way above her head, on account of her yogi-ing on the cardboard on the ground. The sun seemed to liberate her from restlessness. I ventured further, dared to believe the sun's power released some of her selfishness. I imagined, looking at her from a distance, she might seem like a symbol of something: Goddess of Sticks and Trailers, maybe.

I angled myself to get some of the same elixir. Waves of solar energy pulsed through me. A part of me was the head of a pin on the face of the earth. Another part made me the master of my universe, with the forces of nature at my command. Reality dictated I, Dakota Starr Harrison, was stranded in the mountains with a crazy woman.

Everything that unsettled me validated Ray. She had arrived and thrived. No rent, no rules, no responsibility. Ignorance really was bliss. Bathed in the powerful forces of nature, almost certain to starve, possibly to be consumed by soon-to-reach-us forest fires, or eaten by wild animals, Ray's naivety greeted a fresh start.

"We'll do it tomorrow." She cracked open a YT, continuing to be out of step with her ration. "A shade tent, sure. To sleep in. Right. Tomorrow. And I'll wrap some trees with gaudy-puke curtains for some toy-let privacy. I been going in the bush over there. You?"

"TMI, Ray."

She tossed me a can of YT as though we were guys out on the ranch with a couple of cold ones. I recognized her action as avoidance. She'd never sleep outside in the dark.

She pitched her next futile idea. "We can boil water in these cans over the fondue candley-fuel-thingy. You know, to purify it. Then we can pour it into a jug of some kind. We're gonna need a jug to collect it in, after it's been purified." She used the word purified as if she was proud of it, scientific-like.

"Poquito problem," I said. Spanish is such a gentle-sounding language. She looked through me. "Small problem. Where is this water we will boil?"

"Oh, we'll find some, Koda."

The sun had made her deliriously optimistic. I wanted in. I needed to be a part of it.

"Five things," I said. "The ability to read. The gift of sight. Imagination. Being healthy, like not having any kind of horrible affliction like leprosy. And, erm, not being alone out here—like being with you, here." I'd said it and the world had not exploded.

I drew in a deep breath, exhaling long and slow, while watching Ray retrieve the page she'd previously waved in front of me from the pouch in the book, clipped to the heating-pad, attached to the tree.

She placed the page in my hand as if it were a fragile ornament.

DAY TWO
RAYLENE STARR HARRISON IS THANKFULL FOR
1 MY DAUGTHER
2 MOTHER NATURE

3 LIBRARYS
4 PLAD CHAIR
5 MUSICAL TALENT – SONG WRITING

The humour of her fifth helped me un-choke the emotion of her first.

Fourteen

~⌀~

Ray worked ahead of the class, wrapping a group of trees as promised to make a fabric-walled outhouse.

When she'd finished, I limped over and installed the stack of Dairy Queen napkins, and the toilet roll I'd had in my backpack. Twigs made a good roll-hanger and a rock held down the napkins.

Ray'd formed a depression and set up a triangle of sticks over which to squat. Hinged metal salad servers sat on the opened bag of cat litter. I did my business in the hole, then covered my waste with a scoop of litter.

Even at the outhouse, the bugs seemed fewer; either the hint of smoke in the air had moved them on to greener pastures or they'd sucked every last drop of energy from us and were full. Maybe we'd developed immunity, or the diaper cream repelled them.

I spent the rest of the afternoon skimming chapters of the *Scientists in History* books we'd named mini-encyclos. Ray busied herself in and out of the trailer and collecting things from the forest. Eventually, she settled and took a stab at the Sister Gabriella series. Today's survival agenda had been handled and the survival book was page-ready for tomorrow.

We shared two more diet drinks. So much for Ray's math; at the rate we were drinking it wouldn't last long and neither would we. A downdraft of physical weakness and mental exhaustion overwhelmed me, so I used my last bit of energy to climb on to the roof and drop through the hole. My unopened box sat at the foot of my bedroll, safe. But something was missing. My eyes went to the cage.

"Mom?" I interrupted her reading and surprised myself as the *Mmm* sound escaped through my lips. My mind said, no, it's an R for Ray that you're looking for. Without a chance to take it back, I pushed myself back up through the hole and finished my question. "Where's Binky?"

If Ray had heard the M-word she didn't let on; she'd only stared me down while the wheels churned. I waited for her answer, even though I figured the bird was gone.

"I can take it." I said. "Maybe he was old." I slid down the ladder and closer to her.

"I buried him." She said it quietly.

Unable to support myself, due to the problem with my leg, I slithered to the ground making like I had intended to sit. "You didn't tell me?"

"I didn't want you to be upset. Him being our pet and all."

"We didn't buy him at a store. We hardly knew him. And how do you know he was a 'him'?"

"Blue over the beak." She was scientifically serious, not condescending. No "ha-ha, I know something you don't."

"Really?" Of all the things I'd overthought about in my life I'd never considered how to tell a boy budgie from a girl budgie.

"Male. Really. I was going to tell you he died, but you were busy reading. I knew you were attached to him, so I took care of it; spared you the pain."

I went into cold and totally inappropriate mode. "Maybe we should have eaten him."

"Oh, Koda," she said, as if she'd considered it too. "We could never make a cooking-fire in this dry place."

As if on cue, her stomach grumbled. She rolled up a piece of the corner from the page of her book and popped it in her mouth.

"Pica." I diagnosed.

"No." She shook her head and tore off another small piece. "We don't have any pie you silly-Koda-bear."

She didn't get it. Eating foreign objects like wood or paper is called pica. Na-na-na-na-na. I coasted on the energy of superiority for a few seconds—before the realization of mean-ness crept in. My one-upmanship that rendered us intellectually separate meant nothing here. At least she was satisfying hunger. Maybe it wasn't pica at all.

My mind went directly to our differences. Her lack of words and my whatever was the opposite of lack. Usually I was a good opposer, retrieving the right word in a nanosecond. Yin yang, black white, hot cold, Ray's shortage my surplus. Green Jean had nurtured my interests, hours of reading had built a living vocabulibrary, furnished it too, with words like defenestrate, repast, and skive. Spending time with Jean had been like time with a private tutor, a swami, mentor extraordinaire. "A prodigy, you are," she'd say to me. "Do not abuse your gifts."

Just like freaking Yoda, she was.

"So, he's dead," I said.

"In the form we knew him," she replied. "He is part of all this." She swooped one arm through the air. "Nature."

I went around the corner, sat on the bench, and chastised myself for the eat-the-bird comment. If I had ignored the bird's absence I'd already be napping and blotting out the pain in my leg. The sleep would have helped me to avoid remembering Green Jean as well.

What happened to my commitment to get the bird to the boy? What a failure.

Ray stirred, itchy to do more housekeeping, leaving me to think more. What the hell was Koda-bear all about? How could life be so confusing in this peaceful place? Our relationship was as complicated as before, maybe more.

God, Mother Nature, Allah, Higher Power, send me a normal mother. Give me a normal life.

Staying busy took the focus off my leg. A trophy, shaped like a bowling pin, made a great tool to beat the metal around the ragged hole in the trailer roof. It smoothed out and bent well to trap part of the shower curtain.

People's stuff provides information. *Fred Burrow* engraved on a miniature bowling pin, along with the line: *Best Bowler – High Triple – 1992*. Another, *1994 Bowler of the Year*, engraved below a shiny man posed in the bowling position, his golden legs all flaking, revealing some plastic underneath. A commemorative plaque: *Congratulations Freddy-Boy on Another Fine Season 1997*.

Fred had friends and did a sport, of sorts. Photo-imaging him in my head was easy. A guy who never worried about a few extra pounds, waved other drivers in when they needed to change lanes, took kids on bottle drives, and shovelled his neighbours' driveways. People probably remarked about Fred: "Give you the shirt off his back, he would."

"I like Fred." My blurting it out surprised me.

"Meow." Ray looked up at me.

"Meow?"

"Meow, meow, meow." She was scrambling somewhere between boxes of Fred's stuff and the paint drop cloths. She poked her special stick at the previously discovered dry cat food and purred.

"No."

"Meow-yes." Cat food dust escaped into the air as she dipped her hand inside the bag. "Hope you don't have any loose fillings." She purred, tossed a kibble to me, then inserted one into her own mouth.

"I'm not eating cat food."

"We haven't even started on the Under The Sea meals yet," she said.

It was a version of popcorn and movie except there were neither. We ate handfuls of kibble while we stared at the mountain range that surrounded us.

"The fifth peak is definitely a dog." She used her wooden pointer.

"Absolutely canine," I agreed.

"One, two, three, four peaks."

"And a dog," I added.

"Four Peaks And A Dog." We said it together, toasting the naming ceremony with warm strawberry YT.

We had difficulty judging how quickly the sunset would create a lights-out, so we used the candle again.

We decided we liked looking at the stars—from inside the trailer —except for when Ray decided some birds were bats. I hadn't known she didn't like bats. She said she hadn't known either. The heat held in the trailer for a while. At first, we didn't need much more than a tablecloth as a blanket over each of us but, by the middle of the night, it cooled off, and Coat was great to snuggle-up in—worth the occasional jab from the sharp thing in its lining.

I counted the pulsating pain in my thigh like I might the seconds on a school clock in chemistry class. Sleep came to me while thinking about how we should go about finding water. There were two certainties:

1. It would not rain.
2. My leg would not stop throbbing.

Fifteen

R ay was up before me, reading from the *Survival: Improve Your Life in Ten Days Guide.*

"Day Three. Heal Thyself," she called out.

The irony of her words registered as she began to sing in a pathetic rendition of gospel. My leg was no longer a leg. It was something attached to me that required a hip sway to move it. When I hoisted myself out the roof, a nasty pain surrounded the epicentre of the wound. Misjudging the final leg-swing caused the injured area to hit a metal hinge. I yelped.

"Heal, heal, heal, heal." She raised her hands to the sky, swaying back and forth.

"She-He gives us the power to heal ourselves." Exaggerated swaying. "Take the power to heal yourselves." She cut in with another background of "heal, heal," performing the solo with hardly a breath to insert the back-up singers. "The world has the power to heal itself. The world has the pow-wer to heal its—"

Her jaw dropped, mid-lyric, as she watched me drag my leg in an attempted walk.

"It's nothing." I lied. "Carry on, it's got great rhythm. I'm loving the indecisive gender part. Hallelujah! Amen! Keep going."

She remained fixated on my cut-offs.

Braced against the trailer, I traced my hand along the torn edge of denim and lifted back the fabric. The visual exacerbated agony and gave it a name: Yellow Yuck. I had met the source of really disgusting puss-filled pain.

I covered it over, hobbled toward her, and collapsed on a flattened cardboard box close to the one she was planted on. She frowned, and I shot back a dismissive look. Her feet and part of her legs extended past the corrugated edges of her flat-box-mat.

She was over-drinking her YT allotment and rolled one to me in the kid-like manner of pushing a ball along a floor between open legs. I wondered what would happen to her quota when she finished it twice as fast as she'd permanent-markered it. Then I remembered it was Ray and it all made sense again. Mine wasn't mine.

The taste of the YT, and the comfort of the cardboard barrier between the scorched ground and me, helped me forget the pain.

She'd begun reading to herself, a version of quietly mouthing the words and, after I'd stretched out, she decided to make it an official story time.

"Self-healing is para-mountain to…" Slow pronunciation.

"Paramount." I corrected. The author clearly liked this word.

"Like the movies? Paramount Pictures?" She was serious.

"Like really important." I was brief; winced as I changed positions.

"Self-healing is para-mount…" She hesitated. "You okay?"

"Sure."

"Your leg?"

"Nothing with my leg. Leg's fine."

My head was an inferno. I hoped it was because of too much sun.

All I needed to cap it off was the drum to leak through. But it was strangely absent, again.

She hopped up to re-secure the page that was attached to the plastic clip on the heating-pad because it was flapping in a micro-breeze. This gave me time to escape and ease back into the trailer. She could explain Day Three later. I needed to slip into a coma.

I stepped off the chalk-board box-top beside Coat, caught sight of the birdcage on the floor, and reminded myself she'd buried Binky. Confusion struck: why was his little body all rigid and sideways on the floor of the cage?

Fixated on the image, YT puke rose in my throat and went back down in an involuntary gulp. I couldn't tip my head downward to vomit on myself or the trailer floor because my eyes wouldn't leave the stiff little body. I didn't want to touch him but, in my fixation, I planned how to get rid of him. If I could move my arms then I could slide the tray out to brush him off and have him somehow fall into a bag, then the whole situation would go away.

In my mind's-eye-plan the tray wouldn't slide out because his body would be in the way so I'd have to open the cage door and lift him, and I knew I couldn't touch him, and I just wanted to sleep, and my leg throbbed, and it was hotter than ever, and she'd said she'd buried him, but she hadn't and he was all solid and lifeless and strange, and my blood was boiling from climate and emotion.

A howl like none I'd heard before filled the space. It was followed by a heavy sob. Human. Someone was here! Were they lost too? Confusion obscured a flash of "we're saved" by someone who's profoundly upset but has stumbled upon us from somewhere—a somewhere we could return to.

And then my soul plunged when it realized the cry had come out of me.

Ray parachuted through the roof in seconds. I sobbed an accusation about her saying she'd buried him.

"I did. I did bury him, Koda. Oh, him, that's Binky's little plastic friend, Nudgie."

She tried to show me, hold me, hug me, but I resisted. I didn't know Ray had named the toy, but out from behind my tears I was able to confirm the rigid body was, for sure, Nudgie.

In a heated fever I still realized how infrequent "hold me" and "hug me" had been. Funny that I remembered her lack of emotional connection and yet forgot the plastic twin in the bird's cage.

"Koda I'm sorry, I should have gotten rid of the cage. I'm so sorry Koda."

It was painful and warm inside my heart at the same time. She was sorry. She was sorry? Of all the things she could be sorry for, this was it? I was beyond being able to control my emotions—couldn't interrupt the bawling mess of me.

She caught me as I stumbled backward. I was in the alley between Safeway and Carter's drugstore. Even when I opened my eyes to make myself see Ray, I only saw Green Jean lying there. I could not walk away from Jean.

"No. No. No."

I let Ray help me down to the soft lining. Stay here with Coat, I kept telling myself. Do not go down the alley.

Jean had had a coat too.

Back then, I don't know how long I stood in the alley. Speechless, my back and shoulders registered every depression between brick and mortar as my spine froze to the outside wall of Carter's. Eventually I'd moved forward, pushing myself off the wall toward her. How could I have helped her when I couldn't even bring myself to touch her?

After my body had dropped to its knees, I'd forced myself to bend close enough to listen for a shallow breath, but there had been none. My eyes had kept closing for longer than they would stay open. I'd kept wishing for Jean to be okay at the same time as I'd wondered where her coat was. I'd searched it out. It was under her.

My current mindset kicked in. Coat was under me. In the last four years I'd believed I'd made myself forget. But I hadn't. All I'd done was chosen not to remember. While Ray hovered, I faded back to Jean. Hers was a no face. Like in crafting, when making paper, except it was human material, skin, and eye, and lip pulp.

Sixteen

~~~

B ack in the alley, I'd tried to make myself call out. Frozen, I'd
wanted someone to find me there so they could get the pharmacist—sort of like a doctor—I needed an adult to take
over. When I'd finally managed a feeble call, the drug store's owner's
adult son, Brendon Carter, had appeared. He'd bent down in a
controlled way to check Jean, then pulled out his cellphone. I'd
listened to the contrast between the two distinct tones in the three
depressions of 9-1-1.

Sirens within seconds. Fire trucks first. Then ambulances and
police cars. I'd looked around for flames in the alley.

"Fire. Fire!" The trailer was like a soup pot. My insides were boiling. The sirens wouldn't stop.

Ray soothed me with a wet cloth that smelled like berries. "Koda,
it's okay baby." She continued to blot my head with YT.

"Not Swahili. French. Touché. French word. Touch. It's a fencing
term. Not wood fencing. People admit they've been matched in wit.
Not Swahili. Not Swahili."

"It's okay baby."

"Not Swahili." I needed to confess my deception.

"Calm down, baby."

One part of my brain told another part to stay in the trailer. No deal. A massive florescent-green-on-dark-canvas jacketed man had plucked me as if I was a toy in one of those insert-coin retrieve-prize machines. I'd remained stiff and vertical from lift-off to touch-down on a wide, crisscross-patterned bumper. I had thought he was putting something in my hand, but he was prying out a fist full of fake fur.

He'd knelt close, pouring hot chocolate from a thermos into its lid cup, which I didn't drink from, but puked into. The vomit, mixed with the hot drink, overflowed the cup, spilling all over his green canvas uniform. "Didn't." *Breathe Koda.* "Mean." *Breathe Koda.* "It." I'd tried to apologize for the mess.

"So-kay kiddo." He'd wiped the chocolate vomit off me with blue, quilted paper towels before tending to himself. "So-kay huneeey." He'd tried to soothe. I'd kept staring at the canvas weave of his uniform. Real close it blocked everything out.

"Filthy scum." A cop spoke to the firefighter I'd puked on. I hadn't known if he was talking about me, because he was looking at my puke on the chest of the firefighter, or Green Jean. I'd listened with increasing, albeit frozen, anger. Though there had been no fight energy in me to protect either of us, I wouldn't have anyone say bad things about her, so I'd wanted to commit his face to memory, for revenge. But when I did look, his anguished expression matched my own and I realized he was talking about Jean's attacker. His liking Jean allowed me to let down what was left of my guard.

The cop and the firefighter chatted, using words like "gang" and "initiation." "Whatever happened to respect?" The cop had said.

"It's Jeanie." Another cop called out in the kind of crackled voice he might have used if he were talking about a friend of his mother. I'd known then that they would all be nice to her. To her body. They knew her too. Not like I knew her, but they knew her enough.

They relocated me to the cab of a fire truck. High up and out of reach, like a tall hero with a white hat, standing in the alley, making a bold statement, like talking trucks in children's books: I'm not goin' nowhere 'til I find out what's happened. A big, red voice.

Someone passed a grey blanket through the window. I only saw the hand, but a male voice from below asked my phone number and what I had seen. My answer had been that I didn't have a phone and I'd seen nothing. Another cocoa delivery followed. Captain Hot Chocolate climbed into the cab. He braced himself on my first sip. The drink calmed the stinging throw-up in my cheeks and throat. Chocolate swallowable mouthwash.

The truck's window had made a frame around Jean's covered body and allowed a bird's-eye view to the rest of the alley. Six police cars announced the seriousness of the situation. Brendon Carter stood at one end of the alley talking to a cop. The ambulances left and were replaced by white, windowless vans. A crowd gathered behind some yellow tape that had been magically strung like a garland: streamers at a murder party.

Another firefighter climbed up into the cab and made a phone call. I heard him say there were more victims. Then I saw more tarps, the same as what covered Jean.

"Senseless. Four innocent people." The new guy I hadn't puked on spoke to the steering wheel. He wiped his teary eyes on his sleeve, scrambled out, and fell into step with my original rescuer who had slipped away while my eyes were closed from the steam of the drink. They joined a group of cops who were trying to move a dumpster. One of the officers pointed to the edge of the laneway where a woman in a beige pantsuit stood holding a white teddy bear. Captain Hot Chocolate nodded to her, turned, and walked toward my fortress.

"There's this woman," he shouted it up to the window. "She's gonna take you home kay-huneeey. Get some info from ya, okay?" I remember looking at the top of his head and thinking, hey, where's the second huneeey?

He didn't need to introduce her. I'd known she was a social worker. I already owned a crisis teddy.

It had been easy to lie to her when we'd arrived at the apartment: Mom was at work, would be home anytime, I was fine, thank you, bye-bye, thanks-but-no-thanks for Teddy. I'd squeezed through the door, so Ray wasn't visible.

Now, in the trailer, not looking at the cage, only at Ray's close-up face and hair, I decided to go with the final line of the "Old Woman Who Swallowed the Fly" rhyme, *perhaps I'll die*. I rambled phrases from classics Jean had read me and combined them with Shakespeare, something about winged cupid blind, until sleep took over.

Ray stayed, I think, except for when she must have moved the cage, because when I woke, she was there, and it was gone. No trace of a budgie ever being in the trailer, no feathers, no seed. Nothing. Perhaps tossed far into the bush or buried alongside Binky. She must have crawled on her hands and knees and picked up every seed casing.

I cursed my meltdown. We could have used the metal for something, planted the seeds, cleaned up the mirror and used it for personal reflection or for signalling planes.

During seconds of semi-consciousness, Ray seemed to tower above me.

When Green Jean had been murdered, I hadn't told Ray I'd found her. I didn't say anything, even when we went to the funeral. But from my bed in the trailer, in the scorched not-really-grassy place we'd landed, in a super-reinforced-sorta-U-Haul, I garbled out the whole story.

My lips tasted fruity. The damp cloth that had been placed across my forehead smelled like strawberry. The faint scent of windshield washer fluid hung in the air and joined something medicinal, like astringent for acne. "Drink baby, okay?"

"No." I whispered, "Can't waste. Don't waste."

"Drink." She ordered.

I squirmed and pulled on the crotch of my cutoffs; one leg now extremely daisy-duked thanks to Ray. I lifted my head enough to see the exposed wound. No longer yellow, all red and raw.

"I cleaned it. You're sick from it."

"Morphine," I said.

"Wouldn't that be great?" She said it flatly, confusing me as to whether she meant for her or for me.

"No, we have some. Emmas." I used the name she'd relate to and pointed in the general direction of our outhouse. "In the toilet paper."

She ejected from the trailer. Next thing, her fingers were in my mouth.

Seventeen

"You missed a whole day, sleepyhead." She was inside the trailer, fanning me with Day Five.

Tax the best, file behind?

Somehow rubbing my eyes made my ears work better. Relax. Rest. Quiet your mind. A do-over made more sense. "Was that Day Four?" I whispered. It was too creepy.

"Yep, and you did rest so you can still graduate. Today is Day Five. Nourish with breath and water. Today we're gonna get you up, then go find water." A pitter patter caught my attention on the shower curtain roof.

She read my mind. "No, Koda-baby, just pine needles. No rain."

It came back to me in a gentler way. My life. Ray's life. Green Jean. Falling off the earth. Being here. Ray had been thoughtful and dropped the door ramp, thinking I wouldn't be able to climb out the top. She'd put the Strawberry YT in china cups. I examined the saucer, like Green Jean had shown me, checking out various ticks and scrawls on its underside—each a marking of the person who'd been involved in its manufacture—and the stamped words, Royal Albert.

"Mmmm. Morning tea." She smiled at me and sipped.

The drink brought energy and triggered an attitude update. My not wanting Ray as my mother dropped to a lower priority.

We eased through the early part of the day. Me in semi-sleep, Ray puttering with her walking stick. She collected wood, looked at the mountains, and thumbed RNs, mentioning Sister Gabriella, often. She was becoming a superhero to Ray. Ray was responding to the fictional nun's guidance.

"Four Emmas are pretty powerful." I said, zombie like.

"Two." She looked up; squinted at me rather than the sun.

"Four." I said it as if they were members of our family. "There were four."

"No, there were two, Koda. Two pills."

"Four."

"There were two tablets of morphine." She was addict absolute.

The bubble burst. Two for me and two for her. Fooled again. Like watered down formula from my infancy. Marginal care. I did not want to share this smoky breathing space, potential water discovery, or anything else with Ray. I wanted her to disappear into the mountains.

My body and brain teamed up and refused to do anything else; the silent treatment for Ray even though she'd fashioned an excellent bandage around my thigh. My furry friend, Coat, called for me for a nap—a rest of the day nap.

So much for finding water on Day Five. Or breathing good, honest air. There were no wishes on stars, or goodnights. It was all a lie.

I woke possessed by hatred that bred defiance. Day Six. I made it day 666 because that is a devil number and Ray was Satan. Once an addict, always an addict. She'd been so clean the last few years. Now, here in this falling-off-the-earth place, she thought she could truly start up on two narcotic painkillers.

A seed of sick happiness sprouted in my gut. She had fooled her body into thinking it benefited from two pills, only to suffer a reality check that there were no more. My spirits remained high, in a completely slimy kind of way, that her wanting more would hurt her.

Maybe she hadn't even medicated me and kept all four herself. She was a layer on me, like cheap too-sweet icing on a cake. The kind you scrape off because it doesn't taste like you think real butter and pure sugar would. She made me all scratchy. Irrational fears welled up in me that I might swell up with welts inside on a level I couldn't rub off—or worse—induce anaphylactic shock.

If only I could shed her the way snakes shed their skin or scuba divers peel off their wetsuits. I wanted to remove her, apply a nice balm, then try on a more floral, delightful mother.

I rolled over and my leg did not hurt. That made me happy for a few seconds and allowed some future plans to gel. Sure as shit, at eighteen I'd move out. I concentrated to calculate how much time before I left home, then accidentally banged my elbow on the trailer's side. The reverberation spoke to me: it's not a good idea to project the future from a place where you might not have one.

Leave home? Our days ahead weighed heavily in the arms of the Grande Dame of all, Mother Nature. Thoughts of being rescued danced about when Ray blasted in all perky from the hole above.

"C'mon. Up'n-attem, Sweetie. Day Four was heal yourself, and you did, baby. And yesterday we sort of nourished you. We didn't find water so we're a little behind. Still, we can do it. Find water and get back on our program." Nonstop prattle. Not a clue about my feelings, the other two tablets, or worse: that I suspected she'd taken all four. Not a freaking clue. "And today's theme is teamwork." She was relentless.

I became bored and blocked out her voice, then climbed out to see what she'd been doing. My leg, though still sore, had been retied with a fresh bandage of tablecloth remnant. It was a nice touch for a drugeeeee.

She was straightening the books around the cardboard coffee table, cleverly turning over the teacups to keep bugs out. "Can you help me make sure the ramp is really secure?" she asked.

I obliged in silence.

She didn't notice, too busy yapping: "Oh God I need a shower. Oh God I need a shower. I need a shower. I neeeed a shower. Oh God I need a shower." Jekyll-Hyde-ing from housekeeper to whiner.

"I know you need a shower, okay? You've only said it four thousand and fifty-two times."

"You're right," she said. Not shut-the-eff-up. Just, you're right.

"Where are you going?" I called out from behind the trailer as she walked away.

"Shower," she answered confidently.

"What?"

"Teamwork." She called out without looking back, "C'mon Koda, let's find some water. Together." She walked backwards while she spoke. "Wanna use my stick?"

"No, I don't 'wanna' use your silly stick."

"Okee-dokee." She turned, continued to walk, and began to sing.

There was a mother and her kid
And water was their game-oh
W-A-T-E-R
W-A-T-E-R
W-A-T-E-R
And water was their game-oh.

"Wait up." I sounded like a four-year-old. "Wait up."

She substituted a clap for the w, and then, in later verses, for each subsequent letter, eventually eliminating the a, t, e, r until there were only five claps for the word water. Fifteen in total for the third line.

Its ending was signalled by Elton's classic line: *I'd buy a big house where we both could live.*

I trailed behind her determined steps for ages, breaking branches and making nature signs so that we'd be able to find our way back—me onboard the superiority train again because she hadn't thought of that. Some higher power may have been conspiring to put a shower in the middle of nowhere for her—not for Dakota, no—for dear, sweet, Ray-O-Sunshine, but I knew I'd be the one to get her back to the trailer.

It was as if she'd wormed her way into my brain. She picked out one of my thought words and started a new song.

You are my sunshine
My only sunshine
You'll make me happy, this very day
If you please lead me
To some clear water
For little Koda, and me, Mama Ray
…how wonderful life is
when you're in the world.

I wanted to dry heave.

In total we'd probably walked about half an hour.

"Listen." She raised her index finger to her lips and shushed me.

Offended, on account I wasn't even speaking, I breathed heavier. She shushed me again.

"What are you shushing me for?"

"Shhh."

She cuffed me across the head.

"Hey, child abuse," I said.

"Shhh."

"Stop shushing me," I said.

She placed her sweaty, sticky, dirt-encrusted hand firmly over my mouth, and in the observed silence a faint trickling danced around my ears. Holy crap. Call me converted. She *was* the chosen one.

I so wanted Ray persecuted for the morphine violation, but as we neared the gurgling water, I began to forget the last day or so. The best way to deal with it was to turn off the anger switch and pretend there had only been two painkillers.

Not that much farther, the setting had changed to less of a forest-fire-waiting-for-a-spark kind of place.

Water. More than a stream, less than a river.

"It's a striver," she called out.

It was about as wide as a single lane street, bottlenecking in places, faster flowing over jagged rocks in other spots. Mostly it was straight and flat and at some parts it was difficult to tell which way the current ran because it twirled around and lapped over the bits of mountain that stuck up from its rocky bottom. I stood at the water's edge and understood why people kiss the ground when they arrive in a place, or why some hunters kneel and give thanks to mother earth for providing the animals they kill.

"Get in." Ray left out the word "stupid."

Her clothing landed along the bank. When I looked in her direction, she was waist deep, the white bands of her un-sunburned shoulders reflecting off the water.

"Koda! Don't drink it," she cautioned.

"Don't drink it?"

"Yes. I mean, no. I mean don't drink it."

I stooped at the water's edge and splashed it all around my lips and all over my face. Flip-flopped baby steps led me to a knee-deep pool. The shocking cold of glacial melt crept into my legs, readying me to sit. It cooled my wound. Slowly easing onto the rock bottom, the clear, clean water soaked into my shorts and underwear, then my

Carter's t-shirt, until I was immersed to the neck. And I did drink a little.

I waded to shore, too grateful to be cold. The bandage Ray'd tied on my leg held firm.

When she was done soaking herself, she became a human salad spinner, drying off under the sun. I averted my eyes. Other than photos of art and statuary, it'd been a long time since I'd seen any naked body. "We'll bring towels next time," she said, as she re-dressed.

Dripping wet and on her heels, I followed her back to the trailer, correcting her only once when I saw one of my broken branch signs. All the way back, me slopping, and Ray practically floating. After the long walk back, we were tired, but buoyed by the bathing, and by having fresh water to drink.

Ray made a beeline to her office to consult the inventory. Six O'Clock Tree welcomed her with open arms. A flannel crib sheet, burgundy tattered bathrobe, and bottle of bubble bath later, she seemed satisfied. She went to work with a fondue fork, piercing the crib sheet in the centre. I searched out my hoodie, something to wear with the strange crib-sheet-poncho she was crafting me—I knew the robe was for her. My dirty underwear from the knapsack was my only laundry.

Though it exhausted us, returning right away was a good idea. We missed some cues and had to double back a few times. Strips of flannel, shredded from the neck hole of my poncho, made good route markers. On arrival she hung her robe on a bush, then stripped off and waded in with her laundry and the bottle of suds.

"Quick, the bubbles are running out. Give me yours," she demanded.

I tossed her my cut-offs and the T, but not the underwear, choosing to remove and then launder my bra and both pairs of panties in the soapy, downstream residue.

When we were lathered and rinsed, she climbed out of the striver and slipped on the robe. "Okay, Poncho Villa," she said, holding the crib poncho in front of her. I couldn't tell by her pronunciation if she was using an A or an O for Pancho or Poncho—a play on words or sheer ignorance. She pronounced the L's in Villa like those in "stellar," not as they should have, like the letter Y. I stopped myself dissing her more. After all, she'd found water.

She left the poncho on the bank, turned her back to give me privacy, then announced she was going commando.

Undie-less myself, I stretched my hoodie over the crib sheet-toga-poncho.

"These will dry fast." She held up her Fruit of the Looms. "I could've washed your gaunchies too, you know."

"I can wash my own."

"Okee-dokee, that's fine too."

We smiley-walked back. We'd found water. No, Ray had found water. No, Ray had been shown the way as a reward for being such a wonderful caregiver. God's Mother of the Year award. Maybe God was not who people thought he was. Maybe he was a reformed drug addict with enormous tolerance and a disturbed sense of justice. Perhaps the Heavenly Father was not a decent parent to Jesus and had made Jesus' earth parents, Mary and Joseph, leave him in the manger for too long. It might be that Jesus had been fed watered-down goat's milk and had a flat spot on the back of his head.

Holy family considered, knowing we could still die of starvation, at least we'd be clean and refreshed.

"I can't believe I'm so stupid." She made the statement while hanging our clothes on branches.

"I can," I whispered. Even though I didn't know what she was commenting on.

"The water. Boiling. We should have taken stuff there to do it. Now it's too late."

"Okay." It was a lazy agreement. I didn't want to think about anything other than being clean and enjoying a YT.

But the YT wasn't enough. I was exhausted, Ray too. I hadn't wanted it to be me that went for the Cat Granny drink first, but I did, delivering one to Ray right after. It was so sweet it gave me an instant buzz. It set about more cravings, and I browsed the row of Under The Sea meals.

"Pretend it's Dinty Moore stew," she said, sourcing a couple of stainless-steel teaspoons from a kitchen box.

"Dinty who?"

"Okay, pretend it's KFC gravy, then."

Not speaking about it made the eating canned cat food less real. She finished her can then, high on sugar and chemicals, began creating a process. Sniffing what was left of the pink washer fluid, frowning, capping, uncapping, re-capping. "We'll have to find something to pour the washer fluid into so that we can use the washer fluid bottle. See, it's sealable." She gestured by removing and replacing the cap about a dozen times. "To hold the water we purify, and not spill it on the way back. Hey, that almost rhymed," she said.

She began a bit of a "cat came back" song using the words "cap and spill it on the way back" while she emptied the potent smelling cleaner into a paint tray that was layered with off-white, dried paint.

Ray paced back and forth, swinging the empty windshield washer fluid bottle in full arm circles. She was a windmill. I wondered if she was using it to power her brain or get rid of all the fluid. She stopped abruptly, as her pistons fired, and gathered up the empty YT tins, fondue set, and matches into a pillowcase, then the whole lot into the beach bag.

Day Six's header *Teamwork* flapped in a gentle breeze while secured to the heating pad that was wrapped around the tree.

"We did it," she cheered. With the bag of items held over her head, and her staff anchored to the ground, she resembled a triumphant victor in some history book illustration. A character on a Major Arcana card in a Tarot deck, perhaps titled Futile Inventor.

She placed the bag at the base of the tree and secured Day Seven as the light gave in to dusk.

"Working ahead of the class?" I asked.

"Day Seven. Draw on your creativity to create more pleasing surroundings. Want me to bring it over to read the instructions?" She paused beside the book.

"Been there. Done that." The flared edge of my poncho stuck out from under the ribbed waist of my hoodie, drying clothes scattered on branches at the edge of the woods.

My hate was fading a little. She'd done well for Ray. For anyone. "Goodnight, Ray," I said, heaving myself up in as reserved a way as possible so as not to expose my bare butt. Fitting that she was left under the first stars; she deserved a little spotlight under which to shine.

Eighteen

Drawing on our creativity translated into Team Ray dipping a YT can into the striver and setting it to boil over a fondue flame. Three minutes boiling was deemed enough to clear Beaver Fever. One, one thousand. Two, one thousand. Up to sixty, three times.

"You can listen for water," said Ray.

"I thought we were counting from when we see it bubble," I said.

"You don't have to see it bubble. You can hear it."

The first batches were handled carefully, using the pillowcase as an oven mitt, then pouring the "sterilized" water from the YT opening, where the tab used to be, into the bottle. Our first few fills were used to shake the clean water around to clean the inside of the plastic container, even though we'd rinsed out all traces of pink washer-fluid downstream.

When we were satisfied that the inside of the bottle was safe, it still took a long time to fill the container because we drank two cans for every one we put in the bottle. "We should bring the teapot as well next time, to make the pouring easier." Ray acted out her arm as a spout.

"We have a teapot?" I was surprised.

"Matches your china cup."

"I didn't know."

"I was saving it," she answered.

"For what?" A "dizzy me some more, Ray" feeling returned.

"A special occasion."

She burst forth Dixie Chick style.

We'll bring the teapot, for afternoon tea. For we are survivors, Koda and me. You boil the water, I'll find the leaves. A drink like no other, we'll make from the trees.

Insanity lightly seasoned with moments of lucidity. "Good idea," I said. "I like that, making some kind of tea." Then under my breath: hope it's some wonder-drug that cures you of whatever it is you suffer from.

"Thanks, Koda. For your belief in me."

"No problem." It only encouraged her, evidenced by a second verse. Same tune.

I have a daughter, believes in me so,
Right there behind me, wherever I go.

Due to her lack of examples, she completed the verse by humming, and then launched into Girl Scout. "And we should do this as long as possible so that we don't waste any matches; keep the fondue oil lit to boil as much as possible in one session."

"Good idea," I said. We had a mammoth supply of matches, along with fuel, not to mention fish, duck, and heart shaped candles, and two plastic bags filled with tea lights. Comforted by this, the day stretched on into the longest one of my life.

"Survival is boring." I poured tinned water into the plastic bottle, watching the level rise a teensy-tiny bit.

"Yep. It sure do suck, especially when it spills some out of the tab thingy."

"Pass me one of the empty YTs," I said.

I managed to enlarge the tab opening to reach the edge of the tin by using the fondue fork and a sharp rock. "This will pour better now."

"It's like the spout on a jug." Ray was happy.

"Exactly. This way you can save the teapot for special occasions."

"Koda?"

"What is it now, Ray?"

"You're so smart."

My heart skipped a beat. Ray smiled and turned to face the water. She resembled the mother in some shipwreck story. It was easy to imagine her saying, "Hey, kids, come get your boiled squirrel and fried toad legs."

"You can't be thinking… finding water is one thing, but fishing?"

"Oh yeah," she answered. "I'm gonna catch a fish. No. I'm gonna catch two fish. *One fish, two fish, red fish, blue fish*," she quoted Dr. Seuss. I recognized it from Jean's reading at story time at the library. Who knew where Ray'd heard it? She'd never read it to me; the survival book was the first I'd ever heard her read.

"One fish. Two fish. You are foolish." My immaturity fell on deaf ears.

"And because we're not making a campfire, we can cook them in the boiling water," she said.

"It's called poaching."

"Oh no, Koda, I don't think it's illegal. We're starving, so I'm sure it's okay."

"Not that kind of poaching. That kind of cooking-boiling is called poaching."

"Whatever," she said. "We'll catch—"

"We?"

"Okay fine. I am going to catch fishes. Plural. Then I am going to cook them back at our home."

That she knew the word plural impressed me. That in using it she thought she should change fish to fishes did not. But it was the final part of her phrase that threw me. "Our home?"

"And WE will take precautions, clear an area, light the fondue, and dine."

"Bears might come," I teased, even though I had decided we would never have any fish.

"No bear's gonna get our fish. OUR fish Koda. I'm gonna feed YOU and me." The any-painkiller-I-can-find-will-do look in her eyes bore into me. Or was it? It might have been determination.

My pessimism faded. I was being sucked in, buoyed again by the emerging energetic personality I'd never witnessed pre-fall-off-the-world.

A flashback to *The Little Red Hen* had to be ignored. There'd be no fish, so I abandoned any worry about assisting her. I took some time to picture what her method of fishing might look like. Spear fishing, net fishing; maybe she'd build a raft, sail down the striver to a lake, row out and catch the one that had gotten away from world-class casters.

I'd had a fast food filet-of-fish, tuna from a can, fish sticks, and fish shaped crackers that weren't really fish, and I even knew what an Under The Sea meal tasted like, but I had no idea what real fish tasted like.

Ray left the entire purification duties to me. She waded upstream, knee deep, legs apart, then stood still. Her posture made a believer out of me; expected a fish might leap out and land in her hands or sacrifice itself by jumping directly onto the bank.

During the final counting stage, on the third boil, she lay on her side, curled around a large rock that partially overhung the water. Her hands were draped over the edge, elbows bent a little, fingertips skimming the water. She stayed there for maybe half an hour.

By the time the bottle had been half-filled she'd disappeared. For a second it sounded like there might be a bear in the woods, but it was only Ray lugging out a few long pieces of deadfall. She placed them at an angle to the rock she'd curled against, anchoring them in the shallows. When I looked up again, she was in the side position on the homemade ramp, head quite close to the water, resembling someone caught sideways in mid-dive. She stayed staring into the water for a long time.

The next two mornings she left with her silly stick before I woke. Each day she'd dutifully turned the pages. The messages were generic. They basically translated to "get a hobby." She'd left a YT, an Under the Sea meal, and a Cat Granny drink beside my gold and red roses china cup. Her pale blue and pink petit point one was turned over on its saucer. It made our library room look lonely with only one active place setting.

A short distance from our reading room she had started another project: rocks in a circle about three feet across; an attempt to prepare a fireproof cooking area. The concept of Ray in a kitchen was not as unimaginable as it might have been the week previous. I wandered over to Six O'clock Tree and checked out the survival calendar.

Day Eight read: *Feed yourself by finding a passion. Many people overlook hobbies as pleasure for after the real work is done. Significant studies show a serious hobby, a passion, can be a career choice.* I stopped reading and moved on to Ray's note. Tiny printing.

PLEASE MAKE YOUR BED.

So lame, so motherly.

YOUR DOING A GOOD JOB WITH BOYLING. COME TO STRIVER AND DO MORE. GO THRU BOXES AND FIND A BIGGER SHEET TO MAKE ANOTHER PANCHO.

Little mousy, misspelled words.

I wasted the whole day, skipping the boiling—assuming she was doing it wherever she was. I read, and I made the poncho from a much larger sheet, so it'd cover me past my knees. An entire day alone.

She was fearless, a calm clone to my predators-could-be-nearby nervousness. We never discussed how bears or other animals could be lurking beyond the clock trees, or sniffing our footprints on the path we kept carving to the striver. Pretending they were good animal neighbours was my strategy. Who knows what Ray thought. Maybe she was meeting and talking to them like Dr. Doolittle.

It was late. As I began to worry, she came plodding through the trail we had almost formed, a mess of tablecloth lace and a pair of butchered pantyhose tied around her stick. Beach bag in tow, heavy from the full bottle of purified water.

She was mostly silent and chose to stay outside, sipping water, standing in the combined glow of starlight and yellow duck candle-light. Quiet contemplation broken only by a goodnight Koda, good-night Ray.

Nineteen

"Day Nine. Establish A Protective Layer And Safe Boundaries" hung static in our hazy universe. I read it by myself. Ray was gone, again.

It was a scary phrase because it meant tomorrow was Day Ten. After that, what would drive us to survive? What had we learned? Did we deserve to graduate because we had read a set of instructions each morning? I avoided looking toward the heating-pad for the rest of the day.

The *PLEASE MAKE YOUR BED* alongside my eclectic breakfast was the same note as the day before, with an exclamation mark beside the *COME TO THE STRIVER!* to remind me, like a mother might nag, that I'd been slacking. She was exercising her independence—even left the entire kit so I'd know she wasn't doing it. I carved out my own path to our watering hole, finding a less accessible, private spot to bathe and fulfill purification duties.

I chose my time to return to camp by a combination of the sun's position and the level of water in the bottle; I was still back before her.

Ray returned mid-afternoon, a curious smile on her face. She went to her rock circle, lit a candle—without joint consent—and heated some previously boiled water using the fondue frame as we did at the striver. When it was heated, she put it in the china teapot and added some pine needles which she had harvested from Six O'clock Tree.

"Tea is served," she announced. "Fit for the Queen." She poured the infusion, and we each drank a cup of the liquid.

"Another cuppa?" She floated the pot over my cup.

I didn't want to want her stupid tea.

"Sure," I answered, holding out my cup.

Later, she removed the dressing from my leg. "Looking good. I think we should leave it off for a bit, let the air get to it. It's starting to scab." She dabbed it with some astringent for teenage acne; smiling as I winced.

"You enjoyed that," I accused.

"It's so good you can feel it," she replied.

She left about an hour before sunset, a pair of pantyhose stretched between her hands. The lace fabric trailed from her silly stick. A homemade flashlight—a candle in a mason jar—swung from a string on her arm. I almost said something curfew-like, but was still reeling from topical treatment. I checked my leg. The start of the scab was morphing into the shape of a donkey.

By dusk, right before the sun dropped behind the mountain, I was doing a bit of fishing myself, attempting to locate the sharp thing in the lining of Coat, when I heard her screeching. I assumed she was being chased by a wild animal.

For a second, I decided to stay inside, but the next thing I knew I had boosted out and hurled myself toward the ground. Armed with a thin piece of deadfall, I came around the corner, wielding it fiercely.

When I heard her again, I realized she was happy-screeching, and I abandoned the weapon.

"Koda. Koda. Fish. Fish."

My entire heart grew, like the Grinch's when he saw the Whovillians celebrate in the town he'd emptied of gifts, when he saw their goodness shining through their tough situation.

"TWO." She was so damned happy.

She held up two dead, shiny, silver fish about six inches long and three inches skinny.

"Oh my god. Oh my god. Oh my god." I couldn't stop.

"Fish," she panted. "Fish. Fish. Fish."

"Wowzeegood," I said.

She tilted her head, as if it might change what I was saying or how she was hearing it.

"Wowzeegood." I was girl-gone-crazy. She didn't slap me; probably what I needed. My insides were all-a-shiver, proud of her, wanting to eat, and not having a clue what to do, shaking and repeating wowzeegood.

She continued where I left off. "Fishy. Fishy. I have to do something. Fishy. Fishy." She was jittery, yet able to place the fish on the log she used as a footrest.

I passed the fondue fork with the yellow M&M shaped knobby on the handle like a surgeon's nurse might pass a scalpel. She scraped some skin away and there was nothing disgusting about it. She stabbed at the underside, zigzagged a slit, and squeezed out some fish-insides, and there was still nothing disgusting about it.

We lit the fondue base and measured some water into a YT container then dropped little pieces of fish body into it. It was called "all hacked up fish." We redefined the term "candlelight dinner." And I made a major discovery: fish did not taste like filet-o, or sticks, or canned tuna, or Under The Sea Meals. Fish tasted like gold, like rainbows, like meat, like golden-rainbow-ey meat.

When it was all gone, I went to find a place to be satisfied and, for some unknown-to-me reason, Ray picked away at the two fish skeletons in the moonlight.

To the tune of "This Old Man," she sang.

I caught one, I caught two, one for me and one for you, With a knickknack paddy-whack, fish a fish a bone, we are in our nature home.

"Good job, Cap'n Highliner," I called out while sliding into our metal vault.

"G'night, Koda."

I anticipated Sir Elton's finale.

Silence.

Twenty

Day Nine was destined to stay on the tree for a while. Neither of us had ever graduated from anything, so we let the page hang on the tree for days, avoiding the tree by walking a wide swath around it.

Immersed in living, from daybreak to nightfall, we spent the mornings boiling water at the creek. Sometimes Ray broke away from the purification duties and tried fishing, but the early part of the day never returned a catch. At those times I saw her methods, which were relatively simple, yet required incredible patience.

On her side, on her log ramp, chin supported with a little roll of cloth, she held her hands out front over the water like she was doing a modified breaststroke. The pantyhose was skewered on her staff and, with the aid of another stick, the nylon legs splayed out under the water and the waist part billowed into a large opening.

Fishing was like waiting for a bus on a statutory holiday. Ray waited and waited for a fish, any fish, to pass over the mouth of her homemade net, which was ready to be snatched up out of the water using her lightning reaction video-gaming hands. At other times, probably when her back was sore, she shifted positions: sat cross-legged and held the lace tablecloth, tied like a small windsock on a twig frame, under the water. The current blew it out and, by virtue of being dipped in and blown open wide, only the insert-fish and scoop-up was necessary.

Early evenings were prime fishing slots. She caught at least two a night.

Brave as she was, returning when it was getting dark, bedtimes were freak-out times for Ray because of the bat-birds. At those times I'd pull the shower curtain over the hole in the roof, then Ray would re-freak a different kind of tantrum because she wanted the light from the stars. Eventually she'd consent to half and half.

The sky became our clock. Pioneer-like as it sounds, we did certain things before the sun hit mid-sky, other things after, and had a route before and after sunset. We had no idea how long we slept each night, only that it was night.

Ray took to crafting in the afternoons. Once the sun was past the middle of the sky, she'd set up a makeshift easel using my highchair. A piece of thick cardboard balanced on the back part of the tray, and materials on the front part, she'd angle it to face Four Peaks And A Dog and do her thing: attach fish bones to cardboard with white glue.

Ray explained that, in studying the scenery for her art, she'd located an opening well below the third and fourth peak which she was sure would be a natural break where a trail or highway would be. It was eerily high, and way too far away, but I let her have it because her art did look like the range we'd named.

While she crafted, she loaned me her cushioned throne. That's where all the encyclopedia reading happened for me. When that became boring, I began circling words to make new sentences—a story within established text. Between watching the sky and circling words, my butt relaxed in Chair, and my mind invented a total fantasy future, imagining ourselves here in the winter, moving our stuff into a cabin and waiting for civilization to join us.

We tolerated each other as unofficial time rolled by. When we were high on fish and deep in denial of the encroaching haze, life was good. We became better adjusted to each other, like roommates. Her singing was a daily annoyance, only to be replaced by an equally aggravating hum. When she got carried away, she displayed a spastic rhythm in her walky-dance—at those times I simply looked away, like a roomie would ignore a missing beer from her shelf in the fridge.

"Whatcha readin', Koda? Is it good? Read some to me."

" 'Snot a story, Ray." I played the role of a brat, changing "it's not" into booger language.

"Then make it that way, okay?" She completely missed the wordplay.

I squirmed, uncomfortable with her neediness, while she peppered me with questions and sorted through her fish bones. Unless I told her a story, I'd be reading the same paragraph all afternoon.

"Once upon a time there lived a little boy named Isaac. He liked it when his mom made apple pie. One day he was lying on the ground and an apple fell down from the tree and hit him on the head."

"Oh, Koda, the poor little boy, that's not a nice story. That's not what it says."

"He was older. I forgot that part. One day when he was older, not a little boy, an apple fell on his head."

"I don't want a violent story."

"Ray, you once keyed a guy's car and head butted his girlfriend. This was a small bop on his bean with the equivalent of a vitamin C capsule."

Her look translated to "please revise."

"One day Isaac was lying under a tree and a leaf came down and drifted down to the ground and he said, 'Oh it must be Autumn. I hope my mother has made apple pie.'"

"That's better." She abandoned the bones, resealed the glue, and moved closer for the rest of the story.

"Not really," I said.

"Why?"

"Because then we wouldn't have gravity."

"Oh," said Ray. "Sorry."

I turned on an air or authority. "That's all right. We'd have gravity; it's just that he wouldn't have been given credit for identifying it."

Ray smiled and grabbed a paperback. Sister Gabriella's framed face appeared on the cover. Ray stretched out on a cardboard lounger, leaving me confused about having been left in the comfort and company of Plaid Chair.

"You like those the best, huh? There are a thousand more titles," I said.

"Oh Koda, I love Sister Gabriella. The plotline is amazing. And the construction of the one set in Italy is the most realistic of all the Sister Gabriella's so far—even though I've only read a few. You oughta try one, Koda. Like the Italy one. You gotta read that one. There's a character named Maria who is so real."

Plotline? Construction? She was becoming an academic.

She read for a bit, then got antsy and headed to the highchair, flipped over the tray, and stood drumming on it using the flat of her hands. Not bad either. Not dissimilar to the junior drummers Martha got to play at our recitals at Popeye's.

"The piano is a percussion instrument, and you know… Elton plays the piano," she said between beats.

Despite the reference to Rocket Man, her drumming moved me. I relaxed through it, then realized I hadn't had the drum dream since we'd arrived, nor had it broken through during the day. Maybe it was the altitude.

I slipped inside the trailer to tackle the opening of the box. The binder containing the Lifebook was on top. I put it aside—it could wait. After all, I hadn't needed its story so far in life.

Then I moved the tissue paper. The dress was simply too much to ignore.

It was a dead girl's Natural Reflection Global Steps performance dress, until I accidentally brushed it with the back of my hand; then it became mine.

Once the box flaps were fully opened it could have floated. My heart pulsed warm waves through my body. It was as if a missing part of me, sort of like an upgrade, had shown up and was waiting for me to install it.

I knew instantly that it would fit. Deerskin accents, a heavily-woven cotton print in several shades of the kind of turquoise that shows up during pink and orange sunsets, and rows and rows of teardrop glass-like beads on threads, 365 strands of them according to the handwritten card, addressed to me, pinned into the neck.

It was much more than the borrowed dresses I'd always practiced in; lifting one corner created its own song.

When I'd stopped counting every string of teardrops, I got up on our homemade stepping-stool, poked out the roof, and watched Ray get lost in her drumming.

I looked down into the trailer. "Be right back," I said to Dress, and it lay there, quietly, in that patient way beautiful things just do.

I went for a walk to a place where Ray's drumming faded; searched for my own internal rhythm, but it was gone. I sat by the water and cried for no reason at all, or perhaps every reason. I took off all my clothes and stepped into the cold current, baptizing myself in a cleansing to be worthy for the dress that had ended up with me but had been made for a girl who walked in front of a truck. I stuck my head under water and waited for as long as I could, so we could be almost the same, but not the same, because I didn't want to be dead.

When I rose out of the water, I got a solid grip on reality and trekked back.

Ray was slumped in Chair, tipping back a YT. "It's Tuscan wine. And I am Maria," said Ray.

"Of course you are," I said.

"No, I *am* Maria. Seriously."

"Okee-dokee, Maria," I replied.

"You can be Sister Gabriella."

"Yeah, right. Maybe I can solve the mystery of where we are."

"You'll read this one, right? You have to, Koda."

Back in the trailer, I put the dress on a coat hanger and hung it from a crossbeam, then made the three-ring binder that contained the report into a wedge under my rolled dinosaur curtain pillow.

"Is it like Cinderella's slippers?" Ray asked when I hit the ground.

"Were you spying on me?"

"I heard something when I was drumming, like tinkling glass. Is it the package from Edmonton?"

"It's a dress. A dancing dress. You heard strands of beads. Teardrops. Raindrops. Nature Reflections dance style's representation of life." Explaining stuff to Ray put me back in my comfort zone.

"Like what they got at Dollarama? Imitation trash. Rejects. Their stuff is so retarded."

"Don't dismiss the dance or the dress that way. And don't use that word," I said.

"Rejects?"

"You know what word I meant. The other R word. Not only do you insult me and my dance teacher about something you haven't even seen—dance or dress—but you gotta use a word that totally demeans other humans. Fuck, Ray, that's even too much for you. Everybody belongs. Hear that? Everybody. How dare you speak the word retarded? You think your Sister Gabby would use it?"

"Fuck is a swear we both promised Green Jean we'd never use, so you said something bad too."

"Ray, you just don't get it. Fuck is nothing compared to retarded."

"I didn't know."

"No. You didn't know. That's the problem, Ray. You never know. You never think. You never do—and I mean that both ways: you never do think, and you never do anything."

Every creature we'd never seen, but lived on the mountain, knew we'd had a major incident. Even the trees seemed to lean back a metre or so.

Ray collected an encyclopaedia and a dictionary on her way to a spot on the perimeter of camp. I stayed stiff and solid. After a while —maybe fifteen or twenty minutes—I dropped from boiling to simmering and tried to think about Jean's logic and how people don't know till they know. She'd said that educating others is a responsibility, but not something to laud over others. Could it be that Ray really hadn't considered the meaning of retarded and how its use in social circles as a casual insult demeaned people with mental challenges? Had I gone so completely off the charts raving mad that I had failed to see the opportunity to gently explain the word and perceptions of that word to Ray? Yes, I had. Now I needed to fix it.

"Ray," I called out. "Look, I'm sorry—"

"Holy crap, Koda," she said. "Here it is in the dictionary." She began to cry. "Please don't tell anyone how stupid I am. Please. I have a cousin who went to a special school. He lived in a group home. He was the nicest kid ever. Please, Koda."

I wanted to know about our relatives. Here she was opening up about family. But now wasn't the time.

"Ray, I'm sorry I snapped."

"Koda, I'm not sorry you snapped."

"Ray, I won't snap again like that."

"You mean there are other words that are this offensive? And I don't know them? And I might be hurting others by using them?"

Her "don't give a shit attitude" had gone.

"It's okay, Ray. That's pretty much the only one I can think of. And I think it's the worst."

"When did dissing things become my way?" Ray asked.

As far as I was concerned, even though I welcomed her introspection, it had always been her way.

"Amends. Amends. Amends." She spoke it to the sky. Ray turned her novella over so that Sister Gabriella's paper face couldn't see her favourite reader's remorseful expression.

I wet a rag and handed it to her. "I didn't handle that well," I said.

She wiped her face, neck, and hands, then settled into Chair.

"Natural Reflection? And you know how to do this dance?" asked Ray.

"It's not 'a' dance it's a style, but yes I've been in it for a long time, Ray. Too bad you never came to Popeye's."

"It is too bad," said Ray. "I regret that." She was serious.

The best thing to do was flood the conversation with dress factoids: "Martha says it's going to be difficult to sit in—lots of Natural Reflection costumes are. You have to lift the back to sit. Mine has—"

Mine. Mine. Mine. So many borrowed costumes in my past.

The wind swept through and said, "yours, yours, yours."

I choked on some smoke. "It's gonna sing, Ray. It's got three-hundred-and-sixty-five strings of beads—but I don't know how many on each string, they're all different lengths."

"One string for every day of the year?"

"Yeah. Maybe. I guess." I hadn't thought about it too much.

"What music do you dance to?"

"Drumming."

"And what about the drumming?" Ray asked.

"No, I can't hear any drumming right now," I replied, as if it was a normal question, then realized that inside information had escaped from my mouth and sat right between us. She might suspect I was hearing voices. Not that she could phone the school counsellor, but she might decide to lock her bedroom door if we were back in the apartment, which we never would be because we'd fallen off the earth.

"I mean who does the drumming for you?"

Recovery came quickly, telling Ray about Martha's bucket and stick, giving her the names of some Indigenous members who had drummed for us, and some guys from Sri Lanka that she might know because one of them works at the KFC.

"Martha modelled part of the celebration after a Powwow, so she has giveaways at the recitals. But pretty much every culture has drumming. It's a part of all of us."

The dark cloud had not only passed over us but opened a line of communication we'd never had.

"Everybody belongs. It's Popeye's motto—well, the centre's motto. The thing is, Martha takes it further. She learned it from spending time on First Nations territory. I saw it at a Powwow. The dancers gather in a circle and hold a big blanket. The blanket holds all kinds of little things—a deck of cards, a wrapped teabag, a bottle opener, a trial-sized moisturizer—and then a dancer will go into the audience and give a gift to one of the attendees. Then, the person who receives it stands and waves the item in the air and dances in the audience to the rhythm of the dancers. It goes on for a long time. Giving and gratitude."

Recitals of the past popped into my head. Ray stared at Four Peaks.

"Wishes," she said. "I'd give away wishes."

"Well, it's usually stuff you can touch and see. Like a Hot Wheels car or a package of bubble gum."

"That's golden," she said. A tear ran down her face. "Amends. Amends. Amends."

Twenty-One

"I'm larger than a rabbit. I'm larger than a rabbit. I'm larger than a rabbit." This is what I said to the sky, from the ground, as I wondered if the eagle might swoop down and grab me in her talons. How did she know what size I was from way up there. Did she have some kind of to-scale ruler or crosshairs in her eyes? Why didn't I know more about nature?

I took myself high and saw the human me lying on my back halfway up a mountain. "It's okay," I said to Eagle. "I'm not here to compete. And, by the way, she's bigger than a rabbit. Don't be diving."

"I wasn't planning to. I was imagining myself being on the ground and looking up at the sky."

"Wow, snap! That's what I was doing, but the opposite. I mean—"

"I know what you meant. Like we were each thinking what it would be like to be in each others'… shoes."

"Mostly I was wondering if you knew I was too big to kill."

"Why would I want to kill you?"

"You know, prey and all that survival stuff."

"You would taste terrible."

"I thought eagles were wise and symbols of spirit, you know, like Verna Born With A Tooth waves an eagle feather at the beginning of a Powwow at Popeye's. But you're funny."

"Dakota, no one is too big to kill."

"Okay, that freaks me out. And not just that you know my name."

"Everything on the mountain knows your name, Dakota Starr. Hey, you wanted wise, not wise ass."

"So you know a lot of stuff?"

"I know I'd never harm you."

"Can you answer this? Are you ready? Where's the drumbeat?"

"It's safe. In the dream."

"But I haven't been dreaming the dream either, have I?"

"The dream is dreamed, Dakota."

"But what does that mean? Are you going Yoda on me?"

"See, you will, Dakoda-girl. See, you will."

After each morning's boiling I wandered farther. The straying game sometimes transcended to panic, temporarily forgetting where I was. Losing myself, finding myself. Confidence would build then wane. On returning, there would be unspoken ideas between Ray and me—stay or go. Be discovered or discover others.

Our survival skills surged. Cooperation increased. We sustained each other. Rather than hold Mother Nature in awe, we began to take her for granted. When Ray went for fish it was not with anticipation and hopefulness, rather it was with a "see you when you get back with tonight's catch—I'll start the fondue pot." Though we remained cautious about distant fires, we seemed to become overconfident about our ability to survive.

A sort of sassiness made us drop our guard, accelerating the next setback. High on cavewoman confidence, a long wandering from the trailer led me to bushes of smooth, shiny-skinned red berries that spoke to me in juicy voices.

Carelessly ignoring any sensible inner advisor, seemingly forgetting any documentaries or movies where people are poisoned from unidentified nature snacks, I simply told myself these were not mushrooms.

Harvesting as many as my upfolded shirt would basket, I returned triumphant. Gatherer to Ray's hunter. After convincing Ray that I hadn't been shot in the stomach, we feasted by the fistful and, while we chewed, we infused the shirt to make berry-ade.

While we waited for the drink to brew, I wrote off a little acid reflux to gluttony.

"I don't like your pallor," Ray announced. She was studying me through a set of reading glasses she'd found in one of the miscellaneous boxes.

"You finished all those encyclos, doc?" I joked to her professor-like face.

"Either the light has changed, or you are green."

Despite my color, she puked first. Those are all the stats I kept.

To say we vomited violently and repeatedly would be an understatement. That wasn't the worst though. The cramps between heaves were agonizing. After an entire day of being on the dirty ground, we ran out of purified water. We slept outside, not even knowing it was nighttime. At some point we hobbled to the creek and boiled more water. It was only then we managed a few guttural moans. Back at the trailer, several areas looked like a neighbourhood in a slum of a large city that collects its raw sewage in moats and ditches.

"I feel so responsible." My remorse was nearly equal to the physical discomfort. I was totally disgusted with my lack of judgment.

"It's okay." Ray slowly let absolution slip through her lips, exhaling her blessing so as not to generate any energy in forming the letters and speaking them. "Really, Koda, it's okay," she whispered.

When we had puked out all the confidence inspired by our positive accomplishments, we hinted at talking about "talking about going back." Though we had increased our odds of survival by not having daily allotments of Yummy Tummy, Cat Granny drink, and Under The Sea, supplementing them with Stupid Tea, water, and fish, we accepted that, at some point, if the distant fires did not consume us, we would freeze.

"Tomorrow," she said. "Tomorrow we'll talk about going back."

"For sure," I said.

"But we haven't even graduated yet." Ray said it more to Day Nine and the tree than to me.

And then she doubled over.

"Oh God, I'm sorry. The berries," I said.

"No, not sick," she said.

"I'm sorry," I said.

"No, it's pain," she said.

"From the berries."

"No, labour pain."

"From too much work?"

"Not that kind of labour."

"From the cat food or something?"

"No."

"Were you drinking from the striver?

"No."

"We haven't been boiling it long enough?"

"Noooooo. Don't make me say it."

"Say what?" I said.

She cupped her belly from underneath with both hands and the shape formed. She didn't have to say it.

The drum thundered so powerfully I had to hold my ears and squeeze my head so it wouldn't explode.

Ironically, she had dropped to a fetal position. I walked away. A jigsaw puzzle formed in the clouds: sardine cravings, loose clothing, peeing a lot; missing pieces under a table to complete the puzzle I had no box-top picture for.

When I turned around, she'd straightened, walking around like the whole thing hadn't happened. "False alarm," she said. "I'm not ready." She walked toward her fishing gear.

"Hey, come back here," I called out.

She returned with her head lowered.

"Why didn't you tell me?"

"I didn't want to worry you."

"This isn't an 'I don't want to worry you, so I buried him Binky story.' And it isn't a teapot you can surprise me with."

"I didn't want to worry you," she said. "I didn't want to believe it. Pretty much like everything else in my life—except you, Koda. I mean, I know I used to ignore you, but not anymore, not since you almost died." She returned to Chair. "I have a problem. The problem is letting things slide. Even after the cramping a minute ago, I got up and pretended it wasn't happening."

It was like a heavy blanket covered our little place in the world. It covered me, the trailer, and the boxes, and the bench. The blanket of news covered all our stuff except Ray. Six O'Clock Tree peeked under, expressed his shock, then covered me again.

Once again, Ray had created a giant shadow under which I was trapped and couldn't breathe. Vintage-effing-Ray.

"When are you due?"

"I don't know."

"Well, you must have known when—"

"Thanksgiving. The party Carter's sponsored. It's the only time I've—"

"Spare me the details," I said. "Next thing you'll be telling me it's old man Carter—oh gross—or his son."

Her eyes widened on the son part.

"Oh, god. Brendon Carter. He's a pharmacist," I said.

"You know what they say." Ray had the audacity to laugh. "Always the cobbler's child without shoes." She began to sob.

It was all on me, again. I would probably need to boil ten times as much water. Right, if only it was all that easy. Somewhere in all the science books there had to be something.

"Stop crying," I said. "It won't help. There's no U-Haul solution for this, Ray. You've probably got two more months left anyway, right?"

She counted on her fingers from November. "Six weeks, if I don't deliver early."

"Let me guess. No, why don't I ask and get it over with: was I early?"

She nodded.

"When were you going to tell me?"

"I don't know. I did try to. I thought Sister Gabriella could help. I asked you to read the book."

"Have you seen a doctor?"

"Koda, when would I see a doctor?"

"Maybe we'll be rescued before—"

"Let's talk about it tomorrow," said Ray. "Please can we talk about it tomorrow? And make a plan to leave. We'll be out of here before the baby comes. I know we just will."

When Ray "just knew" things, the opposite always came true. We didn't talk about it the next day, or the next. And, like mother like daughter, I pretended it wasn't happening either.

Her thinking about how she didn't have her period must have

combined with some emerging maternal instinct combined with biological awareness. Two days after the news, she appeared with a hand-stitched set of sanitary napkins. "They don't have stickers or a belt or anything, but when you get your period—you haven't had it since we got here have you?—you can use these and then wash them in the striver."

Impressed she didn't call them rags, I accepted them with a single thank you. Then squirrelled them away in a purple bath product basket.

Twenty-Two

During one of the days I labeled as floating days, when we were too fearful to turn the final page to Day Ten, and too scared to discuss the baby's arrival, Ray asked me if it was getting hazier.

"And a smell to it," she said.

"Yeah."

"I can't see the peak beyond the Dog."

"Noticed that too," I said flatly.

"You did?"

"Yeah." I was full of loose affirmatives. "It's obscured by the haze."

"Haze from smoke." Ray connected it.

"Smoke from fire."

"Yeah." She caught a case of my loose yeses.

A strong breeze contributed to our conversation, delivering a telling puff of air laced with smoke. Parked itself right between us.

"There has to be some way out," I said.

There were still moments when I could not or did not believe we had fallen and survived. Flashes of ideas asked me to consider that this was not the real world—maybe it was heaven, more likely hell, or the purgatory between in which eternity would be spent with Ray. How was that different than life on Earth?

"The striver." She pronounced the word as if it was a Webster standard. "Water beats fire. And it's gotta lead somewhere."

"This isn't rock, paper, scissors," I said. "And in which direction would we go? Upstream or down?"

"Down," she said.

"Why?"

"Because downstream always leads to somewhere."

"How do you know?"

"It seems right."

"Sounds better than anything I have," I said.

I looked around us. We wouldn't stand a chance if fire whipped through.

"Wouldn't it be nice if the fire burned to the edge of that tree, then stayed burning to keep us warm all winter?" Ray asked.

"A magic fire you mean. And smokeless? That's an interesting fantasy, Ray. And would there be a 24/7 convenience store right beside it? Let me guess, it would have free food? All the Pixie Stix you could eat, and coupons for the KFC down by the striver."

"I was just supposin', Koda."

"I betcha it can snow here in September. Even August. If we don't walk out, we'll freeze to death."

"Koda, would you eat my body if it was frozen and it meant you could stay alive? I'm not asking, I'm saying, 'eat it, Koda.' I'm telling you now, if we freeze, eat my body. I'm giving it to you."

"Let's not go there, okay?"

"Would you want me to eat yours if you died first?"

"I have no doubt you would."

"What's that supposed to mean?"

"What I meant was, sure, I would definitely want you to eat me."

Telling her I wanted her to eat me was gift enough to take away the sting of my previous suggestion that she'd jump at the chance.

"I couldn't eat you, Koda."

"Well you should," I said. "If it means you would live." There was no pleasing her.

I didn't want to die. We had to get serious about leaving. Then what? If we found a town, it might be harder living there than here. How would we assimilate? The inner monologue was scrambled. Assimilate? As if we'd changed so much that we were like remaining members of some undiscovered tribe.

If only we could look at a map from above and see what the hike out might look like. What if we were close to a town and didn't realize it? Somehow, I knew we were not.

Her stillness closed the door to the discussion of leaving. Tension filled the spaces not already occupied by smoke or haze. I rose and went toward the outhouse area.

"Take the bear-scare if you're going a long way," she said.

"The what?" I decided not to pursue it any more than two words and grabbed her latest invention, a box of broken stuff that, when shaken, sounded like broken stuff in a box.

She had Stupid Tea brewing when I returned. Pine needles floated in my cup and some collected at the bottom when she poured. "I'll read 'em when you're done," she said.

"Okay," I answered.

She always promised to, but never did. Read them, that is. Probably because they only ever resembled a pile of pine needles.

Later the next day, after we boiled, Ray chose to look at the sky instead of gluing bones. She was full of fish and Stupid Tea, and lay like a carefree child cloud-dreaming, except there were no clouds. Her hands behind her head, bony knees bent, taking it all in. "It's the same pale blue as that Chevy Caprice we rode to Saskatchewan in.

We went to Estevan in that Boyd guy's Chevy. Remember that, Koda, or were you too young to remember?"

"I remember I wanted a car seat."

"What summer was that? You were three. Hey, how could you have wanted a car seat when you were too young to know what a car seat was? When you were older you probably heard someone saying that kids should be in car seats and imagined that 'wanting' into the Chev." She dismissed me casually so she could go back to her room full of sky.

"No Ray, that's not the way it was. I mean, I know they're important, but I know in my heart that I wanted to sit in a car seat when I was riding in that car." I made a point not to look skyward.

"Sheesus, Koda, you were three years old."

"Doesn't matter."

"You were too young to know. Too little to want."

"Too little to see out the window. I couldn't see out the window, Ray."

She ignored me.

"I didn't feel safe," I said to the side of her body while she continued to gaze upwards.

"You still here ain't you?"

I didn't like her pretending another voice. Being high on hazy-grey-blue made her accent change. She picked up on my disapproval because she changed her tone.

"You're still here aren't you?" She said it to me, not the sky.

"That's not the point," I said.

"There doesn't have to be a point."

"Says who?" The voice of a preschooler left my mouth.

"Says no one. There doesn't have to be a freaking point to everything."

"Yes, there does." I said it under my breath because arguing with her was fruitless. She'd screwed up. She didn't want to be reminded that she'd put me at risk. Even now, she'd done it to me. To us. It was her fault we were here. And she was going to put another child at risk too. The second she'd stepped into the trailer, with her video games, and hid in Plaid Chair, she'd placed me and her baby-to-be at risk. I wondered if that almost-formed human inside her could hear her, or sense Ray's irresponsibility the day we stowed away. Had the almost-formed-human tried to call out to her? What else had reached it? What did it think of Stupid Tea?

She refused to let me connect my wanting a car seat memory to a review of her parenting. "Well then, tell me, Miss There-has-to-be-a-point, what's the point to all this?" She brought herself up to a semi-sit, opened her arms, and spread them to include the trees, the trailer, Four Peaks And A Dog.

I didn't answer. She was being a pain in the ass. My ass.

"I'll tell you something though." She was determined to make her point.

"What?" I caught myself before stretching the word.

"We somehow came off the road, rolled onto something else."

"Gravel or some kind of dirt logging road." I interrupted, helping her with the basics before she made her point, which I was sure would tick me off.

"Sure," she said, acknowledging my word help. "We came off the road, rolled onto gravel-dirt, and then fell off the world into this, whatever it is—a long flat place in the trees, and you know whaaat?"

"What?" I made it super short, promising myself never again to copy her moronic "whaaat."

"When we did fall into this place, you weren't wearing a god-damned seatbelt and you weren't strapped into a car seat, and you survived. At least you appear to be okay, though sometimes I wonder."

My laughter had spittle in it. In the trailer, I'd strapped myself to the frame, dammit. Winched to the railing with a freaking hoodie-turban-helmet on my head. I'd made sure we were both strapped in. I wanted to go hysterical so she got it, but I knew she never would.

Her "sometimes I wonder" comment bugged the hell out of me— all the time I'd been evaluating her mental state she might have been assessing mine? I stayed sitting on our version of beanie bag chairs, collapsed cardboard boxes filled with drapes and all kinds of fabric stuff. "So, you're saying what? That I went to Estevan and survived, and I fell off the earth and survived?"

Ray nodded. "Same thing really. And hey, another irony?"

I didn't know she knew the word irony, but figured she still might not know the meaning.

"It was just as flippin' hot and dusty there as it is here."

"So, you're saying you knew I would be safe? In Estevan and in the trailer?"

"Let's face it, Koda. I don't have to know. I already discovered you are safe all the time—as sure as Columbus was when he discovered America. You just are. You're a survivor."

That was it. The straw that broke the camel's back. I got up and marched in the opposite direction than the striver. Fast. Forceful steps. I muttered. I stomped. Columbus' discovery was a bit of a mistake, seeing as he was looking for India.

Sweat beaded on my forehead. Wrong about all history, Columbus and my childhood. But she was right about one thing: it *was* as hot here as it was in Estevan.

I moved on. Through. Further and further down the Ray hallway of fame. Recounting failures, sometimes out loud. Like the one time, forty-eight hours after she met Mr. Right, who was Mr. Old-enough-to-be-my-great-grandfather, she became engaged—without a ring. The announcement coincided with a triple windfall of a child tax credit, sales tax refund, and some provincial government give away, which fuelled the impulse to purchase a wedding dress. Seven hundred dollars. Then, by the end of the week, we were back to abnormal. He was gone; she hadn't even known his last name. The huge puffy white marshmallow was suspended from the light fixture in the living room until she found the emotional strength to let me put it in the closet. A few months later, after the lyrics to a western heartbreak were pronounced complete, I was able to wrestle the dress on the bus and bag seventy-five for it at a consignment shop.

Somewhere along Anger Avenue and Rant-a-little-more Road, there were flattened sections where the grass had been bent. Deer beds. Looking at them calmed me. My own space. A secret from her.

I rested in one and used the time to miss Green Jean in the way people miss people who are dead. I used the memories for positive energy rather than sadness, and pictured her sitting in a comfy armchair in the bay-windowed nook of the downtown library, one half of her body being warmed by the afternoon's sunlight. I missed her stories of Levi Jean, her late-husband. And how we'd named Bob, from behind the Esso Station, Oily Bob, and how he hadn't minded us doing that, and then he'd got a job there because of our name for him.

Twenty-Three

I startled. I'd drifted off in the deer beds. It was daylight. I'd have known if a night had passed. For sure I would have woken. And there would have been some temperature change and even dew. I put all my energy to thinking about the signs of morning and night on the mountain. I couldn't understand why I had no recall about what mornings were like. It didn't matter for my current situation—the sun was high in the sky—if a day had passed, then it had passed.

I sensed a visitor beside me. Fearful, I turned my head and there she was: Katie Karma. And why not? I'd been the one who stormed off without paying attention to time or direction. I deserved trouble.

Ray was survivor extraordinaire, diviner of water, catcher of fish, harvester of bounty, brewer of Stupid Tea. I only circled words, rounding them up and spitting them into her face.

No vocabulary would help me now. I had no idea where I was in relation to the trailer.

The degree of fear increased with the passage of time. Body part by body part appeared to recognize that, post-tantrum and pre-meltdown nap, I had not been simply-a-walkin'. No, I'd been moving in anger. Rambling in rage.

I remained prone, certain that, when I stood, I'd feel just as lost.

The predictable "this can't be happening to me" followed as the door to panic swung open. Extra confusion surfaced because Ray and I were already lost due to the stowing away in the trailer, plunging off the world, and setting up a home in the middle of nowhere. Lost inside lost.

I listened for water. Nothing.

I stood. A slight breeze of optimism pushed me to explore a stand of trees.

I kept imagining I'd recognize something at the next turn but, when familiar didn't materialize, anxiety inched in like a burst pipe might force water into a basement.

I was in a small, windowless, concrete room.

The water flooded to my ankles. Then the knees. Soon, I had to tread water. My head bobbed above the surface. My arms worked in back and forth survival. I sucked in the last bit of air. Where was my James Bond kind of escape?

Rather than drowning, I was suffocating in air; the brain saying: "why bother breathing?"

I began panting to let life kick in again.

All of a sudden, the trailer and our stuff and Four Peaks And A Dog looked like civilization, because here in the wild, with no names for landmarks, where walking became stumbling and direction became obscured in a pine-tree-top strobe-light kind of way, there were no geo-human identifiers. Insanity was a step or two beyond the next tree trunk.

The next stage seemed to be acceptance. I wore an imaginary label, one of those red and white HELLO tags people wear at conferences. The kind that needs a name filled in below the greeting. Mine said, HELLO my name is: PATHETICALLY LOST.

I'd heard that the best thing to do when you don't know where you are in the forest is to hug a tree, but remembered the next bit— that someone who knows you are missing will come find you. The search party scenario frightened me. On the first level of realization: we were nobodies to the world. On the second level, which encompassed my current problem, how would Ray find me if she was already a part of Team Lost? We were as lost as each other. I abandoned the "stay put" plan and decided that, since I had no bearings, I might as well lose my mind.

Electing to slip into insanity was gentler than going directly to stark-raving-mad. It allowed me to select the criteria. Choosing from an absurd take-out menu—one item from column A and two from column B—I combined forced calmness with manic talking, and added a side of paranoia.

One way of managing the craziness was to not look up and get dizzy from seeing the top parts of the trees that appeared to crisscross each other under the sky. My focus remained within my own personal height and width bubble. Doing this allowed my mind to slow and, in the relax, it delivered a "good job, Dakota."

I lifted my head a little and watched Katie walk away.

Micro-management was the key. I defined the place. "Base Camp." I spoke aloud and gave it a Roman numeral. "Base Camp I." An official "somewhere" that could be left and even returned to. Calling it something other than lost gave me hope. The naming continued. A tree with a snapped limb became Broken Branch Tree. BBT. "Hello BBT. I will use you as my little leaning place while I name the other items in Base Camp I."

With BBT's support, two trees, similar to each other, made their presence known. "What shall I call you? I know. I'll call you The Twins. Hello, Twins. *Hello, Dakota.* That's *Sergeant* to you, Twins. *Hello, Sergeant Dakota.*" In my folly I'd identified an official location, given life to three things with two names, and spoken for them. The ingenuity alone deserved an elevation in rank.

Between The Twins and BBT I marked out a narrow triangle with my heel. Two long sides and a short bit between The Twins. I could see the triangle in a math book but couldn't remember what kind it was. I addressed my little army, forgiving myself for not remembering geometry. "Not like anyone here is a mathematician."

"Permission to speak, Sergeant," said BBT.

"Permission granted," I said.

"I *AM* a mathematician, Sergeant."

"Smart ass," I said, turning away.

BBT and The Twins chuckled amongst themselves. I sat in my triangle. My stomach grumbled. The soldier in me said that I was okay because I was in Base Camp I, and with that I tied two saplings together in one of my famous "I am here" X's.

I considered trekking from Base Camp I to somewhere. Maybe home, maybe Base Camp II. "Yes, I'll do that. And I'll keep talking to myself. I'll talk as much as I want to. And OUT LOUD." I looked at the ground to steady myself from the giddiness caused by the criss-crossing of the treetops effect. "I'll be moving on soon. Just waiting a few minutes to settle the troops. Give you soldiers your orders. Review the plan." Procrastination alleviated panic.

It all looked the same, tree after tree, except for The Twins and BBT, yet somehow that was comforting enough. "Okay fellas, I'll take my leave. At your posts. Remain on guard." After feeble salutes, and a sigh from BBT, I marched out in style, then plodded through the trees, scaring a few birds up from the forest's floor.

The terrain remained the same for about an hour or so. Then it was time to evaluate another spot for no reason other than it was the place where my confidence waned. "Aha, Base Camp II."

I found a place large enough to sit and reminded myself of the importance of evenly spaced breathing, then chose a tree buddy. "It'll be dark soon. But what-the-hey, people stay at Base Camps all the time. Even spots with hardly any oxygen. Like in the Himalayas. Right? Or the Andes?"

My new host's silence did not stop me. "Civilian?" I asked. No answer. "I'm addressing you, sir. Military or civilian?" Nothing.

"Okay, have it your way," I said. Something shuffled in his branches. "No problem," I said, suspecting he might be a secret operative.

Base Camp II was better supplied than Base Camp I. Lots of pinecones on the ground. "Hey, did you see Mr. and Mrs. Squirrel here?" I asked Silent Spy Tree, but he didn't have a chance to respond because I did. "Red Alert, Red Alert. Whoop, whoop, whoop." I mimicked radioactivity warning signals. "Evil Berry Bush dead ahead. Dead ahead. Whoop. Whoop." I remained seated, shuffling my bottom along the ground in a retreat from the full bloom of berried bushes.

Secret Spy Tree pointed to another pine near Evil Berry Bush. It was missing a strip of bark. I summoned some courage, clutched some berries in a mitten of leaves, and painted a feeble BC II where the bark was missing. It ended up a big red blotch.

My mouth opened, and I let out all my exasperation. A lengthened version of the word "cry" came back to me. After the echo, I modelled another version of pity that came out as a series of "wha-whas." I whimper-stopped, then wiped my snotty nose on my arm. I hiccupped and then whispered the word "okay" about a hundred times.

Communication was important to me, and another hand-sized piece of bark served for my next project. I clicked on a swirly knot part. "Base Camp II to Home Base. Reporting in. Are you receiving? Over."

Missing Bark Tree was clearly military, eager to go on watch. His branches waved about in impatience—implying lights-out. I radioed out. "Base Camp II to Home Base. Bedding down. Base Camp I, do you read me? Over and out."

"Be consistent," whispered Missing Bark Tree. "When you call out. It's either Base Camp I or Home Base. It can't be both. Home Base is the trailer. Is that what you meant?"

"Fuck off," I said.

"Dakoda-girl," said Green Jean. "You promised."

I curled up into a ball of sorry.

A person can only get so comfortable folded into themselves. Squirrels, pinecones, and Ray floated in and out. Had she decided to look for me? Was she lost? I hoped she'd stayed put. That was the best way. She should hug the proverbial tree. Preferably Six O'clock.

The drum announced its presence before sunrise. "Don't listen," said Missing Bark Tree. "That's trash talk." As the sun's first rays warmed me, the drum faded. When I'd been up in the sky Eagle said it was in the dream, and the dream had been dreamed, so why was it back now? Eagle said? Eagles don't talk. What was I thinking? I was never in the sky, was I?

Where the drum had been over the last while, I did not know, even if it was in the dream that was dreamed, it was back now, and I worried that if we ever got out of here, that is, after the "if I ever got out of here," I'd need to sleep in a U-Haul type trailer for the rest of my life so I'd never have to hear it. Maybe the presence of kryptonite was what took it away. I could have a green-glowing ball of it beside me, maybe in a lamp. Could a person buy kryptonite? Was it in a chemistry lab at school? Wait a minute, was it a fictional mineral? I would look it up in the mini-encylos… I had to find my way back, to find out if it was a real thing.

I drifted off in the new day's promise of warmth.

Strange as it may seem, I re-woke renewed and optimistic. Over a breakfast of natural granola—seeds from the ends of pinecones—I punched the knot mark on the bark in an attempt to contact someone. "Base Camp II to Home Base. Come in Home Base. Over. Ray. Do you read me?" I shuffled about a bit and sucked on small branches of needles to get a bit of moisture and flavour, then walked around in tiny circles, calling Ray's name in hopeful repeats.

Having saluted Secret Spy Tree and Missing Bark Tree, as well as radioing my intentions to anyone who might be on the same frequency, I expanded the circles then chose a direction. I walked some more, occasionally transmitting short radio messages, and managing a half-smile, confident I was moving in the right direction. And then, all of a sudden, there it was: Base Camp I. Over and freaking out.

I pictured a waterway about the same width as our striver. But the one I pictured was not flowing—more like a canal of still water with turds floating on the surface. I willed it away, permitting a headache instead of the imagery of having arrived up Shit Creek.

You are a moron, I told myself. No, don't let them see your error. This was a planned return to Base Camp I, to make sure everything was okay and to check that no one else had been there.

"Base Camp I all secure. Over," I said, radioing Base Camp II purposefully.

Broken Branch reminded me: "Slip in and out, Dakota. Better to have control of the mental breakdown. Embrace it. Accept the total ridiculousness of it all."

I used the time to scavenge. Miraculously, I found some cones, forced out the seeds, and devoured them. I rested in the triangle of space I'd defined as my special area, then daydreamed about leaving. Once the decision to carry on was made, I straddled a curved hobby-horse kind of stick named Midnight. At some point I dismounted, and the animal walked alongside me.

Midnight's excellent sense of direction did not lead us back to either Base Camp.

"Good boy," I said.

He whinnied.

He loved it when I reached up past the end of the stick and patted his invisible neck. I loved it too. The wiry-ness of his mane was a complete contrast to the deep velvet of his neck.

The trees began to thin. Time to consult my radio. "Dakota Starr Harrison reporting terrain change. Home Base. Home Base are you receiving? Terrain change. Closing in. Over."

I promised myself it was true. The ground was different. I wrongly identified a naturally crossed branch as my own handiwork, then optimistically roamed in random patterns for ages. Eventually, when I realized there'd be no trailer beyond the imagined familiar landmarks, I considered my soul missing in action and recorded a final transmission. By my calculations it was only early afternoon, but it didn't matter. I was spent. "Dakota Starr setting up Base Camp III. Final destination, Base Camp III. Reconnaissance mission complete."

I placed the radio on a soft bit of earth and cozied up on a moss pillow, pretending it was Midnight's smooth neck. "Soldier down. Down. Down. Over. Out."

From my lying down view I observed that Base Camp III boasted triplet trees and a type of bush I'd not seen before. Base Camp III was a nice place, and I decided I could die there. And, if for some reason I did not quite cross over, I could become the spirit of a crazy mountain woman who granted wishes to wayward travellers, not like the witch in Hansel and Gretel, more like some kind of karmic teenage soothsayer.

Within reach were the longest grasses I'd seen on the adventure. They exposed milky roots when torn from the ground. I sucked on them by the fistful. Cones and twigs of needled pine were scattered around. It was the ultimate in laziness, not having to get up to access moisture or food, meagre as it was. I grazed and napped until the sun set. Not having urinated in the last twenty-four hours was high on my mental list of one hundred and ten things not to think about. The fact my head was pounding rated up there as well. Once it was dark, real sleep came fast and I kept it dreamless even though I was powerless to keep it drum-less.

Birds chirped. Moisture coated my body. The same kind of dewiness overlaid the surrounding grass. I licked my salty arms then sucked a bouquet of branches with pine needles and grass, slightly surprised with my continued survival. I stretched out on my back. The tops of the trees appeared to bend only a little, not as ominously as previous days. A few clouds dotted the sky, and a jet stream snaked the wrong way, rising up instead of across, at the edge of my sky dome. Thinking it might be because I was on the ground, I sat up, eyes lazily following it, watching it dissolving as it rose, like smoke would.

I snatched up the walkie-talkie and depressed the talk button. "Dakota Starr to Home Base, come in. Over. Unidentified smoke at four o'clock. Come in. Over." I stopped myself from making a static sound, realizing the immaturity. "Leaving Base Camp III. This could be trouble or could be a sig—"

Ray was signalling. I did a little jump for joy and moved outward. "Dakota Starr receiving visual. Over." Lighter feet, lighter heart, propelling forward. "Base Camp III secure. Moving Out. Affirmative on the signal. Over and Out." I tucked the walkie-talkie into my waistband and gave the verbal command to my invisible troops. "Go. Go. Go." We forged toward the smoke signal, pausing only to salute the triplets and Lieutenant Bush.

I was mostly ecstatic when I reached the striver. "Home Base. Are you receiving? I have a visual. Approaching perimeter. Over."

The impending homecoming caught up with me. I paused to catch my breath and to don my old persona. Get cool I told myself. Prepare for lecture or welcome.

When I was almost home, I called her name. She'd sent me a signal and, though it had faded, I could imagine how the fire would have crackled when she carefully made it in her circle of rocks. She would have wet branches with striver-water to fan the flames and make smoke. My dry mouth ached for the taste of YT and Under The Sea.

"Raaaaaay."

No answer. Same old same old. Maybe the fire wasn't even for me. Maybe she'd spontaneously combusted. So what if she didn't care. I was home. Coat would be waiting for me with open arms. There would be water to drink, fish to eat, tea to sip, books to read, a calendar of sorts. And I could look up kryptonite. And I would hug Ray no matter what because she had saved my life. I would hug her so long and hard that all the non-love of the past would be squeezed away and we would be best friends forever.

These thoughts were sucked away with one look. It was the longest negative I'd ever uttered: "Noooooo."

The tree-bark walkie-talkie stabbed my midsection as I lengthened my stride. Ray's legs looked extra-long as they stuck out beyond the lowered trailer ramp. I was afraid to even think the darkest thought at the edge of my mind, but it made its way in: Don't be dead, Ray.

Twenty-Four

"*S*arge! *Prop it up and attend to her injury.*" Apparently, the walkie-talkie had a video feature; Secret Spy Tree wasn't a spy, he was a medic. *Use Ray's staff for leverage, a bit at a time, and keep adding books, boxes, and the high-chair sideways, until you can get under it.*

He was right, a box of books and the highchair sideways-tipped were strong enough to hold the ramp above her. It gave me room to evaluate. "What should I do next?" I asked the tree medic through a piece of bark. How crazy had life become?

"It's going to be okay." I said it over and over. The water jug was handy. I angled it to take a few sips for myself, all the while putting the pictures in order. 1. Ray checks circle of stones. 2. Ray builds safe fire (to signal her beloved missing daughter). 3. Ray keeps vigil. 4. Ray walks by ramp. 5. Earth's negative vibes slam the ramp down on Ray. 6. Daughter saves mother in nick of time. 7. Mother smiles lovingly at daughter.

I poured some water on her head, mussing it around with my hand then tipping a bit near her lip. She gurgle-choked. I stopped. "Ray?"

"Koda?"

She attempted to lift her arm, either to touch me or following some kind of instinct to grab those near and drag them under.

"No, stay down. Don't strain." Though the request was soft, she began to cry. I leaned in so she could hold me. Through my own watery eyes, I focused on our closeness. It was like having underwater vision. I was careful not to put any pressure on her, thinking even the weight of one tear might crush her. Over time, she rolled and belly crawled, with my support, out from under the slightly raised ramp and made it to Plaid Chair. She sipped on a YT while I chugged one.

"It's not so much a gash," I explained. "More like a series of deep scratches." The crib sheet poncho made a good sponge for cleaning her shoulder. "For sure it's gonna be bruised."

I took some water over to Midnight.

"You have a staff," she said.

"Not really," I replied. "I mean it looks a bit like your stick, but it's not a stick."

"Well what are you doing to the non-stick?" she asked.

"Watering my horse," I said.

My answer startled all three of us. I gave him another drink, slapped his hindquarters, then watched him gallop away.

When I turned around I burst into tears and ran to Ray on account of she couldn't get up to come to me.

"Koda, it's okay. We're okay."

I couldn't get my words out properly. Between sobs and sputters I managed a "Ray, you saved my life. I wanted to hug you and now I can't."

"It's okay, Koda-bear-baby, let it out. Let it out. Let it all out, baby," said Ray.

I plopped down on a box of books beside her and put my head near, but not on, her chest to measure her shallow breaths. "I'm sorry," I said.

"Don't be. We are safe. We are together. We are here. Let it all out, Koda-bear-baby."

We rested and drank Cat Granny drinks throughout the day. Near sunset she spoke. "I can't get into the trailer. I'll have to stay out here tonight."

"The ramp will work," I reassured her, understanding her fear of sleeping outside. "I'll make it work. I can use the high-chair and Plaid Chair, and keep raising it a bit at a time until it's high enough for nothing to get in. I might even be able to get it all the way."

"It's not safe. It's broken. It fell on me. I'll sleep out here."

"You don't like sleeping outside. I'll fix it," I said, speaking the promise while walking over to evaluate the damage.

As the sun went down, I helped her over the broken ramp and into the trailer. I went outside and poured leftover Stupid Tea directly into my mouth from the teapot's spout before getting to work.

A trio of scented candles lit up the area where the metal had broken—where we'd hammered it when we'd first arrived. A few stolen logs from the bench, angled against the raised ramp, worked to hold it shut. I secured that section with a couple of bungee cords, attaching the hooks to various areas on the outside of the trailer's frame. When it was done, I dragged a couple of long pieces of dead-fall and triangled them between the ground and the door. Flying buttresses is what Jean would have said, pointing out some architecture in a book on the table at the Castell Library. Helper Trees is what I called them. I had no idea if it would hold, but at least it couldn't fall inside and hit us. We'd stay clear of the area, we'd have to.

After I'd inserted myself through our regular roof opening, I spied the bark walkie-talkie, on Coat. "Mission accomplished. All secure. Over and out." I spoke quietly into the toy while watching the rise and fall of Ray's chest.

She murmured my name.

"I'm gonna wake you up every little while, okay? You might have suffered a concussion."

"The signal," she whispered.

"I saw it. I'm here. You saved me." After what seemed like thirty minutes I roused her, then waited a bit and woke her again. Coat beckoned me to snuggle for a bit. The moonless night tempted sleep. A little rest, I decided.

"Morning." She was up close, pushing the word through her dry lips.

The excuse that Coat had seduced me and the sky had been too black, wasn't good enough. I'd not woken her past that second time.

"I am never having kids." I stated it adamantly.

"Okay." She attempted a smile.

"Really, Ray. I'm serious. I am NEVER having kids. Parents are supposed to stay awake and watch over their children when they've had an accident. It could have been fatal. You could be dead."

"Koda, you're not my parent." She cradled her belly.

"How are you feeling?"

"If we could get to the striver, I'd love to soak."

I removed the bungee cords and buttresses—undid all the work I'd done the night before, then slowly lowered the ramp with the help of the deadfall, before leading her out. I put her in Plaid Chair, which I'd dragged to the other side of the trailer. Then I put it all back together without the help of Plaid Chair. Why? I don't know. Because we were going out? I guess it was a version of locking the door. We inched all the way to the creek, a zillion things in the beach bag over one arm, and Ray steadied by my other.

"What's that?" she spied my bark.

I released her and clicked it on. "Home Base receiving?"

"Wicked," she said.

Twenty-Five

Day Nine faded like an old calendar in an abandoned gas station.

It took two days to re-hydrate and fill myself with fake and real fish, and about the same for Ray to heal. We let more days pass, playing them out in our old routine.

We went through our paces in slo-mo due to Ray's soreness and my weakness. When we tramped back and forth, her belly bounced ahead of us.

Ray insisted she do the fishing, so we padded her platform with rolled-up curtains. She said she'd wished she'd padded it before.

Over time, the Cat Granny drinks energized us.

"Koda," Ray whispered, as if the world might be eavesdropping. "We've been here for weeks. I looked past Day Nine. Day Ten has no directions." She fetched the book from the tree, pointed to the inner spine, showing how Day Ten's instructions had been removed from the binding. This left a blank page opposite the page headed GRAD-UATION. We'd let the days go by, fearful of what might be on Day Ten, and whatever it was we were supposed to know for the final day before graduation had been removed. What a crock.

"What do you think we should do, Koda?"

"Maybe let it hang there forever."

"There would have been instructions. Some kind of final exercise. It would have told how to do the ceremony. It's not like anyone wrote in the rest of the book. What shits they were to take out that page." She rifled through the entire text, to prove to me that no one except us had used it.

"It doesn't matter," I said.

"I don't think we should sit around. Let's do a super-uber good day. Then we can genuinely graduate tomorrow?"

"Just another day in paradise, you mean." Only my head was showing as I had inserted myself into our trailer, wanting to lazily mark official time.

"Don't run away from Day Ten, Koda. Let's really do this. I don't want to screw it up." Enthusiastic, despite her injury, that was the extent of her lecture. But it drew me back out.

While she wrote on the blank page to invent a schedule, I realized I hadn't journaled anything for a long time. Her words were printed in the survival book. Other than making circle word stories in the encyclopedias, my writing was all inside my head. If there was a scale for measuring literacy, my reading far outweighed my writing.

I considered the evolution of the personal diary and its use. The little lock, the tinier key, a horse or a cat picture on the cover, or plain, sometimes Bible-like with gold-edged virginal white pages.

The first entry was always carefully written with well-chosen words, in the best handwriting example possible, written with a special pen purchased from under a glass counter at a specialty store —or one that someone like Green Jean gifted you.

That pen that was going to make a writer out of its owner. And that writing started with rich, descriptive, brilliantly crafted phrases written with perfect penmanship, not the diary owner's usual thick jottos. Days later, sporadic entries evidenced poor standards—sloppy script. Not always with the special pen. Often scrawled in anger. Months between dated complaints. Blank pages becoming sad statements of inability or refusal to document. Non-use, signifying the nothingness of every-day.

Picturing those pages now, a quote Green Jean once showed me came to mind. I could bring it back anytime, exactly how it looked in print. Like when you look at someone then close your eyes and see the outline of them in your head and think, hey, does this have something to do with how cameras were invented?

Sometimes I go about in great pity for myself and all the while a great wind is bearing me across the sky.

— —OJIBWAY SAYING

I'd never understood it when I knew Green Jean, but with Ray at the tree, standing with her staff-of-life—just a silly stick—and me hanging out in our reading room, two worn-out chairs on scrub, I began to get it. We knew way more about ourselves and each other than we had weeks ago. More than any other time in our lives, we were learning from our mistakes. The difference between when we'd arrived and now was amazing. We boiled more efficiently, bathed in the right depth and current, and washed our clothes like trained river women.

While Ray was over by the tree, in her office, I told her that, before we graduated, there was something private I had to read. "It shouldn't take too long," I said.

"Okay, I'll do a regular day tomorrow, and you can read your private stuff, then we'll do a super-uber good day the day after tomorrow—that can be Day Ten. Then the day after that we'll graduate."

I believed her. She had become true to schedule. Honest with plans.

Twenty-Six

"Fetal grief," said Green Jean in my dream. "It's like when a person has unresolved feelings from in utero." She leaned against the dumpster in the alley behind Carters. "I'm not explaining this well, am I?"

"Could we have this conversation somewhere else?" I asked. "On account of you being murdered, and all the blood. Besides, I need some time to read my Lifebook. I gotta do it before Ray and I graduate."

Next thing, we were sitting in the comfy armchairs that are positioned in the south facing bay windows of the William Castell Library, but all that was outside the glass was forest. The city street was gone. I noticed we were on identical copies of Plaid Chair.

"If a person can be sad before they are born, then they might remember it after they were born, and that would be fetal grief." Green Jean simplified the statement. "I'm not convinced we are total people before we are born. I mean we can't survive outside the womb until a certain time, even though we have form. But I believe those who are carried to full term, or near full term, remember things."

Jean stared at me in my dream. Then the library closed. We were shuffled out the door with a whole bunch of other people—some I recognized—and in the bottleneck at the door, and on the busy city street outside the library, we became separated. A silver SUV raced by and jolted me out of sleep.

"Fetal grief." I tried out the words.

The sun began to light up the trailer. The stepping-up box had bunched up toward where our heads were, so I inched down and then curled closer to Ray. I fought an urge to suck my thumb and flap my arms and kick my feet. And then the sunrise began warming the sides of the trailer, and the binder slipped from underneath my pillow-roll. I rested the report on my chest.

Ray opened her eyes.

"It's that book I told you about. A Lifebook," I said.

"So, this is your day to read it," she said. She got to her feet, held onto her basketball belly, realigned the stepping-up box with her feet, then climbed onto the chalkboard top, let go of her belly, and pulled herself up onto the roof.

"That's like way more than a chin up, you know that right? Like you are really strong." My voice sailed up to the hole in the roof.

"Take your time," she said when she was standing on the roof. "I'll see you later."

"So, I read today, we do Day Ten tomorrow, and then we graduate the next day?"

Her whole head popped down through the hole. "Duh, yeah," she said.

A typed note slipped out of the binder and onto my bedroll. It informed me, in an insert-name-here generic style, that it had been mandated all children in care who were going to be adopted would be provided a history of their situation. The history would be written into a Lifebook format, so that insert-name-here could come to terms with why they were removed from the care of their parent or parents.

The books were prepared by social workers who specialized in writing narratives that would help a child to move forward.

A handwritten note was stapled to it.

Dakota, I realize that you were returned to your birthmother, but this had been prepared because there were plans for you to be adopted. Even though you weren't adopted, and it is many years since the book was prepared and you were in care, I have discussed the release of it with our board of directors. The decision is that it is your property. It would not be right for it to be destroyed.

In addition, on a personal note, the nature dress sent with this report is sent with deep gratitude that you were willing to receive it. When you dance in it, I believe I'll feel your energy, and I shall remember my precious Destiny Summer.

My mother, Destiny's grandmother, is so pleased one of Martha's favourite people and most creative of students will wear it.

If you can, please have Martha send a few photos.

Best, Joanne Bridgeford

The notes were loose. Everything else was three-hole punched and secured in the binder. A sheet protector encased the first page which was pink construction paper on which a tiny, folded disposable diaper had been secured.

The sticky tabs of the diaper were angled so that the diaper looked like it was already on a baby. Its waistband featured alphabet building blocks. There was a message typed on the pink paper:

When you were a baby you were too small to fit into this new-born size of diaper. Your hair was as soft as the down on a duckling and your eyes as bright as the summer's sunshine. You were absolutely beautiful. You still are.

I puckered the plastic sheet protecter, making the top opening wide enough to slide my hand inside. The diaper had been attached to the paper by a small piece of doubled over masking tape which came away easily from the paper.

I withdrew the tiny diaper and placed it on my palm, imagining my legs sticking out of the leg holes and my tummy coming up above the top part. It was unbelievable I'd been that small.

Ray banging her feet up the outside ladder startled me. I slipped the diaper back into the sheet protector, overtop the pink paper that said how beautiful I was, and closed the Lifebook.

"Here," said Ray, popping her arm through the roof's hole. She released a Granny Cat drink, a can of Under The Sea, and a spoon.

"Watch it," I said. "They almost hit me."

"I'm heading to the striver," she said.

I catapulted her my extra undies.

When she was gone, I reopened the binder to the page after the diaper page.

You were born on October 20th, at four in the morning, at the Royal Alexandra Hospital in Alberta. You weighed 2,585 grams, which is five pounds eleven ounces.

It was hard to pick something in the trailer that weighed about six pounds or 2,600 grams. Anywhere else, I could have gone to a grocery store and read the weight on a bag of flour or sugar.

I flipped back to the diaper page. Did my hair used to be as soft as the down on a duckling? If Binky's mirror were around, I'd be able check if my eyes were as bright as summer sunshine.

Twenty-Seven

Each page was numbered in the top right corner along with a title: Tell Me My Story: A Lifebook for Dakota Starr Harrison.

When we were babies, we listened to the voices around us and watched the people nearby. When we were babies, and were cradled by certain people, we knew that no harm would come to us. We felt secure when we looked into their eyes. We knew we were safe.

When some of us were babies, some people made us feel uncomfortable. We could not relax in their arms because we did not always know what would happen next. We did not always have secure feelings when we looked up into their eyes.

We were very clever when we were babies: we felt, we heard, and we saw a great deal. We knew who we felt safe with. We knew it from feeling and hearing.

At about one year old we began to walk, and say words. We copied what others were doing. We attempted to understand the things we'd been feeling and listening to so far in our life.

No matter what age we might be, we are always learning. Learning about ourselves, learning about others, learning about the whole world.

During our growing up time we might ask some questions. Why is the sky blue? Where did I come from?

Lifebooks answer some of these questions because the information has been carefully gathered from the records of social workers, and from interviews with helpers and family members. If you are a first-grader and someone is reading your Lifebook with you or if you are really old with grey hair and lots of wrinkles, these words in your Lifebook will always have special meaning.

I took the binder full of its typed pages, and my breakfast, outside. With Ray at the striver, I'd be able to get comfy in Chair.

Moments later, Ray emerged from the outhouse area. "No, it's okay. Don't get up. I'm going. I mean I'm really going. I mean I just went poop, but now I'm really going to the striver."

She detoured to a stack of boxes, then appeared with my poncho and put it around my shoulders. "It'll protect you from the sun." She poured leftover Stupid Tea into my teacup, covered the top with its saucer, and smiled.

I pretended we were mountain women, and the crib-sheet poncho was a bearskin.

There have always been happy, helpful, safe families, and there have always been people who have serious struggles. Those with challenges sometimes find it hard to connect with community helpers. One day it would be nice if all families had fun times and safe, healthy ways but, until then, there will always be people who try to help these families and who become involved so that children can be safe.

"Wait a minute," I said. "This is supposed to be my life, not Ray's."

"What?" Ray answered from the perimeter of our tree clock boundary. "You want me to wait?"

"No," I shouted. "Go do your thing."

"Okay, sing, yes. Thanks for the reminder. I love to sing."

I stopped myself from screaming for her to get out of here.

When we are born, we all depend on a caregiver to get us through the stages of being a baby and through our childhood. Everyone is born with a certain temperament or personality and that personality develops further as we grow up.

I figured that if I had been five when I received this, and someone, say like a Green Jean or a Martha had been around to read it to me, then the way it was written would have worked for me in that storytelling-for-little-children kind of way.

Still, I got the point; even held out my hands and imagined them miniaturized. Pictured my hands and feet and arms and legs as tiny as they had been when I'd been small enough to wear the diaper.

Ray's out of tune vocals faded out of range.

The sections were a see-spot-run kind of narrative. A couple of pages each. Every-age words. Okay for a preschooler, but didn't insult my teenage brain. I was curious, too—how would it be possible to stay in once-upon-a-time mode when it came to explaining the shit storm that must have happened for me to warrant a Lifebook?

When I closed my eyes, I saw a tiny me developing. A little curve, spine on the outside, sort of like a letter C. That word I knew from the dream came to mind; maybe it wasn't even a real word—maybe I'd invented it: Fishbaby.

Your birthmother, Raylene Starr, was born on December first, in Edmonton, Alberta. Raylene's mother, Sandra, was born in a town north of Edmonton. While not much is known of Sandra's parents' history, it has been said that their ancestors included settlers and First People who guided the settlers through the undiscovered West.

Sandra's parents had two children: Sandra and Janet. The sisters spent some of their childhood in a small, northern town, then the whole family moved to the city of Edmonton.

Janet, Raylene's aunt, shared that her parents did not provide a safe home. When Janet left to go to a college, where housing had been arranged, she was only sixteen. Sandra was fourteen at the time. But by the time Sandra was sixteen, she had left home and was living with friends or wherever she could find a place to stay.

When Sandra was around twenty years old, she met a man from England named Ronald. He played in a band. When Sandra and Ronald discovered they were to have a baby, they decided to get married. Soon after Raylene was born, Ronald moved away.

A few years after he left, Ronald was killed in an industrial accident.

Basic as it was, it was the most information I'd ever had.

Twenty-Eight

Pages upon pages contained descriptions of places Ray had lived and social workers who had been involved. Concepts of neglect were explained, and social-worker-talk defined. Relationships and names were repeated to the point of my feeling dizzy. The writer must have anticipated lots of questions from a little kid to the person reading it.

It became heavier. Sandra using drugs. Hauling Raylene to parties or leaving her home alone. It was explained sensitively—not like I would re-tell it. Sentences like, *When Raylene was a toddler and pre-schooler, Sandra often had boyfriends who were hurtful to her and to Raylene.'*

All of a sudden, I wasn't hungry for my breakfast. Inappropriate touch, hurtful. I knew what the writer meant: PERVS. PEDOS. ABUSERS.

And I knew the social worker part would come next. Yes, lots of them involved. All trying to help.

At school, when Raylene was told to "pay attention" she did not have the power to help her mind stay sharp and awake—she was sleepy from not having proper rest.

Children who are stressed at home by threats, or experience chaotic lives, have a difficult time focusing. It's the same with an adult—it's hard for a person to learn when that person is in fear. Fear puts a body in a constant state of anxiety. As well as being stressed, Raylene had no one at home to show her the joy of learning or to explain why people go to school.

I remembered when I fell asleep in grade six math class. A teacher dropped a dictionary on my desk to wake me. All the kids laughed. Mr. Chapman. I hated him.

The chapter on fear and tired bodies ended. A lesson in sleep hygiene delivered at a primary level.

The Lifebook went on to describe how Ray got involved with the kind of lifestyle that Sandra had.

Raylene said that she began to use drugs when she was around thirteen, and that she left home at sixteen—in grade ten. She described a kind of restlessness that made her feel she had to move around.

I finished my breakfast, then got up and chose a chocolate YT from my own stash and drank it in three gulps over by Six o'clock Tree. Then I paced.

"Hug me or get back to your Lifebook," said the Tree.

"Come on," said Chair. "I'm all yours. She's gonna be gone for ages."

I did what I was told and learned that when Ray was seventeen she was five-feet-five-inches tall, weighed 130 pounds, and had dark brown hair and brown eyes. Not much of that had changed, but I supposed if I had never known Ray then the Lifebook would be telling me something I didn't know. Fair enough.

After her seventeenth birthday, Raylene became pregnant. She was assigned a community helper who was a student studying to be a social worker. In his role, he became a good friend to Raylene. It is believed he made sure Raylene was healthy and did not use drugs or alcohol during her pregnancy. He drove her to her appointments in a truck she loved to ride in. When Raylene was seven months pregnant, the social work student returned to university in another city.

My own name rang in my ears. And something Ray had said ages ago. That truck was my namesake, a Dodge Dakota for sure.

Sadly, near the end of her pregnancy, Ray went to a party, and she took a lot of cocaine. She became violently ill and was taken to the hospital.

"You were pregnant. With me. What were you thinking?" I went back a generation. "What the hell were you thinking, Sandra? What kind of person were you?" And back one more to Sandra's parents.

Where were all the fathers? And when they were around why couldn't they take care of their children? Were all my blood relatives like that? Drinkers? Drug users? Violent?

Warm and sour, the Stupid Tea still satisfied my dry mouth. Too invested in the book to add more water to my drink, I downed the last drops and then paged back.

An aunt named Janet. She'd helped. There were good people. What made the Janets of the world different? Why couldn't Janet have been my mother or my grandmother? Where was Janet? I wanted to see and speak to her right in that second. I stared down Six O'clock Tree and he moved toward me. It scared me until I realized it was just the wind blowing his branches.

My eyes fell back to the binder. I might as well know how the whole family crashed and burned.

Twenty-Nine

Everything a pregnant woman drinks, breathes in, or eats goes to her developing baby. If she uses alcohol and or drugs the baby is at risk from the dangerous chemicals.

After babies are born, they grow at different rates and do things around the same age as each other, but not at the exact same age. When most children are six, they have learned to feed and dress themselves. When most teenagers are in high school, they have some ideas of what kind of job they would like to do in the future.

When most people are over twenty-one, they show they are responsible by paying their bills, maintaining a home, and working at a job.

Raylene was only seventeen when she became pregnant. She struggled with day-to-day responsibilities.

I 'd be seventeen in a bit more than a year. I could not, for one moment, imagine a baby inside me. Part of me though, could imagine me being a baby inside someone else. Part of that part of me wished it hadn't been in Ray.

"When most people are over twenty-one, they show they are responsible by paying their bills, maintaining a home, and working at a job." I repeated the adult part to the arm of Chair.

I was a bit scared to go on. Maybe it was something in the wind that told me a nasty mess-with-my-head part was coming.

Raylene told the social workers that she had two boyfriends around the time she became pregnant. She said she was not seriously involved with them in a way that she was living with either one of them. One boyfriend was named Terrance (Terry for short) and the other was named Brian. Raylene said she had known both men for a long time and that she often broke up with one, dated the other, and then broke up again. She explained that both men were often violent.

A professional, who knew Raylene and Terry, had the opportunity to see you when you were one year old. She said you resembled Terry.

The writer went on to say that is why there was no father mentioned on my birth certificate. When a woman doesn't live with her partner, no partner need be mentioned on the official docs.

I had the genes from one of those losers. I breathed deeply and chanted a few okays. I made Terry be the better of the two guys.

When she told him, he probably called her a liar or worse: said he didn't want me. Then again, maybe he didn't know I existed, and he'd changed, was all responsible, rehabilitated, was a gazillionaire, and he had been searching for me for years.

"Get real," said Six o'clock Tree. "Read on. Your beginning is coming up."

In October, Raylene began to have signs that her baby would be born, even though she was due in November.

When a woman uses drugs during her pregnancy, her baby can be born earlier than expected. Early babies don't have the fat or insulation required to be in room temperature. Early babies are susceptible to becoming sick from viruses.

The next page was blank and the next one after that was pink and contained only this:

On October 20, the world stopped for a moment and became a more wonderful place.

You were born, Dakota Starr.

And you were absolutely precious and beautiful.

I smiled and read the last line over a whole bunch of times. Then I became sarcastic. "Oh, puleeeease. Write greeting cards do you, Ms. Lifebook Writer?" It appeared that speaking aloud to no one was becoming the norm for me.

But if the book was so, well, pro-me to the point of being ridiculous, why was my lip bleeding? Why was I lingering on the pink page? Why were there warm waves all around my heart? Why was the wind whispering that word? *Fishbaby.*

I brought my knee to my mouth to apply pressure to where I'd bitten.

An eagle circled, maybe that same eagle I'd met before. Her voice more the sound of a little chirpy bird than the sound movies brand birds of prey with. I took a break and watched her until she was a dot over The Dog. I re-read the sentences and wanted to believe that my birth had changed the world, and that I was precious and beautiful.

Six O'clock Tree swayed in agreement. "You were precious. And beautiful."

I shivered.

"You still are," said Tree.

"But if I was so beautiful, why didn't Ray smarten up? Why couldn't she make the changes so I could stay with her? This Lifebook was prepared *because* I'd been taken away her," I said to Tree.

You were born at about thirty-five weeks rather than the forty weeks that makes up a typical pregnancy. The results of a test showed that there were drugs in your body. Raylene said she had taken drugs the previous week.

Your tiny body had to get used to not having those drugs. You stayed in the hospital for two weeks. For the first few days you were kept in an incubator—this is like a little glass bed with a top. The inside of an incubator is a warm temperature like the birthmother's womb. Oxygen is delivered to babies in incubators to make sure that they are given every opportunity to succeed.

You were given medication to help you withdraw from the drugs in your system.

I felt the drumbeat pulse in my ears. "Stop," I said. I couldn't deal with the book and the rhythm at the same time. I went back for another YT then decided I might be addicted to them. I reached for a Sister G paperback, then kicked it off its cardboard table and onto the scrub.

Back at Chair, I carried on. "In for a penny, in for a pound," Green Jean used to say.

The carrying on reading included a whole chapter about drug relapse, professionals, and some legal stuff to make it so that the government would be responsible for me while Ray was supposed to smarten up. Foster parents.

Your foster parents, Sylvia and Roger, came to the hospital as soon as they were told you would be staying with them. You were two days old. They visited twice a day and wore protective clothing so that they could reach into the incubator and touch you. They read stories to you. And when you were able to be outside the incubator, they held you and fed you, rocked you, and continued to read stories to you.

When you were one week old, Janet heard about you through someone who knew Raylene. She flew to the city and came to the hospital. She met with social workers, and she met Sylvia and Roger. Her priority was to help Raylene who had left the hospital shortly after your birth.

At two weeks old, Sylvia and Roger took you to their home. They had taken care of over fifty babies in the past—not all at the same time. They have shared that you were quite shaky and sometimes kind of stiff. They understood, from taking care of other babies, that this was an effect of the drugs and that soon you would be used to getting by without drugs in your system.

*They fed you small amounts of soy formula on a regular schedule.
You slept in a crib in their bedroom. They were attentive and they
rocked you and held you a lot.*

Once I had tofu with Green Jean and Martha. That was soy. Did
that make me a vegetarian baby? Where does soy milk come from?
Soy cows?

It took the writer four pages of gentle words to say that the foster
parents supervised visits with Ray. Sometimes she showed, sometimes
she didn't. But okay, I could see how a little kid would need it broken
to them gently. If I didn't know Ray, or the predicament we were
currently in, I'd have appreciated the narrative more. Part of me knew
I should understand Ray did the best she could with what she had,
and a larger part was pissed at my having been given a crap deal.

"But were you given a raw deal?" asked Six o'clock Tree. "You
haven't finished the book. You're not even seventeen yourself."

"Well, it says here I was stiff; I cried; I was addicted to drugs. It
took a few months for me to get clean. How is that not raw?"

*Sylvia and Roger were an older couple and, in their younger days,
had been members of an orchestra. They loved classical music.
Though they have said they played a variety of music for you
when you were an infant, they focused on symphonies to
soothe you.*

*Sylvia and Roger became used to being with you, and you became
used to being with them. They took you to check-ups at the clinic.
They celebrated when you rolled over, when you lifted your head,
when you smiled. They took lots of photos.*

A new section began. Ray had improved. Every detail was shared of what she did to make changes. The places she attended, the classes she took, the social workers involved. Janet's input. My return to her in May, when I was seven months old. The name of the daycare centre: Tiny People.

When you were eighteen months old, your file was closed.

Thirty

If my file was closed, why was there a bunch more paper ahead? I wished the writer-person had told me my first words.

My mind was on fire with bizarre questions. If I took a lie detector test, and was asked if I had ever taken drugs, and I said no, would it register as a lie, because I had been given drugs?

Shortly after your second birthday, Raylene called her Aunt Janet and said she was sick and needed help.

"Here we go again," I said.

Janet flew in, tried to help. Ray was not totally responsive.

Raylene and you were taken to the hospital. The doctor said that Raylene was under the influence of alcohol and drugs. He also said that you were dehydrated from not having much to drink, and that you had a diaper rash that had formed from not being changed. You had burns on your bottom from your skin being exposed too long to the chemicals in your urine.

Even though you were in some pain, the nurses said that you were still happy.

When you were at the hospital, the nurses said that you played with some of the blocks and you said "puppy" and "Mama," and "hi."

I said the words quietly. "Pup-pee. Puh-pee. Pu-pee. Ma-ma. Hi." How had my voice sounded? Higher than now? Lower? Squeakier? This was a sad story, my sad story, but I found myself, under my breath, repeating: Puppy. Mama. Hi.

I made a sentence: Hi, mama puppy.

Raylene went to a place called a detox centre where she was supervised for seven days to make sure all the drugs were out of her system.

More foster parents, Tina and Bernie. I wasn't used to eating fruit and veg but that changed quickly. Older children around me.

Tina said you liked to eat peas and Cheerios—at the same time. She said you loved to have books on your highchair table, you pretended to read to your teddy bears, and you always had a little stack of books with you, even inside a plastic car you pedalled around in. Tina and Bernie said the other children called it your bookmobile. Your foster family described you as being an adorable, alert child. They said you were so clever.

Ray visited a few times—supervised visits. Then she left for a long-term treatment centre. The writer went into the searches that were done and the reaching out and efforts of many, including Janet.

It came to be known that Raylene had located her mother, Sandra, in Northern Alberta.

The cycle of addiction was strong for both Sandra and for Raylene. Addiction means not being able to stop doing something. When a person becomes addicted, they will do anything to keep doing that something. They may steal. They may lie. They may use the money that has to be used for groceries or rent and spend it on the games at a casino or spend it on drugs or alcohol. Addiction is not like wanting a candy and then realizing that you can't have one because there are no candies left in the bag. It is stronger than that. It is not like wanting more ice cream when an ice cream cone is almost empty. Those feelings of wanting can be strong, but we get over them and move on to other activities, because we know that we will have a candy or an ice cream cone at another time.

I tried to understand why she couldn't stop using drugs and alcohol, just for me. It was sad, yet it filled my need to know about my past.

I clung to Tina's sharing that I was bright. I turned the page. I had to. If I'd stayed on that page and thought about "little Dakota" any more my head would explode. If I took a break, I would break. Incapable of putting a stop to Ray's pain, which became mine, I repeated what the page header said: *Tell me my story.*

"That's right. Tell me my story. Do it fast. Get it over with. Screw this Lifebook. I'm damned if I read it and damned if I don't."

Six O'clock Tree agreed with me, his uppermost branches nodding. Possibly he was bored with the same theme, or he felt that the sooner it was over, the sooner I could move on.

Thirty-One

Miracle of miracles, Ray resurfaced a new Ray, according to the writer. She started visiting. She was involved in positive activities… compared to the activities she had been involved in.

Tina and Bernie wanted the best for Raylene, but they also knew that it was difficult for parents like Raylene to make long-term changes.

Foster parents find the right balance to prepare a child for change and yet have the child feel welcome and at home in their "temporary" home. Sometimes temporary becomes so long that more changes take place, and the foster parents and social workers have to help the child get ready to move on—not to return to their birth parent or parents.

Social workers know that there is a time to look for a forever family for the children in their care. They found a couple named Brenda and David who wanted a little girl just like you.

There are some people in the world who live life to its fullest. They receive the gift of life and embrace it. They come with names like Janet, Bernie, Tina, Sylvia, Roger, Brenda, and David. They see rainbows and joy where others see sadness. They see beauty in everything. Brenda and David knew that they wanted to share their lives with you.

The next dozen pages explained that I had lots of visits with Brenda and David. They took me to parks, a petting zoo, and shopping. Apparently I slept over at their house a few times.

They had created a bedroom for you, and a playroom. They organized a celebration for when you moved to their home. A moving date was set.

I turned the page and this was all it said:

That is your story, Dakota. It is certain Raylene will always love you. She wanted the best for you. Your adoptive parents have committed to remaining in touch with Raylene if Raylene would like that.

It is hoped that when you read this Lifebook, you will be able to understand the circumstances that led to your being removed from your birthmother's care.

Enjoy your life, Dakota. Every day is a gift.

"No, this is not my story, it's mixed up with someone else's because I'm here with Ray, not in some fancy house with adoptive parents. Something is wrong."

I turned the page. Another note.

Dakota: originally your Lifebook ended at this point.

Normally, it would have been delivered to your adoptive parents and they would have been able to decide when to read it to you or give it to you. Of course, this didn't happen, and the Lifebook—the actual binder —was locked in a file for a long time.

There are reasons for this, which you will find out in the rest of the book which I have completed all these years later.

Let me recap, before I finish the book in the style of the other writer.

As the time neared for you to have a goodbye visit with Raylene, and to move into the home of your adoptive parents, there was a tragic event. After that, your Lifebook stayed with the social worker until she retired, then she passed it to someone else.

A new social worker initiated a meeting and received permission to go into the archives and add some information, then send it to you. That was when you were about seven years old.

Unfortunately, there was a mix-up and, though it was supposed to be updated, the Lifebook was filed again (and found weeks before I contacted you). You will find below the catching up that was done, as I said earlier, I've continued in the style as the original writer. Hope this isn't too confusing.
　　– Joanne B.

But the adoption did not go through…

Three days after you moved in with Brenda and David,

so they could be like foster parents with a view to adopt you, Brenda suffered a stroke. She died before she arrived at the hospital.

Her husband, David, was heartbroken. He still wanted to be your dad, but he was grief stricken.

Tina and Bernie immediately stepped in so that you could return to their home and the routine that you were used to.

In the meantime, Raylene had completed six weeks of residential treatment with the only time away from there being the supervised visits with you. Rather than leave the treatment centre, she opted to stay in and complete six more weeks, visiting you only on weekends.

During this time, Sandra died from an overdose of drugs. Janet and Raylene attended a service in Northern Alberta. Janet has said that this, combined with all the support that was in place, gave Raylene the strength and willpower to leave her lifestyle of drugs behind.

You were moved back to live with Raylene. There was lots of supervision from the community resources in your neighbourhood—a large organization housed in a former gym, in which people from all specialities come together to help one another. You began preschool there, and the retiring founder of the organization, Jean Standish (wife of Levi Jean, I believe most knew her as Green Jean) became involved as a private volunteer, a role I am told she went beyond.

It is important for you to know that David arranged an educational trust for your future. Raylene was advised of this by letter, but the records show she did not acknowledge the letter. The paperwork was placed with the law firm McLennan & Company in Calgary, Alberta.

This Lifebook is also unique in that it had an ending which was interrupted and then was filed, and then found and refinished with a second ending.

Write a thousand more chapters of your Lifebook by living each day to its fullest. Dance under the rainbow that is forever above you. Every day is a gift.

NOTE: The photos taken of you in foster care are in the archives of the Child Services Office. I've enclosed contact information for you to retrieve them.

Thirty-Two

Wow. Another father who never became my dad. I could have and I would have totally glued macaroni on a can for that man.

How horrible, his wife dying like that after she was so close to becoming a mom. My mom.

But if she had not died, then Ray and I wouldn't be together.

The problem had always been that I never quite knew how to frame Ray and her ways. Now I had some reference.

It was too much.

I focused on the final lines of the second ending that should have come to me when I was younger.

Dance under the rainbow that is forever above you. Every day is a gift.

My closed eyes squeezed away tears. I built a wall in my throat to stop emotion. Grief for an adoptive mother. Sympathy for an adoptive father. Gratitude for Janet. A mix of confusion over Ray. Administrative appreciation for the social workers.

"Go inside," said Six O'clock Tree.

I pitched my head toward the trailer.

"No, in here," he said, a branch curving to where his heart might be.

I sunk into Chair and closed my eyes and imagined myself under a blue sky. My entire braincase featured a rainbow—the book's ending. Its paler double arced overtop. The colours were vivid, like a bold illustration in a child's picture book. I attempted to dance in my thoughts, but even in imagination my feet were cement.

The clunk of the book falling, and rattle of the cup and saucer, brought me out of the rainbow spell. It fell open to the final page: another pink cardstock inside a sheet protector. My birth date as the header. The book had started out with that date and a diaper, it ended with poetry. I supposed, because of the title, written for me.

The Twentieth Day Of October

For many, love is a heartbeat, a muscle, nothing more.

Never comparing its rhythm to ancient drums played ceremonially on riverbanks while fallen cedars ride wild rapids.

For some, love means childhood.

A youthful phase, of rainy days.

Ending with certainty at eighteen years.

For others, love is matter.

A scientific feat.

No playtime or hooray-time.

No melodic beat.

And to a few, love's fragile pulse, purrs a pre-emptive tune, not long enough for lyrics.

Cloudy with the probability of grief.

The backpack is heavy, and the sun burns even in frigid temps.

Each sweltering step higher, the load seems greater.

But true love's altitude refreshes.

Listen to the gale.

Its sonnet for you.
Hear it roar.
Heart-pounding powerful sounds, reaching great distances yet
gentle enough to be a whisper.

The trees blurred. Everything around me began to spin. How long had I been holding my breath? Who wrote that for me? A social worker? Was it an original? Was it copied from somewhere and not attributed? It hurt to believe something had been written for me by a stranger.

That it was the final page was a good thing. I couldn't have taken another; didn't have the energy to even turn to another one, let alone read anything else, though there was a line at the bottom of the page.

I tasted salt. When had I started crying?

Was this what it took to break me? A piece of poetry? What happened to clinical reports and facts on a spreadsheet? Who thought this was a good idea?

What was I supposed to do now? File it all away and carry on like I didn't know all this shit?

Ever the follow through-er, I pushed myself to capture the line at the bottom of the last page, far removed from the poem.

Note to therapist: when you have read through this with your client, or
instructed the adoptive parents on how-to, please contact the depart-
ment of social services through request form 45-B-47 for further
information.

I heard my own voice inside my head: "You have got to be effing kidding me."

Where was the caution at the beginning? Apparently, this was to be worked through with a professional. I looked to all the trees, put my head in my hands, let the binder fall, and waited for total meltdown for having taken in too much, over too little time, without supervision.

The breeze kicked up. Dust swirled. I stayed inside my cupped hands. Paper rustled. The tears kept coming even though I remained silent. I cried more than a lifetime of them. The wind turned pages, threatening to tear their fragile three-hole anchor. I pretended not to care. Let them blow all over the mountain. Let sixty-five kite-pages take to the air and travel all the way to Four Peaks And A Dog.

Why ridiculous wishes come true and meaningful ones do not, I have no explanation but, as if on command, the wind strengthened. It got darker inside my hands. I shivered and peeked between my fingers. Clouds blanketed our site. Nature shifted into overdrive and rifled through the pages. I lowered my hands and watched mother earth's weather liberate a chapter one page at a time.

My story was being torn apart. My life was falling apart. It took a swan dive to land and shut the binder, then a chase around the clearing to capture all the escaped pages. The last two I had to trap with my foot to stop them from getting away.

Nothing was ever easy. The tops of the trees agreed, swaying and bending, pointing to their own destiny.

I put the binder sideways in Chair, then went and washed my face. I was taking the third of a promised ten deep, slow breaths which I hoped would lead to clarity, when the wind dropped, and I felt Ray's approach.

"Hey," said Ray heading toward the circle where she cooked the fish over the fondue and boiled water for Stupid Tea. "Magic of all magics, they were biting this afternoon."

"Hey." I roused and took in her profile of a cook in a wilderness kitchen.

"Good book?" She gestured to Chair.

"Not a bestseller. But better than that Tuscany Sister Gabriella trash."

"You haven't read a Sister Gabriella. And you need to read the Tuscany one," said Ray. "Want some tea?"

"Think the fish were biting more because of the clouds and the windstorm?" I asked.

"What windstorm?" asked Ray.

"It swept through here, all clouds and menacing."

Ray looked up into the afternoon sky, all blue and sunny. "Like, no. It's a scorcher, babe," she said.

It seemed part of me had moved in a parallel universe with another weather system.

Thirty-Three

Day Ten involved an inventory of the YTs. Four each. We packed them away, deciding to substitute Stupid Tea. Two of three fish Ray'd netted the previous day were gobbled up, the third stuffed into the peanut butter jar. I remembered my new food discovery of pinecone nuts, and scouted some.

We cleaned the camp, including the bathroom. We rearranged our chairs. We shook out our bedrolls. We bathed. All in the name of an uber-good day.

When we'd finished dinner, staccato conversation replaced star watching. Did we do a Day Ten? Yes. Were we sure? Yes. We could turn the page and graduate.

"Okay, tomorrow we celebrate with double Cat Granny drinks," I said.

She began planning. "And tea?" she asked politely.

"Stupid Tea," I replied.

"The only brand worth drinking."

"Superior blend of Stupid Tea," I said.

"SBST." She abbreviated quickly, much to my amazement.

"Fish?" It was like she was checking off some kind of menu in the book.

"Of course," I answered.

"Fondue-eeed?"

"Fonduey-dueyeeeed," I stretched her version of the word, and continued. "And chocolate mousse with strawberries. And Champagne."

"Don't," she said. Instant sulkiness.

"Don't what?"

"Make it less than it is." She was upset.

"Chocolate mousse with strawberries and Champagne make it less? I thought it would make it more." I instantly regretted the sarcasm.

"You know what I mean, Koda." For a second her expression was pretty much one of a disappointed parent mid-grounding. "And diplomas," she said. She was done with food and onto administration.

"How?"

"There's one in the book." She held it up and showed me.

"But we need two."

"You can have it, Koda. I don't need it."

"Well let's see which one of us actually graduates," I said.

"If only we knew what we were supposed to do to graduate. Do you think I carried out all the instructions?"

"Oh yeah, Ray. You went way beyond, especially at the start when you did all that inventory." I was serious even though it may have sounded cynical.

"You mean I fizzled at the end."

"No. You were good at the end too, what with jingly bear thing, and the Stupid Tea, which isn't stupid, Ray, it's pretty good. God, Ray, look at how amazing your fishbone picture is."

"You think?"

"I don't just think, Ray. I know. God, Ray, you sent smoke signals."

"I think you did well too, Koda."

"My heart wasn't in it like yours was."

"You mean you did it because I wanted you to?"

"At first."

"Then what?"

"Then I was okay with it. It did give us something to focus on and to work with."

"So, we need two diplomas," she said.

"Apparently."

Ray took a piece of the onion skin paper, one of the ones that prevented a potential graduate from looking ahead, and placed it over the existing diploma, then, using a Sharpie, began to trace. I could almost hear it bleed onto the real diploma underneath, rendering it a poor original.

Ray wore her determination forcefully, a cloak of tension. While she continued tracing by candlelight, I curled up inside the trailer on my nest. A sharper than usual scratch was all I needed to take the pointy hidden thing to task. Enlarging a tiny hole in the pocket and fingering through the lining, I snagged the end, sensing something trailing behind, a chain of not so sharp things, and drew it back through the inside of Coat and out through the pocket. A bracelet which, in the limited starlight, sparkled pretty brightly.

Sleep came with me clutching the bracelet. When I woke to daylight and saw Ray beside me, I remembered to remember to listen for the drum. And because I had to remember to remember, I realized it wasn't there, again. Maybe the trailer was kryptonite, and maybe kryptonite repelled the crazies. And I had forgotten to look up kryptonite, but I didn't want to because I really wanted it to be real.

Thirty-Four

Morning sounds were becoming far too familiar: birds, dry pine needles raining on the shower curtain, Ray's singing. The wind stirred up more noise than usual as it played with everything from loose grasses to cardboard box tops. My palm held an imprint of gemstones, the bracelet inches from my elbow. I snatched it, taking it in to affirm it was real—not real as in authentic gemstones, but real as in I'd found a bracelet that, perhaps years ago, had slipped through a pocket and into a lining. The golden thread holding deep blue sapphires snaked across my hand like a living, jewelled caterpillar.

A human trumpet interrupted my pocketing the bangle. A royal da-da-da-da. She was too much. She trumpeted again, her way of calling me. I periscoped out of the roof.

A poinsettia tablecloth, corners held down by rocks, had become a red carpet, spilling out from some random point in our flat grassy outdoor room to the highchair podium area. She stayed off the carpet and raced to me, gowning me with a dark blue shower curtain.

I winced "Ray, you're strangling me."

"Sorry." She spoke to my neck, loosening up where she'd caught my throat skin in a plastic shower curtain ring.

Ray hurried to the stage, avoiding the homemade runway. When she beckoned for me to advance, I indulged her by taking small slow wedding aisle steps. She handed me the onion skin copy—the higher quality document—then gestured for me to sit in the highchair.

"We are gathered here today to recognize the outstanding work of this young student. We invite you to a special sunset ceremony this evening at… well, when the sun sets. Congratulations Dakota Starr Harrison on your accomplishments."

She extended her arm and, because I remained stunned, she swallowed up my hand with hers in a Dean of the University of Four Peaks And A Dog handshake. She smiled. I smiled back. An owl on a mixed-up schedule hooted, which was completely appropriate, like there was a fan out there.

When the presentation was complete, she left the stage, a cue to me to find her diploma and gown to exact the same ceremonial courtesy that had been given me. I stepped out of the spotlight, located her diploma—the non-onionskin one that I knew would be illegible from the Sharpie bleed through.

I bought some time by asking her to mingle with the crowd, which she did by mimicking conversation with imaginary attendees, like fellow students, their parents, teachers, and ghosts of the past. My pocket was empty. I made a beeline for the trailer and caught the shower curtain robe on the roof opening.

The bracelet sparkled against Coat's lining. Its design dazzled me, taking away all the poky pain memories. The dark blue imitation or real sapphires strung and interspersed with diamond-like crystals, or real diamonds, invited me into the deep sea. The gemstones were cut in slightly skewed rectangles. When I squinted it became the mirrored pieces in a blue and white kaleidoscope. It was the most elegant jewelry I'd ever seen. For a moment, I wanted to believe it was my graduation gift.

On my way to the podium, I straightened the carpet and tore the back cover from a mini-encyclo that had been left out on one of the cardboard box coffee tables. Ray'd cloaked herself with a white tatted cloth made for an extra-long table. It trailed behind her looking quite regal, for an out-in-the-wild, manage-with-what-you-have graduate. I straightened my own robe.

It took some sorting out: an insert-name-here from a canned form in my head, a search in my mind-catalogue for an appropriate line of poetry. Artistic. Creative. Innovative. A deep breath transformed me to actor and musician. I trumpeted the exact same da-da-da-da so we'd each received the same fanfare.

"Greetings." I would not allow my voice to shake.

She looked at the ground before facing the invisible audience. It made it easier to contain my emotion than if she'd faced me. "Oh, one sec, I'm sorry, I'm new at this." I bent the four corners of the encylco cover to make a cap, frisbeed it to her, then unrolled her diploma.

"Ladies and gentlemen, esteemed guests, faculty and student, it gives me great pleasure to present this diploma to—"

And there, amongst bled permanent markered dots, was her complete name. Raylene Starr Harrison. I reinforced my position, staring at the imaginary audience, too uncomfortable to look at her.

"—to present this diploma to Raylene Starr Harrison."

We continued to throw ourselves off balance with emotion, quickly glancing at each other. Long stares only when we knew the other was looking elsewhere.

"When you first joined us, here at the college of the Peaks, you embraced the environment, met the challenges of the classes, and demonstrated success." I turned a bit and caught her blushing.

Ray settled herself into the highchair as if it was an oak throne at a hundred-year-old university. She was completely into the entire circus. And I kept reminded myself I didn't like circuses. But myself didn't want to listen.

"Some examples of meeting the challenges were your experiments with making tea—surely an enterprise you could continue and take into the business world. Well done." I glanced oh-so-quickly because of my lumpy throat. "Fishing. Again, stellar results. You basically took inventory from the first lesson and ran with the course."

I found it hard to believe where this was all coming from because it was true, and I meant it. I wanted to say all kinds of things, including that she'd made this place a home. I ended up blurting out, "You showed up in the... in the forest of life."

I got right into the ceremony, gesturing for her to rise, completely abandoning how ridiculous we must have looked. She'd managed to clip the book-cover to her hair, four folded corners wrapping nicely around her headframe. "I hereby award you with the highest honour this educational institution can bestow on its graduates, that highest honour being the Peaks Bracelet." I dug into my pocket, retrieved the bracelet, and placed it across her wrist.

Her jaw dropped. Her expression a mix of confusion and surprise; a "where did this come from?" combined with pride and happiness. Recipient joy. If only I'd given her things in the past, she might not have taken so much.

Securing the bracelet required touching, and when our hands brushed, I quickly drew back, not taking the time to close the additional clasp. But the bracelet spoke up and said it didn't ever want to be lost again, so I gestured for Ray to lock it into place.

I intentionally exposed myself to smoke, then inhaled it; let it burn deep in my throat like an imagined cigar. Better to choke on fumes than sentiment. Do not feel too much, my inner voice reminded. I rubbed my hand against my shorts to get rid of the skin touching sensation, and wished for a paper cut—noticed my thigh didn't hurt. Wanted it to.

Without enough time to figure out how to wind down my speech, I panicked a little, but she was over the top happy and took over. "I am so proud to accept this award."

She blew my mind by having an acceptance speech ready. But the pressure was off; my not having to speak anymore was a blessing. My inner Koda said, *Look into her eyes. Touch her.* But I couldn't. Wouldn't. Didn't.

She faced the crowd, standing proudly. "I couldn't have done it without a fine teacher." She gestured, seemingly to mother nature. "And such wonderful peers and support." She looked at me. A geyser erupted from my heart to the back of my eyes, allowing a waterfall of tears to cascade inside me.

"Thank you." She stepped away. When she came toward me, I dodged her hug by passing her the spotty diploma. We oohed and aahed over the bracelet as she double secured it. So perfect, deep blue jewels with micro chandeliers between, like it was custom made for her.

"We should mingle some more," I suggested. She nodded and walked the red carpet to the general area of crushed grass around our trailer. I gathered up the Christmas tablecloth and watched her robe fall from her shoulders to reveal the rear view of a fit woman. As she folded the white cloth and bent down to return it to a box, I realized my mother was quite tidy. Maybe a little anal.

I sat on what was left of the bench to examine my diploma. Ray dismantled the stage she'd made. In a lean forward, I watched her. She kept looking at the bracelet, stealing moments, admiring how the light danced off the various facets.

She caught me. "I'll see you at the sunset dinner then."

"Yes." Awkward, but trying to be upbeat and casual. "Good ceremony," I added, not wanting to be too mushy.

In comic relief she stretched the width of the panty-hose fishing net over her head like a bank robber, pulling it down to cover her face. As quickly as she'd started, spontaneous-silly turned quickly-serious. She snapped off the mask to examine a snag near the waistband.

She waddled away, heading out early toward her fishing hole, singing inspired-like to a simple tune: A home. A home. Gotta love a home. A muffled third line ended with the word roam. Ah-ha, a rhyming song. I pictured her singing it in the creek and wished for her that we could stay here forever, and that people would sort of move here to join us. We'd become a town and she could become its leader. I'd have a store and trade bags of Stupid Tea in packages made from softened tree bark. The tea would be called Blossoms of Nature. There'd be a family who discovered a source of clay and made pots from it; I'd meet their son. We'd have children. And those children would be so safe even though they were adventurous like the ones from Three Chimneys in the English story called *The Railway Children*. There'd never be the need for social workers to take them away.

A crack of a branch brought me back to reality. I rolled my diploma tightly and popped it into my backpack that was hanging off the side of the trailer.

The knapsack reminded me of packing and moving from other homes we'd lived in. That triggered wanting to spread bread with peanut butter and jam. I wanted the basics. I wanted food. When we'd first had the fish, I remembered it tasting like gold might if gold was edible. But now that we'd eaten a lot of fish for days on end, it was just fish.

The afternoon proved perfect for napping, daydreaming, and indulging in Chair time. Still, there was something in the air. A post-ceremony, pre-dinner something. I questioned if the completion of a half-assed, home-made, wrongly interpreted ten day program done over many more days than ten could bring about the same energy as a bachelor's degree, or produce the same sense of accomplishment as receiving a diploma for an online workshop on building your own website. We hadn't finished high school. We hadn't even done a non-credit course.

The graduation ceremony had shifted something. My senses were more alert than ever. In the city, I'd known change was coming based on eviction notices. The change that I knew was coming was more powerful than a midnight-run-away to another apartment.

There was a dark patch the other side of the striver. Change was wrapped in that rogue cloud and was drifting toward us. I had no idea what form it would take, but it was as if I knew it would visit before bedtime. "Are you bringing a welcome guest or a party crasher to our graduation dinner?" I asked it.

"Didn't you hear who the keynote speaker was?" asked Six O'Clock Tree.

"Maturity is coming," said Three O'Clock Tree.

"I still don't know if that's a good thing or a bad thing," I said.

Thirty-Five

I set a pretty table, draping a pink curtain over the box in the library room. The most appropriate candles available were purple tapers, which I planted in pebble-filled YT tins. Ray was all giddy-happy with the effort. Our graduation dinner was made even better because she forgot to sing a promised grad song.

After dinner, Ray moved over to the highchair and began drumming. It was interesting how nothing surprised me anymore—about Ray's competence and that she wasn't doing it to impress anyone.

The patient sun delayed sunset, suspending time. The energy cloud drifted closer.

Intuition led me to the trailer. My heart moved me toward my calling. I knew what it was like to surrender mind, body, and soul to dance. I'd done it hundreds of times. But this was more.

Ray must have known the energy cloud was there too. She'd laid out my dress—its fragrant leather accents scented the trailer.

"You told me you'd be right back," it said.

The dress wore me.

Ray drummed. I emerged carefully so as not to damage one thread.

She continued to drum—something raw with smooth segments. I moved past our dining area to the scrub, only the weight of good responsibility on my shoulders; breathed in as if wearing only feathers.

On the mountain, the strings of teardrops and raindrops swung back and forth but did not make a sound, like they knew it wasn't time to start yet.

I retreated to Popeye's, the large gym that doubled as an auditorium. Martha opened her arms to everyone in the audience. She announced my solo. Justin, one of the janitors, leaned on the emergency exit door, stealing a smoke. Paul dusted his drum ever-so-softly.

No, it was Ray. Where was I? Where was my new dress?

Despite the gym being over capacity, everyone sat quietly. No drum in me and no drum from Paul, I walked to the middle of the room, a little nervous because I was not dancing, knowing they were all watching a teenager in a dress with all kinds of decorations on it. A costume cobbled together from the excess in the wardrobe room.

At the recital, I wondered if some people might question whether I was walking regular-like or if this *was* the dance. Some guy said, "Holy shit, is this it?" And a woman said: "Shut the hell up, Herb. Show some respect."

Kyle, a boy I liked, waved to me and I got all fluttery inside.

I let the new dress access my memories.

BOOM I was back beneath Four Peaks And A Dog. Immersed in the earth, a part of the mountain.

The beads responded. Their shiny sides rubbed together in an energetic conversation.

BOOM Ray hammered the highchair again. She opened her mouth. Her throaty chant cut through the air like a primal scream from the first person on earth.

Dress was an envoy to nirvana. As its ambassador, it invited me to join sacred bliss in a place that gave supernatural powers to history. I might as well have been in these mountains a thousand years ago.

Silence. Beat. Silence. Beat. Beat. Silence. The pattern changed as Ray made the drum take on a melodic form. The music of a single instrument sounding like an orchestra.

Dress told me not to worry about Ray's journey.

My body remained on the piece of scrub between Chair and the circle of rocks, but the trinity created by my mind and soul with the entity and entirety of Dress edged toward the mystery of the universe and closed in on the certainty of love that's born from gratitude.

The tapestry of us lifted an official step, over the fescue and down into the valley of dance.

All of life's tears moved with me through a vortex—time unravelled as if a thread from Dress had caught in the whirling. I carried all of life's rain in one droplet in my hand. All of life's love swayed to make waves that rippled around the world.

Ray and I remained connected through rhythm. From some distant hill came the comfort of her drumbeat.

The jingle, tinkle, ring from Dress surrounded me like a protective aura.

I went alongside a river, lighter step, lighter step, sometimes teasing the water's edge. I was buoyant and rode the currents of endless flowing water while looking up toward a blue sky mixed with evergreen treetops that could make someone feel lost in the forest. It was all smooshed together, the then and the now. I was free.

Turning, twisting, gliding, I was a single mountain to the west, the beads on my dress singing like warm Chinook winds breaking through the coldest of winter days. I became the stream flowing along the valley on a warm spring day when bears stirred out of hibernation.

I was a bison calf teetering beside its protective mother in a thin stand of trees. I was a leaf bursting out of its bud, holding a caterpillar, sheltering a bird, turning golden in an early fall, a salmon struggling upstream.

I reached the ocean by riding the wind.

I was the atmosphere above the clouds, higher than planes fly, at the point where sky turns to outer space. And I was earth, deep, deep, with buried bones of ancestors, tangled roots and stones.

The eastern sun woke me and made more music: Arctic chill and blizzards. My hands opened and became snowflakes. They retreated and I was drought, hope, then rain.

The earth's ancient voice lowered. Her spirit called me home. Three beats from Ray, two steps from my feet, so close to the ground they barely cleared the dust. I dropped in a bow to the great creator: in awe of the power of it all.

A surge of appreciation filled me up and overflowed. Love that had circled the globe poured into my pounding heart.

As Dress's aliveness retreated, she coaxed me to walk away from bliss, then pulled me and pushed me because I didn't want to leave.

"You are enough," Dress whispered.

"You are needed," said Destiny Summer's grandmother.

"Go girl. You're killin' it sistah," said Destiny Summer.

I opened my eyes. In the closest stand of trees, Green Jean stood beside a woman I inherently knew was Brenda—my adoptive mother to be whose stroke had changed the course of my life and landed me back with Ray.

I rose from the bow, then turned and landed in Ray's outstretched arms. She pulled me close. She held on to me so long, like Green Jean used to. I remembered how Green Jean's skin had looked up close, like Martha's: a bit of weathered leather, as if she'd ridden the wild rapids of the river of life for ten thousand years. Ray's was softer. Clearer. Fresher.

The baby kicked from the squish of our hug, but Ray didn't let go.

When we separated, my insides messaged me. We'd be okay. We were okay.

Thirty-Six

I got used to Stupid Tea. Though it tasted mostly like hot water, the pine needles gave it colour, which affected my taste buds.

Ray seemed to believe that anything that came from, or near, pine was safe. She poured it, and I drank it. It was an extreme limit to which I went so that I could experience her doing something for me.

Each afternoon Ray brewed then poured from the gold and red rose teapot into the two china teacups. Ray's blue and pink china, which had a cross-stitch sewing pattern called Petit Point—a fact confirmed under the saucer. The undersides of all the pieces sported small symbols scattered randomly in unreadable little brushstrokes, accompanied by the Royal Albert emblem. Ray suggested the china might be monetarily valuable.

She mentioned we could take the tea set and some of the other junk to an appraisal even, like one of those they set up for television —a stuff in your attic type of show. This reminded me we were about as far away from the *Antique Road Show* as Mars—we were more likely to experience interplanetary travel than arrive at a town hall to have stuff that wasn't ours estimated. On the other hand, it could be accessible to places that evaluated old stuff, if we were not here. It brought the world closer and took it further away all in the same blink. I tried to define isolation. Even in solitary confinement there would be people around—criminals next door, guards, cooks, and cleaning staff.

The tea routine was insane, but it satisfied by creating mood and ambience. "Teatime in Britain," she'd announce. I'd answer with an "awright mate" which seemed more Australian than British. We kept our pinkies up, crossed our ankles, and placed faded Christmas napkins across our laps. Theatrics aside, the formality saved us from complete madness.

The day after graduation, Ray pronounced Four Peaks complete. After the unveiling, she began a self-portrait on the backside of a Clorox box. With the change in creative subject, she also expanded her reading genres—scanning the indices of the encyclopedias and other non-fiction for interesting topics—reading ferociously, lips moving a mile a minute. Not the box I'd buried the Lifebook in.

I had never seen her have such a good run of functionality, even when she had gone back to school for upgrading, during which we'd fought like crazy until she'd quit, and I'd resumed control.

I considered, in our life below Four Peaks And A Dog, that we'd moved beyond a struggle for power. Her newfound competence did not seem to get in the way. I no longer feared her with the same paranoia a lead actor might of an eager understudy. It was the start, I think, of each of us claiming our own roles.

In the past, though I'd hated it when she did crazy things, it had kept me employed. The more unpredictable she was, the more secure was I—even if it placed me at risk because of my age. Now I could look at some things a little more objectively, and with some humour. Even the "the wedding dress and the octogenarian" chapter made me smile.

Watching her as an artist, inventor, and innovator caused a shift in my Ray-lens.

"Whatcha wanna do today?" Ray asked. She seemed disappointed not to have a theme hanging on the heating-pad tree. We were three days post-grad.

She stared at me, then blurted, "What is our purpose?"

"Here on earth, like all people, as in purpose of mankind? Or us here in this forest, the whole missing in action thing?"

"Either. What are we here for? What do we do?" she asked.

"We watch the river?" I pronounced it with uncertainty to the point of becoming a question. In asking myself, "myself" replied internally. *Sometimes we do a lot. By the time we boil, have teatime, and I read mini-encyclos, and Ray reads Sister Gabriella adventures, and catches and cooks fish, the day is over. We are immersed in living day-to-day. A version of paycheque-to-paycheque. Hand-to-mouth.*

"I don't know what we do, Ray."

"I fish."

"You wait for fish to swim into a pair of pantyhose."

"It's a net."

"Oh. Sorry."

"And it takes patience. Not only a net. It's a series of trapping scooping bags," she explained.

Lethargy 101 and Advanced Mario Brothers, that's what I wanted to say, because I hadn't completely lost my memory or my sense of sarcasm. I chose the safer road. "Skill and a tool. That's actually quite impressive, Ray."

Chimpanzees made tools. I'd seen a documentary where an ape had inserted a long blade of grass into a hole to collect ants.

"You really mean that?"

"Definitely. Toolmaker and skill." My brain appeared to have two filing sections, past Ray and current Ray, which dovetailed with a mocking Dakota and a respectful Dakota.

"Maybe we should gather some wood."

"For what?" I probed.

"For building a cabin," Ray added weakly.

"A cabin?" Days after graduation, by my calculations almost a month in the wilderness, and she'd become Mike Holmes, master carpenter.

"Okay we could build something else. We did build a sort-of-bench," she said.

We'd rarely used it. The image of us sitting on that sort-of-bench, enveloped by the approaching disaster, played in my head. Two corpses leaning against a trailer, dead from smoke inhalation and scorched by fire. Decomposing to skeletons only to be discovered decades later—a tumble of logs and a pile of bones near sheets of metal with some strange kind of "cave" paintings—the Full House Moving Boys. What a forensic nightmare that would be. A palaeontologistical puzzle. The imagined scene was interrupted by a thicker version of the same breeze that had been blowing our way all day.

Ray coughed as she rose and headed toward her art, gathering it up and storing it away, like a protective mother. "I can't see as far," she said, looking up and around.

"The fire's getting closer," I said.

She scowled. Nature was disappointing her, getting in the way of her plans.

I sniffed the charred air, and I got a bit frustrated about why we'd bothered building a bench and organizing a camp.

The few clouds that formed looked irritated. They collected near Four Peaks And A Dog in a tight meeting, leaving the rest of the sky an ominous greyish blue. It was as if they'd absorbed bad news and become noxious. Perhaps they were signalling animals that could read them: RUN FOR YOUR LIVES!

The cloud-knots hung around late in the day, when Ray was fishing, even when the rest of the sky turned navy then black. Lightning struck in the surrounding mountains, then closer. No rain. No Ray. I pulled the shower curtain all the way over and waited inside, telling myself it made no sense to tramp to the striver to find her.

The thunder was an all-encompassing, constant roar. The wind so fierce and flashes so bright I became disoriented, convinced that lightning had struck and deafened me. I examined my fingers and noted they were not smouldering stubs seen in cartoon disasters, so remained hopeful for the return of my senses.

My fear increased, and the only way to move on was to try to figure out a way to check if the roaring sound around me was thunder or deafness. The laziest and most non-medical test I could think of was to wish for not being deaf, so I closed my eyes and wished.

The thunderous sounds receded, like waves on a shore when the tide is going out. Silence enveloped the trailer. I struck the wall. Crinkled some paper. Passed each hearing test successfully. I mouthed a word of thanks, grateful my wish may have come true.

The no rainstorm picked up strength again. Some of the ramp buttresses fell. I expected the door to fall open and invite the lightning inside. I imagined myself in a huge conductor as the flashes and sounds increased.

Between the tides of wind, thunder, lightning, and no rain, my sense of smell kicked in. Double citrus of bubble bath and candle announced Ray's return. I stood on the box to peek out. Somehow the storm didn't seem as bad as it had from inside the trailer. Her candle was aflame inside its holder and silvery, scaly food jiggled inside the net held over her arm.

"Scary eh?" She made a voice like a ghost. Only her torso and head were visible by shaky candlelight.

"Uh-huh," I whispered in relief, confused as to where her fear of the dark had gone.

"We're gonna die," she chanted in a horror show voice, then got herself and her belly through the roof and whipped the shower curtain top over.

"Shut up," I said.

Thirty-Seven

Breakfast conversation was all about the future.

"Ray, it'll get so we can't breathe. We have to head out." The storm had moved through without a drop of moisture.

"Sure, we'll take the Chevy." She paced over to the sign she'd made the previous day: *Day 4,576—The Invention of the Wheel.* The topics came from the mini-encyclos. We'd themed nothing around it. She slid the cardboard flap off the clip, turned it over, and wrote *Early Man Discovers Fir'.* Topped it with *Day 27,000.*

"Very funny," I heckled.

"I don't wanna die here, Koda." She flopped down on Chair.

"We won't, Ray. We're gonna walk. We're gonna head downstream and downstream and downstream."

"And what's downstream? Fire could be downstream."

"Downstream may lead to somewhere. Off the mountain."

"Lame," she replied, forgetting it had originally been her suggestion.

"We won't be fighting a current if we have to wade through it."

"True." She livened.

To me, the striver was like a safe road. We could fish, boil, and drink our way to Sometown, Canada.

Being active made life better and stopped Ray from spontaneous death chants. Emotions were mixed. Taking action to walk out: good. Leaving the stuff that wasn't our stuff: bad.

It took work from sunup to sundown and then some, but that kind of productivity was satisfying. With the weight of making the decision lifted, the getting ready to move on seemed easier.

The picture was too fragile to pack out. "It's too precious to ruin," I said. I really meant it. "Leaving it here is best, because if we end up not too far from here, we can recover it later." I think that's why we lowered the ramp and stacked everything inside the trailer, in case we could come back and get our stuff another time.

If she couldn't take her picture or Chair, I wasn't going to try to work my dress into our packs. It was only fair.

She shrugged her shoulders and put the Four Peaks collage between two cardboard box flats, then looked longingly at Plaid Chair. "Don't gloat," I whispered to Coat.

When the peanut butter jar was crammed with cooked fish chunks, the windshield washer fluid bottle full of water, and the last four YTs packed within our rolled linens, we had our final meal, filling up on the remaining Cat Granny drinks and polishing off the final Under The Sea.

Then I climbed onto the roof to double the shower curtain. When I leaned off the edge, to hoist logs for securing the shower curtain, I spied Ray. She was expressionless and drained of colour. I rolled out of the way so she wouldn't see my share of fear. Right before the final log was in place, I pulled back a tiny piece of rubbery-plastic and spied on all the boxes inside, down below—wanted to cry.

"There, there, don't worry," I said to it all. "You're protected from the elements."

"You comin', Koda?"

"I'm comin', Ray."

The knapsack held triple-plastic-wrapped matches along with candles and fondue fuel. Coat resembled a large creature rolled into a tight bedroll. Ray made a similar animal by stuffing bedding and supplies into pillowcases. We knotted the hoodie at the waistband and cuffs, stuffed supplies into the arm and torso compartments, and then secured the bulging sleeves to my backpack. The windshield washer fluid bottle dangled from the outside of it all. We could have decided to boil water at the end of our first day of walking out, and not have the additional weight, but we knew we should hydrate on the way, and Ray pointed out that stopping to boil would take time.

Ray invented a head-hip carrier from the tackle box so she could use one arm to balance things on her hip and, if needed, move it higher to keep it above water. "It's my hippy-head," she joked nervously, trying to ease the sadness of our departure.

"You are a hippy-head." I teased.

"I am a strong woman from Four Peaks And A Dog." She used a warrior voice.

"Hippy-head." I taunted some more.

She took it well, made a song out of it, something about hippy-head, carry a bed, heavy as lead, better than dead.

As we secured each other's loads, I experienced déjà vu—a "moving house again" mixture of anxiety and anticipation.

We waved goodbye to the Dog of Four Peaks. A few more personal snapshots were taken from various distances. Finally, we slipped into our own footprints on the worn trail to the striver.

Sharp bushes lined much of the water's edge. We chose the wetter path of the shallows. From time to time Ray shook the box jingler and chanted something like, "Bears get the hell away from us." Other times she sang the "Teddy Bears' Picnic" song: *If you go out in the woods today…you'd better not go alone,* a disconcerting nursery song from some other child's past.

While Ray exorcised her demons outwardly, mine were directed inside. We'd had all this great stuff—more than we'd ever had in real life—and some of it had history, though not ours. It came to carrying only a few mementos, the rest of our stuff, like battle-dead, left behind for logistical reasons. It was unfair.

Thirty-Eight

We trudged downstream, sloshing out at sunset. We hung my thin flip flops and Ray's runners on the ends of branches. A little chilled from being in the water, we would have liked to have started a fire, but dared not. The only heat was provided by a single tea-light candle in a can. We ate from the supply of fish in the jar and disciplined ourselves to sharing a can of YT.

Not wanting to open everything, we unwound Coat and huddled side-by-side, each placing an arm in a sleeve, forming a two-headed body. We wormed our way to the ground, like conjoined twins might do, and curled into sleep.

When we woke, we figured we'd been gone over twenty-four hours including our sleep time—so strange to be internally recording time away from a place that was, in itself, a place from which to record time away from our original world.

I was still thinking too much when Ray stirred in her half of the coat. "We gonna keep goin', Koda?"

"Good morning to you too." I slipped my arm out of the sleeve and opened the jar of fish.

We packed up, rolled up, and moved on. Downstream. One step at a time. I had expected the haze to clear, but it wasn't clearer or cleaner. With no idea how many miles we'd walked—Ray mentioned a million—we pushed ourselves late into the afternoon and then spotted a place that resembled a manmade camping spot that was missing only the metal cooking grill and site number.

A blue shower curtain—stretched between overhead branches—formed a roof over our bed. One of the puke-coloured curtains formed our bottom sheet, and Coat became our comforter. Elated and full of holiday spirit, Ray found the energy to fish and, a fat one later, we boiled its body and dined, leaving the day-old mix in the jar, in the creek, to stay cold.

"Goodnight, Koda-baby," Ray sang. Our dirty bodies were tired and banged up. After one day and one night on the trail, Four Peaks And A Dog looked pretty good.

It was a silent night. Gone were the flapping Themes of the Day from Six O'clock Tree. Past-nights had held the protection of metal walls. There was an absence of bubble bath smells and other stuff of our lives that melded together to make our scent. Boxes filled with creativity were two days behind us. But for each other, we were all alone.

Ray hid in her sleep. Even though my eyes were closed, sleep did not come in those first hours of dark. I pulled up Coat, but all it did was blanket me in fear. Sleep visited much later, when it was no longer welcome, in the form of scary dreams with grey ghosts from which even a seasoned nightmarer would recoil—but no drum. The mystery of the missing drumbeat continued, but there was no time for detective work or analysis. We were in the survival business.

I heard the rain before I felt it. Nightmares were quickly abandoned. A royal downpour teased. Delayed like aircraft waiting to land, it couldn't be felt right away because it had to pass through the trees before it wet us and the ground. Ray slept through the initial weather change and I, engrossed in looking up and around the shower curtain roof, forgot to wake her. One drop at a time the water forced its way through the forest canopy, then came looking for the ground like wet arrowheads.

Ray sat up under the plastic roof.

"Rain," I cheered.

"Rain," she said softly.

After a time, we celebrated by taking turns being human umbrellas. When we were thoroughly soaked, we went back under the tented shower curtain and shivered.

Relief enveloped me. Ray too. The lifting of impending doom an accused might experience when a guillotine jams.

We ate all the fish-mix, then collected rainwater in the oily jar. Water inched up the windshield washer fluid bottle and gathered in two angled YT tins.

The weather system blurred when afternoon ended and dusk began, no boundary between grey day and grey evening. It rained, it poured, and painted the world wonderfully wet. We slept a while, and for me it was a welcome, dreamless, thick sleep-soup.

When the rain eased, and we were both cold to the core, we discussed the merits of having a fire. Such a turnabout to not want fire then to want it. So much mental deliberation in rain-soaked brains.

During our shivery discussion we kept an eye on the water level. In places the waterway resembled a raging mudslide. Forest debris, like deadfall and tree branches, was carried up and over the current, bumping and jamming. The place had taken on a whole new look as foreboding as its former self, just a different mood. Another tempest.

"I'm serious, we need a fire." Ray took charge. "It won't make a new forest fire. We're drenched, and you're shaking."

"Okay, a small one." I shivered.

We chose a spot a few feet from our tent and became the best scouts ever, weaving anything dry through anything else dry to make kindling. Three tea lights caught the home-made fire-starters. By slowly adding larger pieces of wood and twig we created a heat source to thaw our stiff bodies.

We heated our anatomies in sequence. When the butt was cold the tummy was warm. When the feet were thawing the head was chilly. Eventually, the heat penetrated our entire bodies and we were comfortable. When we were all dried out, hunger and thirst teased. Instead of doing something about it, we wedged ourselves, as comfortably as two people could, in a mustard-purple-colored-floored, tree-trunk-walled, shower-curtain-ceilinged room. And it began to rain again, our fire a smoky mess, blurring the space around us.

"Do you think all this rain put out the fires around Four Peaks?" Ray poked the curtain tarp and a huge rain pouch exploded up and into the space around our campsite.

"I do," I said. "Forest fires wouldn't have burned through all this water."

"Then I think that makes a difference to our plan."

"Huh?"

"We go back," she said determinedly.

"We don't go on? Downstream? Somewhere to find a town?" I began to ramble.

"I don't think we've prepared the way we should have. I thought we'd have found something by now. The rain's given us the opportunity for a do-over. To get stronger. Pack more food."

"We could build a travois," I announced. "When we get back."

"A trav-what?"

"Like a flat sled. To bring out more of our stuff." The idea of it not being able to go in water or between trees hadn't occurred to me. I was too focused on wanting to haul out all the stuff that had become ours.

Thirty-Nine

Our little fire was out, but Coat kept us warm. More rain forced us inside in more ways than having to stay in the tent because of weather.

At first, we played twenty questions and spoke only of superficial topics, like the trash shown on the covers of sensationalist papers: "Chihuahua in Guadalajara speaks to reporter." That kind of stuff.

When the weather eased from raging downpour to a shower, Ray tried to fish, but the water was murky and the current powerful. She said it wouldn't have worked anyway because all the fish had been swept away.

We lit the fondue base to boil water. We infused pine needles in YT cans that we pretended were our china cups. Ray's raised pinkie generated a memory—a postcard on our fridge when I was a child: *Ladies at High Tea at the Empress Hotel.*

"Remember we had a post card from the Empress hotel in Victoria?" I asked.

"No," she said.

"That means yes. It was on our fridge for a while. It said love J."

"Don't remember."

"Was it Jane or Jerry?" I sat back, eager for more story, leaving out that I knew it was the Janet I'd recently learned about. Better to have her set me straight on the name.

She was bored too; nothing to distract us other than the occasional slosh of water over the creek bank caused by a log surge.

"Four," she said calmly.

"Four?"

"Four too highs. No, five." She pointed as another piece of deadfall collected in a log jam on the other side of the striver. "Five. Too highs. Five so far, today."

"Cool." I demonstrated fake-impressed on her naming the arrival of debris in order to forward my agenda. "The postcard? Jane or Jerry?"

She made eye contact and took in a deep breath. "Before you were born, I was..."

She'd never started a sentence with that before. "You were what?" I pushed too hard and she took her mind back to the water and waited for wayward branches.

"Six. Six too highs."

"Before I was born you were what?"

"Messed up. After, too."

"Ray, I know stuff happened. I'm not trying to press any buttons." I wasn't about to throw the Lifebook in her face. "It's that I remember the postcard when you said ladies at high tea."

She smiled and her face softened. "Auntie Janet," said Ray.

"Auntie Janet," I repeated.

"My mother, Sandra, had a lot of relationships. The difficult child. The bad one. Janet was the good one."

I clamped my mouth shut with my hand. Janet and Sandra. Sisters. Exactly like the Lifebook had said. One is Ray's aunt. The other one Ray's mother.

I hurried her along with my free hand until I had to speak. "When did you last see her? Janet, I mean."

"Whoa, Koda. Don't go thinking family reunion okay? Before you were born, way before, I stayed with Janet for a while. Then I split. And she was around after, too." She dropped her shoulders and her face became less intense. "You look like her Koda. You got her eyes. The family nose too." The declaration relaxed her more, and she smiled at me.

"The family has a nose?"

"Everyone has a nose, Koda."

"Tell me more."

"Uncle Ron. He was in the Navy. That's why she moved to Victoria. There's a base there. They had three kids." An interesting expression came over her face, like she had a phone to her ear and had made a connection.

"You have cousins? We have cousins?" She appeared to be speaking about a functional branch of the family. I liked where it was going. The Lifebook hadn't said anything about Ray's cousins.

"Relax already. Three cousins, James, we called him Jimmy. William, he was Billy, and Jennifer."

"Jenny or Jen?"

"No, always Jennifer."

I kept matching things up with the Lifebook. Ray's version was quirkier. Janet's boys had nicknames and Jennifer did not.

Ray's steady, deep breaths pushed the pause button on our conversation. I tripped into what it would be like inside her head, organizing her life story. Reorganizing her life story.

She fidgeted with the strap on her tank top. "My mother, Sandra, always had guys around, and they were more important than me. Janet was always trying to help, but her helping never did any good. There were too many drugs. Too many men."

She looked toward the water. "Eleven," she said. "I was eleven when my grandmother, Irene, died."

All of a sudden, her expression, which had seemed kind of sorry for her mother, became visibly hateful. "What a piece of work. My grandmother, Irene. I was too young to know that then."

"Your grandma?" I knew it from the book, but didn't want to confuse her by saying I knew because, in truth, I didn't know everything.

"Officially, yes. But I never called her that. My grandparents were horrible to my mother," she said.

Ray was trembling. I inched up and wrapped Coat around her, fur side in.

"Thanks, Koda."

She folded her feet and body into a tight tuck even though her belly had grown quite a bit. It was like she was a super fit pregnant woman that would one day have a baby—but I didn't want to think about that "one" day.

"Eventually, Janet told me what had happened. And when she did, I put it all together with things I remembered my mother saying." Ray rubbed her neck and chin on Coat's fur, then took a deep breath.

"Sandra going bad meant she'd been raped when she was a little girl. Assaulted by a family friend, and not once, Koda; not that once is okay, once is not okay, lots of times, Koda. Even though once is not okay, okay?"

"Okay." I said, feeling like okay was a dirty word.

She continued to tremble beneath Coat, rocking slightly.

"After the…"

"Asshole guy?" I helped.

"Yeah. After him, she told her parents what happened, and they didn't believe her. They said he was a church-going guy, so it couldn't have happened."

Ray stared at me. I nodded my buy-in.

"After that it was all downhill. Sandra was basically farmed out. And to boot? The jerk still came for dinner. Janet said he never tried anything with her, but that she never let herself be near him or alone with him. If he stayed after dinner, to read the Bible with my grandparents, she'd push her nightstand against her door. At least that's what she told me. And I believe it, Koda, because I figure he knew he'd already burned one of his bridges by molesting Sandra, so he'd better watch out with Janet. Maybe they would believe it if their other daughter came to them and said something."

"That's big, Ray."

"Irene had croaked already by the time Janet told me. My mother was gone then too." She rocked back and forth with her arms wrapped around her legs. "You know what, Koda? Janet figured they knew, you know, about church-guy. Yet still, every time Sandra was in trouble, Janet said they turned the other way, spouting a bunch of crap about the devil and evil. They'd joined the church when they'd moved into the city. Still, a bottle of hooch under the table and in the nightstand. Phonies."

She continued rocking. The sound of each raindrop was discernable—the rest of our world silent. She pulled her stick closer and began examining the surface, then took in a long deep breath after which her stone expression melted.

When the colour in her face was restored, she said in the most sincere way, "She wouldn't have got it, Koda, even if I'd have known it all, and had been able to tell her I understood. She was way too wasted. And Janet had a family of her own, with me in the mix too. She'd done everything she could. She was exhausted, Koda."

"She was probably filled with all kinds of guilt, your grandparents treating them differently," I said.

"I never thought of it as being guilt."

"Could be. A sort of twisted appreciation for not being the one he'd violated."

"You're so freaking smart, Koda." Ray had stopped shivering. "That guilt probably hurt as much as what church-guy did."

We breathed in and out for several minutes, letting nature envelope us in the way that it had for weeks.

"My mother's legacy, a drug addict who died from an overdose, and a daughter destined to follow in her footsteps. A kid who lived on the street. My turn to go bad."

It was a heartfelt disclosure. I kept my head up, eyes on hers, and dispatched a caring message from my heart—wanted her to know I wasn't judging her.

"I know I haven't been the best parent, but I would never not believe you." She stared past me. "If you told me anyone had touched you, I would believe you to the moon and back. And then I'd murder them in cold blood."

I squeezed my eyes and my lips closed so as not to cry.

"Twelve too highs," she said, dreamily.

I pushed my arm near hers and held her hand in mine. "No," I said. "You're not bad."

She squeezed my hand. Her magical bracelet settled between our wrists, glittering without any help from the grey day.

"Janet took me in. More than once. Before you were born. When I was young. Well, I was a handful of trouble. The second time I was a bitch. The third time, I left, saved her the trouble of kicking me out. Later, she worked hard to help me with you. After you were born, she was so helpful. I got stronger because of her. But then I got lazy, and never got myself together to thank her."

"She sounds like such a nice person."

"She was. She probably still is. I haven't done enough to keep in touch. At first, she did keep checking on me. Then over the years, I suppose when she figured I was back on my feet with you, she left it to me to get hold of her. Sheesh, she must have been so tired of flying back and forth. You know, drugs are like little gremlins that run around inside your body and find the weakest spots. They are good at helping you forget horrible things that happened—that you don't know if you dreamed or not. My mother had a lot of boyfriends, you know. And I was pretty young. I remember the freedom of after-school art classes and not wanting to go home. Home was out of control. Eventually, I was out of control too. You can't be a tall and healthy tree when you've had drugs. Just look at this forest. There's nothing weak about it. It's not on drugs."

"Wow, you're right."

"Know what, Koda? Even though I wish I didn't have the history I have, and I wish I hadn't used drugs, if I hadn't left Janet's when I was a kid, then screwed up big time, you wouldn't be here. And I wouldn't want to ever make it so you weren't here."

The pretty powerful realization used my gut as a chair and reclined its huge self into my heart.

Ray's face softened, maybe a spark of family energy.

"Can we see her again? Ray, can we look her up?"

Ray's smile was of happy remembering tagged with an unspoken trailer: if we ever get out of here.

"How many cousins?" I asked.

"Thirteen. Fourteen," she said.

"Wow," I said.

"Fourteen too highs. Holy crap, we need this water to calm down," she said.

"Thanks for everything, Ray." I meant it, even though she hadn't answered the cousin question.

"That's not everything, Koda-baby. But I tell you what."

"What?"

"If you shut up, I'll make you some Stupid Tea."

Forty

The flow calmed and the mud settled. Ray returned to fishing at sundown, albeit without her ramp. We ate and stocked the jar, grateful for pantyhose, lace, fondue forks, YT cans, and candles. Without them we would have starved.

Then hippy-head and daughter began inching upstream, chatting about stuff at Four Peaks, chirping about everything except the elephant in the womb. We remained in good spirits, even though progress was slow because we moved against the current.

It took a whole day longer to return than when we'd packed out. When we hit the familiar surroundings of our boiling point, we smiled nervously. Half an hour later we were Home Sweet Dysfunctional Home.

The shower curtain was drooped over the hole in the roof, but had not fallen into the trailer. I spoke first. "We'll have to figure out when to leave again. You know that, right?"

"Bears manage out here." She said it hopefully.

"Bears hibernate. And they have fur coats."

"You have a fur coat." She went out on a limb, as if we could survive.

"It's fake."

"I know that," she said. "I just wanna believe."

"Me too."

"Hey, we might be found by someone who checks if the rain put out the fires."

"Plausible," I said, wanting to become a believer too.

There were more bugs than before. They celebrated on us. We were reluctant hosts, dabbing the stored pink windshield washer fluid over our exposed parts. We willed something to happen, storytelling to each other that some "someones" would come to check on the post-forest fire conditions. We would welcome them, returning with the someones, somehow, to somewhere. It was crisis mismanagement at its best. In anticipation, we set the cardboard box for tea, including empty YT cans for our guests.

A small campfire highlighted our first night back. We tried a method we couldn't have risked before, roasting fish on sticks. We sipped Stupid Tea until way past dark. At bedtime we put wet boughs on the fire so as not to perish by the flaming-enemy we'd feared and run from. It was safe-smoky.

Snuggled down in our beds, a tiny chill suspended itself above. Inspired by some freak collision of Disney and jazz, she crooned.

Summertime.

It was a rich female imitation of a jazz standard.

And it's been a hot one so far.

Ray reached the lowest of her range.

Summertime, do-dooby-do-da-do-da-da.
  Some- ah -times, I miss the tender touch of your hand,

And I think of you, like you are near,
Even though-oh-oh.

Going deeper on the oh-oh.

You are far.

A new low.

So far.

An octave higher. Such an eclectic mix.

So far.

An octave lower, followed by an intended flat in her medium range.

Faaaaaarrrrr.

Then a lounge act's close.

G'night everybody.

Total fanjazzmic immersion.

"Good night, Ella," I whispered. She might have been starting to sound better or maybe she was the same and only sounded that way because I'd not heard another living soul for a while. I tackled the question in a fitful sleep.

Forty-One

"Hey! Hey! Hey!" We waved, shouted, and hollered beneath a moving dot. The helicopter was high and angled toward another mountainside. It entered our sky from one side and went out the other.

"Which direction did it come from?" Ray asked hurriedly, as if recording the details for some kind of cartography course. "It could help us know which way to walk out."

"Looks like downstream." My reply was steeped in sarcasm.

"There are no creeks in the sky." Ray was truly serious.

Another one, or the same one, flew over and we waved a crib sheet, and tried flapping Ray's crimson robe. By the time we'd figured out how to reflect light on a piece of tin, the chopper was gone. We flitted back and forth, waiting for it to return. Nothing. Ray made tea.

"How do you think they did it?" Ray began.

"Who?"

"The pioneers. Settlers. People who came here with 'nothing' and made all the things that make up towns and cities."

"I guess they foraged and hunted and gathered. Built stuff."

"We built a bench."

"We did," I said.

We took turns asking questions and saying what explorers might have done: fire, animal pelts, fur for clothing, meat from the same animals. Ray decided containers could be made from dirt and water made into clay. She began a bout of uncontrollable laughter when she described a buffalo hip socket as a "hop sicket." The discussion of joints led to architecture of log cabins.

"I don't think they used nails. They sort of notched the logs, didn't they?" Ray asked.

I pictured bearded mountain men felling trees and constructing a cabin, head-scarfed women feeding them.

She continued. "I like that word, notch. Notch, notched, notchy." She was full of energy. "So, they had shelter, water, food, blankets, and they could notch. That's how they did it."

She was happy with her conclusion. It appeared she'd escaped into her own little world. "Who was first man and woman here. Not like chimpanzee-turned-man. But first person to set up life?"

She *had* been reading the mini-encyclos.

"They were Sasquatch," I explained.

"Very funny. Seriously, who were they, Koda?"

"Oh Ray, pul-eeease. Look around. We are the first people here."

All my arm flapping and gesticulating didn't faze her. "C'mon, Koda, I mean here in Western Canada, the Rockies, or other mountain places. They would have survived."

"That's just it, Ray. They. There were many. Many hands make easy work or something like that. Many penises make…"

"Dakota Starr Harrison, the baby might hear," she said.

"Hey, penis is not a dirty word. I didn't say cock or dick. What I meant was survival means more than two females. Some males. An actual gene pool."

She covered her belly with her hands as if the action covered the baby's ears.

"Don't go all Sunday School teacher on me, Ray. You know, something's happened to you here. You've become something quite mother-like."

It was the first time she'd acknowledged the pregnancy since she'd told me. I'd wanted to pretend she wasn't pregnant as much as she had, maybe more. I'd worked hard to keep it that way, but it scratched at the walls of my brain, and it bothered me because I knew the universe was expecting me to embrace a career in midwifery.

"We have stuff," she said. "So, we could be quite far ahead of them in that way." She completely discounted the need for population.

"Them. You mean the notchy generation?"

"I love that word. Can we be notchy?" Ray asked.

"Sure," I said. "We can be notchy but not crotchy, okay? I don't like the word crotchy."

"We are notchy, not crotchy," she announced.

"Ray, don't even use that word to say what we're not."

"I didn't even know there was a word 'crotchy.' You made that up."

I explained my theory about charity pants: how they probably are never washed before donation, so I'd always used extra laundry money to wash them because I didn't want crotch mono.

"Dakota, there is no such thing as crotch mono."

"You would rather deny it," I answered. "Expose your privates to the gusset, and use the quarters for candy."

"Not anymore. That was then, Koda-baby."

I almost believed her. That if we were able to return, instead of dying out here, she would never again spend the laundry money for candy.

It was something I would come to accept—her transformation.

Just as the fall could not be believed, but had to be, Ray evidenced miraculous change.

I tried to define us. Stood and orated like an official of some kind. "We are strong-thin-women from Four Peaks And A Dog. Like the swinging pendulum on a clock-of-life we went from one life of city-poor to a strange lost-rural. We are headed for a place to settle between the two."

"Our identity." Her voice was gentle and approving.

"Our mission statement," I said.

"I know what a mission statement is. I know it from the Salvation Army and the Freedom Counselling Center." She raised her hand like the keener in a classroom.

"The Salvation Army." She fake-cleared her throat. "An international movement, which is an, er… wait a minute, I know, I know it, knew it… movement which is an evangelical part of the Universal Christian Church. Its message is based on the Bible. Its ministry is motivated by the love of Christ. No, God. Love of God. Its mission is to preach the gospel of Jesus Christ and to meet human needs in His name, that's with a capital H, Koda, in His name without discrimination."

"Sheeshus, how do you know that Ray?"

"Some things, Koda, they stick."

"No crap."

"They all had mission statements. All the agencies I've been to over the years. They're longer than mottos and shorter than…well, they're longer than mottos."

"Impressive."

She shrugged off the compliment and went on about us writing ours out and having it up on a wall.

"What wall?" I asked.

"The trailer's got walls. The heating pad clip works on the tree. We have options."

Ray's gaze stayed on Six O'clock Tree for a bit too long.

"I'll take philosophy for a thousand, Mr. Trebek," I said. She turned her head and concentrated on me. Her remembering agency stuff and energy around wanting a mission statement of our own had petered.

"It's not Mr. Trebek anymore. Alex Trebek passed. He was Canadian you know. I loved him. Oh, not in that way. I loved him in the way a daughter wishes for a father. The whole time I was pregnant with you I watched Jeopardy. He was such a brave man. And so passionate. What an incredible grandfather he would have made, huh?"

"We're still alive, Ray. Can you believe it? We get up each day, go to bed each night, in those beds you made. It's amazing." I hesitated a bit on the word "it's," almost saying "you're."

"I'm grateful for you, Dakota."

"Don't."

"I'm grateful for you, Dakota."

"No. Please don't start."

"I'm grateful for this life. I mean *this* life. This last however many days, weeks… this thing we've made here since we arrived. This you and me thing."

"Close to real," I whispered, of the relationship thing we'd made since we arrived.

Teary as she was, a deepness appeared in her eyes. Nothing to do with the pregnancy—her hands weren't even near her belly anymore. The look she cast upon me was serious, without any trace of immaturity or selfishness. There were wrinkles each side of her eyes, and each side of her mouth; nothing teenagery about her. She, the mother, looked right into me, the child.

"My gratitude list's changed, Koda. I mean you're on the top an' all, but now there's new stuff."

"Yeah?" I croaked, not wanting to cry.

"It's kinda weird. Don't know if you wanna hear it."

"Who else is there to listen?"

She hesitated. "I don't know if I can get it all worked out."

"Then don't."

Reverse psychology worked, even though I wasn't meaning it to be reverse psychology.

"Learning," she said. "And remembering about learning. I think I knew some of this stuff before. Learning is two, it's after number one. One is you. Two is a whole bunch of stuff about learning. A learning stew. But one is definitely you Dakota Starr."

She let me pretend there was a bug in my eye. She poured Stupid Tea while I used the bottom of my t-shirt to clean away my tears.

Over supper, we decided that at first light we'd make an amazing plan to head out again, do a different take on the packing, and start downstream. I wished I could blink and, when my eyes opened, we would find ourselves two days downstream, where we'd turned back; pick up where we'd left off.

She went to bed early. I stayed up to deal with a cracking scab on my leg.

Forty-Two

Something creamy was seeping through the leg scab. Lint had started to adhere to it like bugs to sap. I decided to slide into the trailer and get some homemade bandages from my knapsack. Back outside, I lit a candle and spilled the contents of the bag onto the highchair's tray.

Two blue Emmas skittered across the plastic. I stared at them in disbelief. Two from the four must have worked their way out of the toilet paper roll before I'd hung it in our outhouse.

The scornful accusation, "two for me, two for her," or the more severe: "four for her," deadened the leg hurt.

If she hadn't been sleeping, she could have said, "See, you rotten child. I only found two. Two for you." But she was oblivious to the sun having set, the wind turning the pages of a mini-encyclo left on Chair, and my discovery.

Hating myself overpowered the throbbing, the primitive conditions we were living in, the lies we'd told ourselves in order to survive in this place, the bizarreness of it all. Nothing about our past life, current life, and perceived future seemed relevant as I held the two pills. Whatever had sustained me until now was gone.

I slammed the door to self-respect hard in my face and decided the sticky seepage from my leg was pure poison leaching out of my ungrateful body. I placed the pills in a page from the closest book, and folded it around them. Once they were in my pocket, I returned to the trailer and sobbed myself to sleep.

They were still there in the early morning, like a street drug purchase. Ray slumbered in her narrow bed. I set off at a fast pace toward the water and, once there, stood as close to the edge as possible without getting my feet wet. I dug into my pocket, pried them out of the paper, then made a fist like an imagined prize-fighter might. From a mound by the water's edge, I wound up like a pitching machine and released into a powerful throw.

The throw failed miserably—the tablets simply dropped to the ground because they'd been kind of stuck to my hand on account of all the fist squeezing.

Plan B entailed kicking them into the water, but was botched on kick one because I missed, and aborted on kick two since mid-kick I made a decision they might be useful. As I rewrapped the filthy tablets, I realized it would be disrespectful to release them into the wild—*trees shouldn't take drugs.*

I tracked back, climbed up onto the roof, and looked down inside. She was curled like a thin kitten with a bulging belly. I returned the pills to the side pocket of the backpack and decided to take care of overlooked business. First: the practical, to get a good look at the leg, and clean the oozing scab with something as close to disinfectant as I could—probably Stupid Tea. Second: to revisit my gratitude list. Third: to prepare tea for Ray.

While the water was set to boil, I chanted: "One. Life. *This* life. Two. My mother: Raylene Starr Harrison. Three. Green Jean. Four. Every book in the world. Five. Meeeeeee."

I stripped pine needles for the brew. "Is that bad?" I asked an invisible creator. "To count myself on a gratitude list?"

Facing Four Peaks And A Dog provided absolution and filled me with peace. I turned to the circle of rocks and paused. "You idiot," I said, punching myself in the head. "Moron." I moved closer to the rock circle where the boughs sat overtop of ashes from our fish-stick cookout. "It rained. There is no threat."

Fire had dominated our temporary life. Ray'd made a small one during the forest fires to rescue me from the woods. We'd even hiked away from it. We'd returned to home away from home because it was gone. And we'd talked about how the first settlers survived with it. I shook my head at my brainlessness. I hadn't thought to build a big signal fire when we'd returned.

"You made—" she said, as she popped out of the roof hole.

"Tea." I finished her sentence, holding back the excitement about how we could make intentional smoke signals in a deliberate and consistent pattern. First, I wanted to make tea. For her. I decided that once she was enjoying her morning cup, I'd make my presentation that our rescue was a match strike and about a thousand bundles of sticks away.

Planted in Chair, legs over the arms, she began singing a simple country tune with a southern drawl.

Oh, we are two chicks from Four Peaks And A Dog.
We made a bench from some sticks and a log.
We never go farther than creek-side nearby.
We drink Stupid Tea and we look at the sky.
The sky. The sky. The sky. The sky.
We wish we weren't here, but still look at the sky.
Oh, we are two chicks from Four Peaks And A Dog.
We tried to hike out in the haze and the fog.
We did a rain dance and now here we are.
We stare at the sky, at the moon and the stars.
The stars. The stars. The stars. The stars.

We wish we weren't here, but still stare at the stars.

"We wish we weren't here, but still stare at the stars." I joined her on the last part. Couldn't help it.

She started again by humming. Perhaps she was going to repeat the first verse. I didn't get to find out.

Oh, we are two chicks from Four Peaks And A DOOOOOOGGGG!

Forty-Three

"We need an RN," she called out.

"There are no Registered Nurses here, Ray. Breathe. You're delusional."

"No, the Romance Novels. Sister Gabriella," yelled Ray.

"You're hallucinating, it's me, Dakota," I said.

"No. Sister Gabriella delivered Maria's baby at the ruins of a Tuscan castle," said Ray. She grabbed the paperback from down the side of Chair.

She pushed the book at me. "Maria was pregnant with Demetri when she ran from Paulo—she was sure he'd cheated on her, but he hadn't."

"Save your energy for breathing, Ray," I said, refusing the book. All those encyclopedias, and it was a Sister Gabriella romance novella that was going to help us? Ray thumbed the pages and slid off the chair. I grabbed the flattened cardboard boxes and used the seat cushion of Chair for her pillow.

She thrust the book at me. "Near the end," she said. Then she took off her sweatpants and underwear as casually as she did when she went into the striver.

While I found the chapter titled "Blessed Delivery," Ray got down on the cardboard ground-bed I'd made. I kept skimming the pages; it did seem like the nun from the convent in the Tuscan hills knew exactly what to do. The problem was, as I read, the words went into my head and then straight out again.

I considered the irony. Ray had found a self-help book and turned it into a lost in the wilds survival manual. Now her fate was linked to a scene in a romance novella of the Christian variety and it would become a medical manual.

"Coddeeeeeeeeeoowwwww."

I read aloud: " *'It's all right Maria, you're safe now. Your baby will be fine. My name is Gabriella and I'll help,' said the novice.* "

Ray calmed.

"Novice?" I asked.

"That's a nun learner," said Ray. "But the Mother Superior could have totally boosted Gabriella to nun, because Gabriella was the best, even though she always got into trouble with mysteries, but Mother Superior had an axe to grind with Gabriella because—"

"Ray, enough already." I went to secure a couple of containers of water.

"No, Koda. Gabriella was the best. Smart, like you."

"Let's hope she was a super-nun-midwife," I said. A cold sweat broke out on my forehead. I began to tremble. This was all up to me, again. Well, me and fricking Sister Gabby.

We estimated her contractions were about two minutes apart. She kept apologizing between the pains.

I read silently: *It's all going to be fine, Maria, said Gabriella.*

"It's all going to be fine, Ray," I said.

Then a gush of clear fluid came out of Ray. It completely soaked the cardboard bed.

"My water broke," said Ray. She rolled off the wet cardboard and began to stand.

"Ray, don't, the baby might drop out," I said.

She looked at me as if I was the crazy one, stood, then began to pace.

I read ahead. Sister Gabriella had grown up on a farm, wanted to be a vet. I read the same page four times and still couldn't remember a word. "Let's get you into the trailer," I said, racing to grab a couple of shower curtains to put over our beds.

Amazingly, she got in through the roof—at least she was out of the dust and pine needles. She reclined and bent her knees, letting them fall to either side.

"Oh-my-freaking-God, I see the head," I said.

Ray's cries of pain drowned out my words.

"No, don't move. It's okay, I think this is normal," I said when she stopped screaming.

Silent reading: *Maria took her place on the bed. "I'm going to wash my hands, just breathe and relax between the contractions," said Sister Gabriella.*

"I'm going to wash my hands," I said, book in one hand, the other pushing onto the floor.

Ray grabbed my ankle as I climbed on the cardboard box step.

"You've got to let go." I said. "I have to go and disinfect my hands." I shook her off. I used some of the water we'd saved in containers, rubbed some astringent between my palms, and went through the inventory to locate some more drapes and tablecloths.

I returned and continued to silently read: *Gabriella spoke gentle words to Maria, to soothe her. "How long have you been having these pains, blessed girl?'" "Oh, sacred Sister, I'm so ashamed. I've failed you. I've failed everyone.'"*

"How long have you been in pain?" I asked.

"All day," said Ray. "Not this severe. On and off, weaker than this all day, maybe even yesterday, but I had been moving rocks so thought it was muscle aches, not muscle contractions. I've made such a mess of things, Koda."

"*Now look here, I'm not going to cast a stone—we've all sinned.*" *Sister Gabriella took Maria's hand in her own.*

"Now look here," I said, ready to deliver Gabriella's "cast no stone" lecture, then changed my mind. "No, I mean look here, catch this wet cloth for your forehead."

"*Let us welcome this child into the world with a prayer of hope and forgiveness.*" *The novice made the sign of the cross.*

"We don't have a hope or a prayer," I whispered.

"Koda, I'm sorry. It was a one-night stand. I didn't drink or do drugs, I swear."

"I know, Ray. It's okay."

"It was one of those things. I wanted to be held. It was stupid."

"It's okay, Ray. Let's get through this."

"I should give the bracelet back."

"Ray, relax. You've done this before, right?"

"A long time ago, and it was different. You were an easy baby. I'm so sorry."

"Ray, get a grip." I wanted to bathe in her apologies, but there was a human head about to shoot out at me.

"I'm a failure."

"You're human."

"You're a super-hero daughter."

"I'm human."

"The baby's coming. Owwwwww." Ray writhed in pain; bit the wet cloth.

Silent reading: "*Maria, now you're going to push gently between the major pain okay?*" *Sister Gabriella's voice echoed in the chamber within the ruins.*

"It's okay, Maria, try to push gently between the major pain, okay?" I said and turned the page.

Ray didn't seem to mind my calling her Maria; good thing because I was too confused between the narrative and reality. I continued from the book. Word for word. Loud, so Ray could hear me. "*Oh, Maria, you're so strong. God chose you for this journey, and will not forsake you. This holy child will have a sacred role in this world. Maria stay with me okay?*"

"Yes, Sister," said Ray

"'*Heavens, Maria. Hallelujah to the gift of life.*'"

"Thank you, Sister. I'm sorry, Sister."

"'*Oh, Maria, God is not upset with you, and I am his humble servant. We are all his children.*'" I stopped reading aloud, but continued speaking. "Oh, God, could this get any weirder?" I said.

Ray panted, gripped the trailer's inner frame at a floor joist behind her head, and tightened her body.

A human head emerged from between Ray's wide-spread legs. I found myself holding each side of a wet, sticky, ball with thick black hair. I didn't want it to drop onto the shower curtain. "Whoa, the baby's head's turning in my hands," I said.

"You're doing great," said Ray.

I needed to look at the book, but could only bend my head down and turn the page with my nose. "I can't read and deliver this baby at the same time," I said.

But I didn't need to read, not right then, because Ray pushed and a shoulder came through and then *sploosh,* out came the rest of a real baby. It slipped out of my hands and skidded a bit on the shower curtain. It wriggled, a tiny human-once-tadpole sliding about. I managed to wrap a piece of fabric around the infant and push the whole package up toward Ray. A thick, bloody rope prevented me from shoving the baby all the way up Ray's chest.

Ray sat up a little and clung to the child while I bloodied the pages of the RN. I read out loud again, "'*Gabriella held the baby with two hands, neck and head tilted at forty-five degrees to let the fluids drain from the baby.'"*

I snatched the baby back and did that. The baby let out a gurgle. I returned the anchored baby to Ray, its head still tipping down.

In the book, Gabriella told Maria they needed to cut the cord.

"Oh my God, I'm not made for this," I said.

"I'll do it," said Ray.

While she somehow balanced the baby, she tied some fabric around two parts of the cord then, using a sawing motion with the blade of craft scissors, she cut the part between the two pieces of fabric.

Surveying the mess was my first step to cleaning up.

"It's a boy," said Ray. She smiled directly into my half-brother's mucus-covered face. She rewrapped him in the cloth, then put a damper on my clean-up plans by telling me to stand by.

"There's more?" I asked. Then I remembered biology class. The placenta that had nourished the baby during the pregnancy was at the other end of this science project. It had to come out, but naturally. I tried to remember *The Miracle of Birth* movie at school, but animation is not the same thing as real life.

It was Sister Gabriella to the rescue again. The author's penchant for full detail had probably saved lives. I read to Ray.

"'Your baby is beautiful,' said Maria. 'Now I need a little more help from you. We're going to wait a little while for the placenta, so stay where you are, and keep the baby warm.' Sister Gabriella revisited her memories of the farm and the many babies she had helped deliver. For a few sad moments she wondered if she should follow her spiritual calling to the Lord and instead go out into the world, have a baby of her own, but she knew she was needed here with Maria. She told herself she would think about her life later. She said a short prayer to ask forgiveness for worldly thoughts, especially those impure ones about Antonio the baker. She considered, for a moment, that might be why

Mother Superior was holding back on providing full permission for her to be a fully-fledged nun. 'God Bless Mother Superior,' the Novice whispered."

"I told you she was amazing," said Ray. "She loved Mother Superior even though she was an evil bitch… but really, Mother Superior's just jealous of Gabby's youth." The blanketed mountain child squirmed and squeaked. I kept reading to them both.

"Sister Gabriella placed a bowl below Maria's passage of life, then began to firmly massage Maria's abdomen and pelvis to help slow down the bleeding. Yes, she could tell it hurt, but it was necessary. Sister Gabriella was patient—she had time to think about the animals on the farm, of Marco the young man who helped with the chores, and the single kiss he'd given her before she left for the convent. A tear rolled down Sister Gabriella's cheek. She wanted to confide to Maria that she wasn't sure about her vows, but Maria's body interrupted and delivered the placenta."

I readied myself for it all. Ray called out, and relief filled the air that it would all be over soon. But Maria hadn't called out. Ray was clearly in pain, like she had been when the baby had been making his way down the birth canal. Ray leaned back. I got the bowl ready for the placenta. The writer had not written enough about the placental part. I dared myself to look.

"God help us," I said.

"Koda, you don't have to do Gabriella any longer," said Ray before pain caused her to hang onto her new-born and convulse backwards.

But I wasn't doing Gabriella. I was doing me. Another head had crowned. A second baby. I braced myself for a repeat. In a nanosecond I made myself understand I could do this again. But, in the next second, as a tiny grey body was ejected, I wanted to throw up. My body began to tremble. This was no celebration.

"It hurts so much," said Ray. "What's happening?" She was flat on her back. The live baby on her chest.

"No, stay there," I said. "It's okay. I'm not used to this. It's, it's, it's…"

"Sister Gabriella said the placenta has to be delivered," said Ray. "I remember that, but there wasn't much detail. She didn't say it hurt like hell."

I knew this baby had not been alive for a little while, but I forced myself to jiggle it a little. No amount of CPR or sophisticated machinery in a hospital would have saved this child. Now that its physical body has presented, its soul could be re-shelved for another creature. I looked through the hole in the roof. Blue Sky. As if on some mystical cue, an eagle passed over. I told myself the bird would carry its spirit to another living being, then gathered my strength for deceit.

Pretending it was a placenta, not a baby, was the best way to handle the situation while the actual placental material was delivered. I massaged some more, in case I'd missed anything.

"Ray, stay here," I said, placing another drop cloth over her tummy and knees. Stay there and look after baby. I'll deal with this end."

The swaddled baby, content on Ray's chest, squirmed. My half-brother. All alive. At my knees lay my half-sister. All dead.

Forty-Four

It played out as a song of sorrow with actions instead of words:
Ensure the dead baby was concealed within the bloody fabric.

Get Ray to promise to stay put.

Climb out the top of the trailer.

Remove all the wood holding up the ramp door.

Drop the ramp.

Enter the trailer.

Smile at Ray.

Remove the pile of fabric that contained the baby—don't drop out, dead baby.

Find a private spot.

Wrap the dead baby in a white tablecloth.

Place in a solid-sided box that had held bathroom products.

Put the box by Six O'Clock Tree.

Re-enter the trailer via the ramp.

Smile at Ray.

Begin bundling more bedding.

Haul it out.

Ignore the dead baby.

Look for Eagle.

Revive the fire.

Separate the bedding into two piles. Burn. Wash.

Ignore the dead baby.

Look for Eagle.

Check on Ray.

Insist she remain resting.

Build up the fire.

Ignore the dead baby.

Look for Eagle.

Make Ray a cup of Stupid Tea.

Keep her warm with clean blankets.

Build up the fire.

Ignore the dead baby.

C'mon Eagle, where the hell are you?

Watch Ray sleep.

Watch my half-brother sleep.

Visit Six O'Clock Tree.

Look for Eagle.

Build up the fire.

Look for Eagle.

When the fire grew large enough for a funeral pyre, I soothed myself with Stupid Tea. I added more fuel and dragged a dead-fallen tree across it, then collected the box.

"Now," I called to the sky.

Eagle circled, I walked onto the edges of the fire and across the log bridge that would soon catch. Between the licks of flames, some three feet high, a section of my flip flops melted. I placed the box at the end of the fallen tree, right at my feet, then turned and balanced my way outside the rock circle.

I couldn't smell anything or taste the normal tastes in my mouth, but I was still me. If she *had* to be dead, then I had to handle it all.

The fire blazed.

The Eagle's cry rained on us all.

It circled. It cried.

I collapsed into Plaid Chair.

Ray slept inside the trailer, ramp down, with the alive child.

When I next looked at the sky Eagle was gone.

Fatigue consumed me.

I startled. "Ray?"

"I'm on my feet now. A bit unsteady but I needed some air, and to pee."

"You can pee that soon after birth? What about the whole birth canal urethra thing?"

"It's all sort of natural," said Ray. "Hey, you cleaned up good."

"You too," I said.

"I've got to make some pads," she said. "You know, Kotex-ey napkins."

"I've got those ones you made for me. I'll get them from the purple box."

"No, you tend your fire," she said. "Why so big?"

"Some of the blankets had to be burned. Wasn't hygienic to keep them around."

"Koda?"

"Yeah?"

"You should consider becoming a nun."

Her knees wobbled, and she took herself back into the ramp-down trailer.

I followed her in, stroked the little baby and, when I did, a shiver ran through me. Would it be like that every time I was around him?

I looked back out to the fire. A nun? A midwife? I was a fricking undertaker and funeral director.

"Whatcha thinkin' then?"

"Oh, Ray."

"C'mon. Give me some vintage Dakota. A lecture? Some words of advice? A correction? I can take it because we made it. We're alive."

"Oh, Ray, I got nothin'."

"What shall we name him," asked Ray. "Demetri?"

"How about Ranger?" I couldn't believe I blurted out my dream dog's name.

"Ranger it is," said Ray.

"You're kidding me."

"You delivered him so you should name him."

"Well, it is better than Demetri. But you'd go with that?" Then I remembered she'd named me after a truck. "I wasn't serious."

"But it's nice. We're here in the forest, and he's like a forest ranger. Ranger Starr. Let's give him a part of us shall we? He'd be forest guy by day and protector under the night sky."

"I'm gonna check the fire," I said.

"You've been obsessed with it all afternoon," said Ray.

"I want to make sure everything is incinerated. The bloody sheets and stuff. Disease and environmental concern, you know." My half-sister had become stuff.

In a final act, I raced to Dress and tore off one string of teardrops.

I flared the fire for a final time, hoping it would reach the temperature for bones to burn—if not, they'd end up underneath more embers and charcoal.

What I noticed was that some of the wet wood made the fire smoke the same as Ray's little one had when she signalled me. But I needed this fire to get hot, not wet. There was a body to burn.

I decided, though, when this ordeal was over, I'd collect more wood, make a larger fire, and create a massive smoke cloud by sacrificing saplings; enough fresh growth would surely create something that would show up in the sky and then Eagle could carry it to some curious forest officials.

I drew a little heart on the side of my dress box—decided to draw one every day that passed—so there would be, when we got out of the forest, if we ever got out of the forest, a way to calculate the birth day by minus-ing the hearts from whatever day we got out.

"Today is August the something," I said as I kissed the string of teardrops and tossed it into the flames.

And a drum sounded. Not the dream one in my head. One that shook the forest and threatened to rock-slide the whole mountain. At that moment, my half-sister became August Starr.

Green Jean and Brenda waited in the stand of trees by Six O'clock Tree. Jean's hand rested on the shoulder of a girl who was hit by a semi because she took too much ecstasy. They turned and carried away August Starr—in Brenda's arms—dropping the scorched string of beads on their way into the forest. I know it was through blurry eyes, but I saw them and watched them.

Ray comforted Ranger with lullabies and, without knowing, she eased my grief and blotted out the random drumbeat which had returned. I heard verses and choruses of cradlesongs from a distance and realized I'd fallen asleep outside in Chair—I'd stayed up tending the fire, again.

Ray's voice came closer and, when I opened my eyes, she stood with the baby tied to her front with a sash. She handed me a jar of chopped fish.

"Hey, I should be doing that," I said.

"People have babies all the time," she said. "I'm fine."

Then she squeezed in beside me on Chair.

"I need to do laundry. One day old and look at all the messy curtain-diapers." She sounded like a mature mother.

"Hey, there's a disposable diaper in my Lifebook. I could trace it and make some. Plus, he can use the one in my book."

"If you like," she said. "But he doesn't need to poop on your stuff. Besides it's trendy to use cloth."

She slipped Ranger out of the sash and rolled him on to me. He curled into me, as if he were a sloth clinging to a branch. His chest rose and fell. His eyes opened and he locked eyes with me then blew a bubble.

I avoided looking at the smoking memorial because, every time I did, the drumbeat returned.

"Ray, rest first. We can both go do laundry. I can make him some diapers from some of those dinosaur valences."

She reclined on flattened cardboard boxes while I stayed in Chair.

"I know now might not be the time," I said, "but there's something I ought to tell you.

Forty-Five

Ray was inside the trailer, fixing something on Ranger's crib. Though it was warm, I slipped in and sat on my bedroll.

"I think I might be going crazy," I said.

"I don't understand."

"A drumbeat. It's in my head a lot. It was there all the time before we came here, and it went away, but it came back when I was lost. And then it went again. And then Eagle said... I mean and then it came back last night, and today."

I waited for her to tell me that, at my age, some girls hear drumbeats, and that others hear bells; some both. Something she'd forgotten to tell me. A rite of passage for teenagers. *Silly Starry, it happens to every girl.* But she didn't.

"A drumbeat? You're sure?"

"Yeah. Really."

"What are the other signs? The signs of you going crazy."

"The sounds in my head. Isn't that enough?"

"Voices?"

"Crap no. Not yet. The same sound. A drumbeat, kind of." I

269

began thinking the drumbeat wouldn't be that bad compared to what she'd suggested.

She said a few okays which I recognized was her way to trick me into saying more. It worked. "And a dream."

"A nightmare?"

"No, the same dream. Even though I can't remember it, I know it's the same dream. Like a whole bunch of need-to-know information in a kind of weird-twisted way that I remember but I can't remember."

She stopped rolling fabric and sat back on her own bedroll. I'd scared her. I tried to ease up.

"It's a dream. Longer than a cartoon, but not as long as an old movie."

"What's it about?"

"That's the problem. The only thing I remember is that it's important."

"How often, Koda?"

"The dream? For as long as I can remember. At least when I remember. The drumbeat when I'm not sleeping—well, not so long. How weird is that? It went away when we came here, but like I said, now it's back."

She lifted herself and leaned on her elbows, squinting. She was either confused or she was ready to rescue Ranger from the psychotic daughter. I cleared it up for her. "The dream has been for a while. Not too long ago, I noticed the drumbeat, that is also in the dream, is with me a lot during the day."

She butt-shuffled closer, but not too close, deciding I was some kind of freak that she now needed to surrender. She had Ranger. She didn't need me.

But where would she take me or send me? What place was there, to give me back? Who would take me? A call to a social worker, a stay in a foster home, a group home, no home? I would live on the street, in a dumpster, or a refrigerator box behind a grocery store. She stared into my eyes. Compassion there. She was in it for the long run, crazy daughter and all. She'd visit me at the asylum if it came to that. Bring me cookies and magazines and stuff that I couldn't hurt myself with or on.

"It's too often to be normal. It's one thing at night in my dreams, but in my waking hours, it's over the top."

She tucked some blankets around me, even though I was fully dressed. "Dakota, we can get help."

"Oh, I don't want that kind of help." I pictured brain probes and sterile room.

"You need help, Dakota, if this is messing up your days. Not to mention your nights."

"Promise you won't tell anyone. If we get back."

"I can't make that promise."

"Promise," I demanded.

She nodded.

"Okay, I was hearing this rhythm part of the day. I worked through it; sometimes it was there and sometimes it wasn't. It went away for the most part when we got here, but it seems to be coming back. And I know it has to do with the dream."

"Right, the dream you can't remember."

"The dream I can't remember. Except for at the end when I know in the dream that red bowl and yoghurt is coming.

"Do you have any ideas what it means Koda? Any suspicions? Oh no, it's me. I didn't do enough, did I? Oh, Koda, I'm so sorry."

"Ray, please, you did fine. Wait. Hang on."

The earth was shifting under me.

"Oh my god…Ray! I always thought the sound was from a drum but, I mean, I know a drumbeat sound. I mean how long have I been dancing? I so-ooo know the drum. But oh my god, it's… it's… a heartbeat with attitude."

"There's something wrong with your heart? Like that missing beat stuff what people get pacemakers for?"

"No, it's not my heartbeat. I don't need a pacemaker. It's just that… Wait. Ray. This next part won't make sense."

"What?"

"It's yours."

"Mine?"

"Yeah, yours."

She reached out to grab me, but I squished myself into the wall of the trailer.

She touched me anyway; one hand on my forearm and the other cupped behind my head. She totally squished Ranger between us. The head cupping produced waves of healing that flowed into my neck and through into the rest of me.

"Face it, I'm a freak," I said to her arm that was holding me against her chest.

"We'll need to go see someone. A professional. Because if you're screwed up it's because of me."

"You promised," I said.

"No, I didn't. Not in the way you're saying I did. I have responsibilities. Let's calm down. Think this out. You have to get help. I mean we have to get help."

"Why do you have to be so responsible now?" I asked.

"Dakota Starr, be serious."

"I am. Look, this is the first time I've talked about it. I only this second figured it out. Maybe I'm wrong. Now that I have, maybe I can do something about it that can make it stop. I mean it stopped the whole time we've been here till a few days ago. Maybe now I'll start recalling some of the dream. Wait! I hear it now!"

"Oh my god, Koda, I hear it too."

"It's escaping me. Like that alien in *Alien*. It's gonna come out of my chest. Raaaaayyyyyy!"

And then Ray was up on the stepping-up stool, fighting to get past the shower curtain.

"Don't leave me," I cried.

"Shit, we're trapped in here, we need to get out there and wave," said Ray.

By the time Ray was able to push through the curtain and get on the roof of the trailer, the chopper was a dot in the sky.

"I'm sorry, Ray. If I hadn't come in to tell you about my problem, I'd have been out there." I slammed my fist against the wall inside the trailer.

Ranger started to cry.

Ray slid back inside and started to nurse him. "No, Koda. You were right to tell me. We're okay. We're survivors."

"Maybe the pilot will know it's not an abandoned site," I said.

"But might think we're some kind of trappers who want to be here," said Ray.

"We still have to walk out, don't we?"

"I need a week to get some strength back, and then we're outta here," she said. "I'm making a strong sling for him, and a pack from his bed."

"One week," I said. "I can be ready."

"You really think it is my heartbeat?" Ray asked.

"Uh-huh. It's exactly like I heard when you were beside me, before the helicopter came." I said it shakily.

"That's pretty powerful," said Ray.

"Ray, you're pretty powerful."

"We'll make a dream catcher," she said. "Green Jean showed me how."

"We don't need one, we're going to be walking out. I'm good. Ranger needs you."

"You need me too."

"We all need each other." I said it quietly, so that she wouldn't hear me, and I pictured everyone in the world holding hands around the globe. The way Martha had described it within her dance.

"You know what, Ray? I never had it in the trailer. I had it when I was lost in the forest. I had it out here when I slept in Chair. I never have it when I'm sleeping beside you."

"Maybe that's a good thing?"

Forty-Six

Ray made a dreamcatcher with twigs and pinecones and string and sparkles, finishing it before we went to bed.

From that first sleep, the dreamcatcher floated above us where the birdcage had been. I like to believe it caught the bad ones, filtering only good ones. No drum.

"Excellent results," Ray said. "And just think, therapists get paid for this."

I wanted to say, *The drum dream and drumbeat didn't happen when I was in the trailer with you, anyway*, but she was too happy, and I was too eager to believe in her magic. I let out a "We'll see."

"No. It will be every night, no matter where you sleep," she said.

"Okay," I said.

"Good. Let's move on. A dreamcatcher for you, now I'm gonna make that pack I talked about. Where's that cardboard box with the really thick sides? The one with the stiff edges?"

The strong sided box. The box that had bathroom stuff in it. The coffin. August Starr had been in that box. I'd burned it. I'd burned her. Would every conversation lead to something about the other baby?

She moved in and out of mothering Ranger and me, and fishing, and Stupid Tea. An inflatable foot bath became Ranger's cradle.

The second night with the dreamcatcher, Green Jean came to me and reminded me about fetal grief. She kept it simple. She and Brenda, my adoptive mom that never got to be my adoptive mom, had Destiny, the girl whose dress I had been given, and August Starr, my half sister. Ray had me and Ranger.

In my dream, an uninjured, white-winged Jean stood in the alley behind Carters. She said: "The great wind has taken pity away. The sky is yours. The earth is yours. Love is yours."

That's when I knew I'd never have the drum dream again. And I knew that somewhere deep inside me I would find a ritual to settle myself into myself.

I began to collect wood to burn into a massive smoke-signal fire. The funeral fire was a thing of the past—all the charcoaled wood holding cooling ashes. I was glad Ray didn't ask about my fuel collection. I wanted to surprise her with creating our way out before we walked. I figured it'd take two or three days to collect enough wood to build and maintain a fire that could send smoke signals so far that the helicopter would return. I'd stack it all just beyond Six O'clock Tree; tell her right before I lit it. No one would be able to ignore my signals. If, before I was ready, she somehow she decided we were leaving, and heading to the river again—and I didn't think there was much chance of that, she was loving life—I could buy a few days extra by faking sick. I woke and decided that I'd go deeper into the woods, near the vertical wall, to check out if there was dead-fall there.

She was brewing tea when she screamed my name, or something like my name. Oh god, she was going to die from some toxic thing from having given birth in the wild. Or maybe she'd fallen, and if she had Ranger strapped to her she could crush him. I hadn't got the fire restarted yet, let alone big enough.

I shot out of the trailer roof, shimmied partway down the ladder, then leapt to the ground, rolling to protect the impact on my ankles.

Ray's image blurred into the foreground. She hadn't fallen. Ranger was okay. She simply stood and stared west.

From the path we'd trampled back and forth to the striver, there emerged three human forms. Apparitions, like heat waves from pavement—a movie scene where aliens appear on the horizon and walk toward the camera.

If this were our movie, this is where the orchestra would have burst in, all the instruments joining. If it were our movie, the orchestral soundtrack would likely have been a twangy guitar.

"Nice hiking boots," said the tallest one, staring at the singed flip-flops on my feet.

Even though they were uniformed in khaki forest service issue they asked no official questions, at first. It was as if they believed we were on the mountain by choice. Our situation was never described as a rescue, and they weren't the type to consider hero status.

In all the rescue stories I've since read, people jump and cheer when their heroes appear. But a lifetime of uncertainty, and the closeness we felt to nature, had combined to dull any of that animation. We were Ray and Dakota. In the moment. No hysteria. Mountain mellow.

Matt was super easy going. Carl, the tallest, often tagged his co-workers with comfortable teasing. Over our Stupid Tea and their re-hydrated food, we discovered Brandi (with an i) and Carl were married and had made it their priority to match-make for Matt.

When we'd kind of explained how we'd arrived, they told us that our smoke had been spotted from a tower. The helicopter had confirmed it wasn't a new forest fire.

I detached from their lively conversation; the pyre I'd built for August Starr to go home would take us to our new home as well. I wouldn't be able to surprise Ray by purposely engineering our rescue.

On the positive side, I wouldn't have to spend days collecting and hiding wood, on the negative side the fire that saved us would always be the fire that killed a little bit of me.

Mountain mellow continued in that our rescuers explained that since there were no reports of missing persons, that there had been no search and rescue, therefore there'd be no reporters when we got back. Ray shared that no one had known we were going away, and that our being here was a decision, all hers, made from desperation.

Our story of stowing away seemed to invoke more "hey, great sense of adventure" versus empathy over poverty or Ray's impulsivity. Beyond that, the three of them seemed incredibly proactive and practical. They passed around Ranger, then Matt fished a hoodie from his knapsack, then fashioned an insulated baby carrier. He wore it on the front of his body and carried the little guy around. "Same kind we make for injured or orphaned baby bears," he said.

Their ways were smooth. Their gestures easy. Each of them handled a subject. Carl told us how we could leave—by helicopter—as they were scheduled to meet one the next day, not too far from our camp.

The pilot, Jake, expected Brandi, Carl, and Matt. He'd get Ray, Ranger, me, and Matt. Brandi spoke of how she and Carl would stay behind to prepare our stuff for a cargo lift—that Jake would want to use the opportunity for training. Matt seemed to be the future accommodation specialist—discussing logistics with Brandi and Carl. He seemed to be planning to use his local boy status with relatives in a town called Fieldstone Ridge. It was like a support group, right there in the forest, without any framed mission statement.

The best thing was, we weren't being judged. And the next best thing was that Ray seemed receptive. Matt smiled away our unspoken fears and offered advice, including how we'd need to get used to eating a little more each day. He filled us with a cheery hopefulness, his confidence contagious.

It was too close to a romance novel. Sister Gabriella, reuniting Paulo with Maria, and having him meet his son, Demetri.

But I was Dakota Starr, not some novice in an Italian convent.

Something else bobbed about, something inside me that kept messaging from my heart to my brain. Matt could identify with our past—what little we'd told him—maybe more. That we'd skipped out on rent, moved a thousand times, lived off welfare cheques. I saw it behind his eyes. But there was no judgment or pity, just a knowing something about us. He looked at me the same way he looked at the baby. Softly. He looked at Ray with a more mature version of soft—respectful for sure, and curiosity. Ranger and I were children. Ray was a grown up. No, Ray was a woman. A strong woman.

The three of them were genuinely impressed with our survival. "I'm writing a manual for the department. It's a collaboration between my people—the Cree—and my employer." Matt had such a gentle voice with no trace of authority or ego. He occasionally rubbed his hand across his shaved head as if expecting hair. "You're gonna have to share some of your secrets. Like this tea, here." He sipped, then did a childish "mmm good" smile. He was hitting on Ray, without knowing he was hitting on Ray, in a tender, playful way.

After sunset, Brandi and Carl showed me all the pictures on their cameras—nature, nature, and more nature—and Matt sat on the ground off in the distance with Ray and Ranger and a few candles. Eventually we all came together for goodnights, and the conservationists unrolled their sleeping bags, announcing it'd be better to start out the next day. It was strange, having company.

Once inside, I whispered ever so slightly to Ray. "I feel like they're…"

"Lookin' at us?" She was quiet when she spoke.

"Yeah. They're nice enough. And we're gonna get outta here, but…"

"But now we don't have privacy."

"It's kinda scary, you know. The unknown. What *is* gonna happen, Ray?"

"Dunno, Koda," she whispered.

"Ya think they can hear us?"

"Dunno, Koda."

"Are we gonna live in Field-Whatever-Ridge?"

"Dunno, Koda."

"Ray!"

"Keep your voice down," she whisper-hissed.

We were silent for a few minutes, then she spoke. "Our last night and I can't even sing you to sleep."

"At least there's something to be thankful for," I said.

She adjusted the angle of her body, shifted her head around the cardboard stepping-up box, and drew close to my ear, pulling a table-cloth over our heads, Ranger and his inflatable foot bath bed included. She began to hum. I squirmed a little, knowing I needed to keep still because they could hear our movements.

To the tune of the Tin Pan Alley classic, "Hello! Ma Baby," I suffered through

Goodnight my baby
   Goodnight my baby
   Sleep tight tonight because
   No more tomorrows in this mountain heaven
   Sleep tight-y tight-ey
   last night-y night-ey
   see you tomorrow morn
   I will be up at dawn

And then she told Ranger that he was a guest listener, because this was only a lullaby for Dakota Starr.

Last night, tonight. Those words so bittersweet.

When Ray started snoring, I wished I could too. Instead, I went up on the roof of the trailer and watched the night.

Even if there had been no moon, I could have found my way about, that's how home this place had become. I eased down the ladder and grabbed an empty YT can from the stack we had, scooped up some ashes from the large fire circle, then squeezed the top of the tin together to seal it the best I could.

I whispered to Matt, who was or was not watching me, "I have to do this."

Forty-Seven

They had their own mini-fire going near their fold-out one-burner stove close to where their sleeping bags had been deployed. A twirl of that smoke snaked its way over the hole in the trailer's roof. The aroma of coffee came along for the ride.

Two china cups and three metal mugs of java took the chill off the morning. Brandi and Matt went over some kind of checklist while Carl snapped photos. "Better Gnomes and Gardens." He chuckled between his words.

"They're for your eyes only." Brandi made sure to avert our fears.

Matt offered Ray and me a protein bar. "Slowly, remember? Nice 'n' easy. Like hiking a long incline. Little bites. Lots of chewing. Like the hare and the turtle. Slow and steady wins the race. Don't wanna get sick? Don't stuff your face."

He was repeating his words in rap when Brandi cut in. "Sheesus Matt, I'm pretty sure they get it."

When he stopped laughing at his race and face rhyme, Matt took on a dreamy tone, reminding Ray of soup he could rehydrate for her later.

"Lu-uv soup," said Carl, nudging me with his elbow.

We were caught in a whirlwind of chatter. A part of me ached for silence, and the rest of me begged for them not to stop talking.

Ray popped Ranger in his sling, then tried out Matt's hoodie carrier for comparison. She settled on both; double security for the kid.

Matt fanned the campfire with a fresh branch. "Way smaller, but pretty much like what the fire-tower watcher would have seen when you had a fire going, or when you put it out, or whatever you were doing to it," he said through the smoky puffs.

"Burning a baby," I whispered.

"The firewatcher thought it might be a plane crash. That's why Jake came to check it out," said Brandi.

"The same Jake who's coming to take us away from here?" Ray asked.

"One and the same," said Matt. "He'll fly over a bit later, then he'll go do something to give us time to get there."

"Today?" asked Ray.

"Plenty of time to take a slow walk there and be out before nightfall, if he flies over in the next hour or three," said Matt.

"Today," said Ray.

"Probably today," said Brandi. "That's the plan."

"No," said Ray. "I don't think so. I can't go today."

I looked down on Ray from the hole in the top of the trailer. For the last hour—since the "can't go today"—she'd isolated, sitting on Coat on my bedroll, unresponsive to everyone. Even Ranger was trapped by her breakdown, involuntarily soothed by Ray's rocking back and forth.

"Same as last time I checked," I said to our rescuers. I slipped back into the highchair. Matt was perched on a box of RNs, Brandi in Plaid Chair, Carl next to her on its arm. "Gnomes and Gardens," said Carl. "I shouldn't have made that joke. I didn't mean to hurt her."

"It was a trauma response, like I've seen from some of my fellow soldiers. It wasn't you, Carl."

Matt stood and retrieved the pot from the forestry-issue stove and topped up everyone's coffee except his own.

"Drink. Stay where you are while I'm gone. Don't bother her," he said.

"What if she comes out?" asked Brandi.

"She won't," said Matt, then he looked at me. "Koda, would you boil some water please? I won't be long." He walked off, taking his empty mug into the bush in the direction of the striver.

We sipped. No one looked at the trailer. My breath slowed. The goldenness of silence warmed me. I used their little stove and boiled our water in one of their pans.

He was gone ten minutes, maybe twenty. I kept the water on simmer. He joined me beside the stove. "I want to ask Brandi and Carl to go for a walk. Is that okay with you?" Matt asked. "What I'm saying is, I want to speak to Ray with as much privacy as possible. I would be here, so would you—and the baby. But I won't do that if you don't feel safe without Brandi and Carl here."

"You and her were talking last night for a long time. That's not something she does—socialize comfortably. If you think you can help her, then it's a good idea. She can't live in the wild forever."

"Is that a yes?"

I nodded. He went over and spoke to Carl and Brandi. They picked up their packs and called out a loud "see you later." Ray had to have heard.

Matt took a handful of pine needles from his mug and dropped them into the simmering water. He held his empty hand in front of my nose. "Inhale," he said.

Beneath the pine there was a peppery hint, not quite enough to make me sneeze.

He gestured for me to show him my palms, then placed a second pinch of needles onto one of them. "Like this," he said. He rubbed his hands together then held them flat against his face and swept them downward toward his neck.

I copied. "Wow, that's amazing," I said.

"Nature's wet-wipes," he said. "Sometimes they're a bit sticky. You can unstick them with the steam from the tea."

I held mine above the pan, then stroked my face again. He did the same.

"Stir." He handed me a twig.

"But it's only pine needles. They don't need mixing. You're making Stupid Tea."

He crumbled a dark material over the water. "With an extra ingredient from the bark."

I stirred in the bits until they dissolved. "Do you know what's wrong with her?" It was a begging more than a question.

"Pikwâstan," he said. "She is broken. Broken by the wind."

I held my finger to the air.

"Not that wind," he said. "It's kind of like the current from helicopter blades. She fears it will kill her."

"But people just bend down. Right?"

"Not that kind of death, Koda."

I pointed the twig at the mixture. "Is this supposed to save her life?"

"Koda-bear, do you know what the Plains Cree are known for?"

"How did you know to call me that? She calls me that."

"Koda, short for Dakota; you remind me of the Kodiak bears of Alaska."

"They sound scary and friendly." I tapped the twig on the side of the pan.

"The Plains Cree were here first. Did you know that?"

"I know the land most of us live on was once First Nations Land, so it's important to recognize that. People announce that at the beginning of graduations and stuff—territorial acknowledgement."

"I'm impressed."

"I learned about it at Popeye's. Well, it's not Popeye's, it's a friendship centre—diverse membership."

"Ray told me last night that you go there."

"Did she tell you she doesn't?"

Matt took another pinch of pine from the mug; did the hand rubbing thing and freshened his face and scalp.

"And I've been to a few Powwows. I dance. Did she tell you I dance?"

"You dance at Powwows?"

"Of course not. But I've seen the dances there. I dance in the studio. At Pop— the friendship centre. I do a kind of fusion that's influenced by Indigenous dance."

"What has she told you about her ancestors? Which would be yours too."

"Besides that she believes Elton John is a distant relative? An aunt in Victoria. Nothing. I have this Lifebook. I've only read it once, but it might hint at something 'northern Alberta-ish remote-like.'"

"The Plains Cree were spread over a massive territory; lots of communities living in harmony with what each geographical area gifted them."

"Like this one?" I asked.

"Not quite this high, but for sure in some spots like foothills. Their lifestyle was focused on bison, and on gathering plant foods. I'm mostly of Cree descent. In the beginning of colonization, there was a lot of mixing of settlers and Indigenous people—hey, it got some European explorers in tight with the Chiefs, by marrying their daughters. Then there were more mixed partnerships over time. Some chose to stay on the land reserved for the 'Indians.'" He used two curling fingers as air quotes. "Others tried to find themselves in the towns and cities. It wasn't easy or smooth. Especially when there was a forced forgetting—an abundance of abandonment."

"My erm, friend-sorta-godmother, Green Jean, said something like that too—advantage by marrying into tribes. My dance teacher said dance went underground—as in not being allowed."

"It wasn't. For a long time, like decades, children were ripped from their parents' arms and taken to residential schools where they were not allowed to speak their language, or keep their braids. Even with a truth and reconciliation process, the scars remain. The spirit in me recognizes your mom is of mixed ancestry, as are you."

"She confirmed it?"

"Her heart did."

"The heart language is a thing? It's an unspoken word thing?"

"Koda, the mouth can lie. The heart cannot. Answer me this: when you got here, did she seem to know what she was doing?"

I started stirring again. "You know she did."

"When she arrived here, her ancestry stretched out its arms to her and she embraced it. She may not realize that, but it is what happened," said Matt. "Now we're threatening to take it away from her. Again."

He grabbed a hoodie and used the cuff to hold the handle of the pan.

"Let me find her special cup," I said.

He poured two cups of his Stupid Tea plus and gave me one of them. "I'll move the comfy chair close to the trailer so you can listen. It's important that we're a team." He was already zigzagging it across the scrub. Then he covered Ray's cup with Ray's saucer, and stood at the bottom of the ladder.

"I've got this," he said.

I staggered backward in relief. Someone other than me was going to take care of a crisis.

Forty-Eight

ansi," he said when he was in the trailer. I knew from Popeye's that loosely meant "hello, how are you?" I waited for Ray's heart to speak to him in the universal language of mind your own business…tell him to get the eff out.

"Pikwâstan," said Ray.

I spilled a bit of tea meant for my mouth. I knew that word. I'd learned it minutes before from Matt. How did she know broken by the wind? Why was she saying she was broken by the wind? The stove was too far away for her to have heard us.

He asked her, "What part of you knew to make the tea? Hands? Head? Soul? You knew it was nâtawihowin—healing medicine."

There was some cup and saucer clinking from inside the trailer. "This tastes different than mine."

"Not everyone adds bark."

"Where are your braids?" Ray asked.

"Jake's mom has cancer. A bunch of us shaved our heads."

"But the hair is sacred."

"So is Jake's mom."

Her teacup clinked against her saucer again. Ranger squeaked. Ray spoke: "I'm not going back."

"Your spirit already knows there's a journey ahead," he said.

"Koda says the snow will be coming soon, but the forestry could check on us."

"A lot of gear. A lot of visits. And you'd still freeze."

"You know the wind will break me the moment we leave this mountain. Out there I'll fail Koda, again."

Outside, in front of me, all the ashes from the funeral fire chased each other in the circle of rocks, and the ones in the squeezed-shut YT can were sad because they couldn't come out and play. Plaid Chair held the space I needed, held me down so I didn't interfere, held me tight so I didn't cry. Chair kept messaging Coat to hold Ray.

Matt spoke again. "What if you could live on another mountain. With a town close by, and a river, and a garden, and your spirit could flow between both lives."

"I'd say you're a coyote. A trickster."

"I said something like that to someone who told me I could live freely. But I do live freely. I live on that other mountain. I go into town. Sometimes I have a drink at a local watering hole. Once in a while I've been known to stay in bed all day and feel sorry for myself. Other times I hike to glaciers and watch them calve. And I work in the forest. And I teach at a university. My spirit is free in all spaces."

"I am not you, Matt."

"Do you remember when you told me last night how you listened for water?"

"I can't hurt her again."

"Do you know the word: iyiniwak?" asked Matt. "It means distant. It means ancestors. Our ancestors know the way to the water. Where are they saying the water is now, Raylene?"

"They say Gitche Manitou. Matthew! How did I know that word? Where did that come from? Why did I just call you Matthew?"

"Kisê-manito," he said. "Ask them what it means."

"Gitche Manitou. The great spirit. The great mystery. Some call it God," she said.

There was movement. I thought maybe Ray was coming out. Matt said, "Good idea, that coat is a perfect place to rest. Come on Ranger, let's get some fresh air little man. Let's go see your big sister."

Outside the trailer, but inside me, the Stupid Tea Plus began to polish the dark spots behind my eyes.

"Mamâhtâwisiwin," said Matt down into the trailer.

"I don't know that word," said Ray.

"The way of appreciating one's relationship to the mystery. Tapping into the mystery, Ray. That's what we're doing, right, Ranger? Always tapping into the mystery."

Matt passed Ranger down to me, then scrambled to the ground.

"Thank you," I said.

"Ay-hay," he replied. (Thank you.)

He moved Plaid Chair back to the grouping and poured himself a Stupid Tea Plus.

"You take Chair," I said, passing him Ranger.

Matt snagged a paperback from the top of a box where he rested his mug.

"It's a Sister Gabriella novel," I said. "Ray likes them."

He turned it over and read the back of book description.

"What if Jake flies over and then goes and lands wherever it is he lands and Ray is still sleeping, and hasn't come out, so we can't get there?" I asked him.

"Then one of us will get over there and let him know to come back another day. Carl's a fast hiker."

"And how many times can that happen? The another-day syndrome?"

"Picture it all happening perfectly. Because it is," he said. "And on that note, when Brandi gets back, will you let her look under that bandage? She started out as a medic in the armed forces."

"It's okay. I can wait."

"For another day?" he asked.

I had run out of words and so I took comfort in the ones in the mini encyclos. Ranger would need to eat at some point, so she'd have to come out, or we'd have to lower him into her capsule. Matt proceeded to read Sister Gabby; soon, he appeared more immersed than me, one hand turning pages, the other holding Ranger like a football player holds a pigskin.

"Greetings," Carl called out and closed in fast. "Matt, you gotta see this." He waved his phone. "Penstemon strictus. Tons of them."

"They're a kind of native aster," said Brandi to me. "He's into flowers. Not the surprise bouquets from the florist kind, though." She turned to Matt. "But he's right, there are a lot. Buffalo berries too. Lots of them."

"They should be called bear berries, since that's what keeps the bears fed," said Matt.

"Here," said Carl. "I got a picture of them too. They're these little red berries—"

"No. Don't want to look," I said. "Ray and I know what they are."

"Aha, yes. A bit sour. Can make you poop and puke for sure. Kind of like the asters, they're not deadly poisonous like their cousin the foxglove, but they can make you puke too. Good you didn't find them," said Carl.

"We haven't seen Jakey yet. You?" Brandi directed her question to Matt.

Ranger squawked.

"Hey little man, are you hungry?" asked Matt.

"I'll climb up if you pass him to me once I'm up there. Then I'll float him down to her," I said.

But there was no need. As I looked at the trailer to plan the baby shuffle, Ray pulled herself onto the roof. "I think someone is hungry," she said.

"I waved her toward Chair. He likes having his tenth meal of the day here," I said.

Ray smiled. "He does eat a lot doesn't he?"

Matt guided Ray to Plaid Chair just as the chopper's buzz resonated in the distance. I watched Ray's legs become jelly. She teetered, and Matt steadied her and got her seated.

"Here's what I think," said Carl. "I think you warriors need a lot more food energy. You're missing some vital minerals. And iron, especially with having the baby, yours is probably pretty damn low. It's amazing what you've done here given what you don't have."

Ray spoke: "Thanks, Carl. That may be partly right. But I know I have some fears to get over. I'm so sorry about what happened earlier. It's only fair to say, there could be, erm, more expressions of fear from me. If there are, I'm sorry ahead of time. When I've fed Ranger, would you guys mind watching him while I have some private time with Koda?

Carl made soup. Brandi went into debate mode with Matt over natural medicine versus big pharma. Each time they mentioned a conventional medicine, Carl called out a flower name. "They all started as plants," he said. No one mentioned Jake would be at their meeting point in four or five hours from now. If any of them checked the time to keep track, I didn't notice.

I stared at the can of ashes until Ray nudged me.

We walked side-by-side. She made a pitstop at the washroom. "Show me where you went that first day, when you tracked the gouges in the ground," she said.

I took her to the vertical wall.

"We fell off the earth," she said.

"It's time to get back on it," I said.

Ray nodded.

"But you're not saying, you're just nodding. That's not saying."

The closer we got to our homestead the slower we walked.

"We're going to have to dismantle that toy-let," said Ray.

Forty-Nine

Matt insisted on carrying out Ray's fishbone picture. Before he wrapped it in a tablecloth, he noted its likeness to Four Peaks. When he attached it to his pack, it sat high. He had to change his posture to protect the bones in the art. He insisted on us carrying out anything else that was important, in case Jake had trouble getting it all. Ray chose the survival book. Dress told me Jake could do anything, so I chose Coat. At the last minute Ray substituted the survival book for the dreamcatcher she'd made. "It's essential," she said, patting Ranger's butt through the sling-carrier on the front of her. "Paramount to our lives."

After a chorus of see y'all laters, we left with the slightly hunched Matt. I looked back, like when we'd left before, except there were people there with our stuff. I kept turning, until only one distant frame remained in my sightline.

Once we crossed the striver, Matt directed us away from it. Ray pointed in the opposite direction to show Matt where we'd tried to walk out.

"Good job you tracked back." He looked downstream. He was an open book—concern registering on his face. "Pretty long walk to nowheres."

The land opened up a bit: fewer trees and more cragginess. Two protein bars and a jug of water later, we reached a spot that, to me, looked like everywhere else. Matt checked his fancy compass that had all kinds of readouts on it, and made a sharp turn. Then he pulled out a tiny, basic compass. "Yep, still working." His smile could have warmed the entire cabin that Ray had imagined.

"The only thing I have from my childhood," he said. "Jimmy Simpson gave it to my great-grandfather, and 'son' on and 'son' on."

"You sure you know where we're going?" asked Ray.

He pointed ahead. "Less than an hour. Half an hour if we stop yapping."

She turned in the direction he pointed.

He handed her his prized heirloom.

I stood a bit behind, resting. My leg was giving me a bit of trouble because we'd walked a long way.

He steered her head to the left as if to focus her on where we were aiming. While his hands were still either side of her head, he leaned in and whispered to her. Then the film-of-life slowed, and I watched his body sway.

His knees buckled, and he dropped to the ground.

The tablecloths fell away from Ray's art.

Fishbones from Four Peaks And A Dog burst from the cardboard, sailed through the air, became needles in haystacks.

"Don't move." I shouted to Ray. "Keep your head where he pointed it. And don't move the compass either."

Everything attached to me fell away in a shrug. I was at Matt's side. Ray remained frozen.

Though it was Ray and Matt and me in the wilds, my friends from being lost showed up.

"Check for a pulse," said the tree who had been the medic when the ramp was down on Ray.

And I was on the ground. "Stay fixed, Ray, while I check Matt."

Matt's pulse was strong and even. He was breathing as if in a peaceful sleep. Despite little pieces of the rocky mountain beneath us poking through the scrub, he had no visible cuts from the fall. I got ready to roll him on his side because I'd seen that at school when a kid in grade five had an epileptic seizure. "Stay, where you are Ray, okay?"

"I'm staying, Koda. I'm staying."

He was heavy, and part of me didn't want to see if there was blood underneath him in a big, life-draining pool.

"One, two, three, roll," said the tree medic.

Matt relaxed into a fetal position. His breathing even.

"Ray, he seems to be reasonably fine except for the unconsciousness." I stood and evaluated the ridiculousness of my assessment.

"What direction does it say I'm looking toward," she said. "I haven't moved my head. All I did was close my eyes, so when I open them, I need you to look at them and see where he got me to look," she said.

"The compass will show us where you were looking, but good idea, just in case you drop it."

When I'd determined Matt had intended us to go southwest, she unstrapped Ranger, placed him on the ground, and directed me to put the compass next to him.

"From this spot," she said. "Southwest from this exact spot where Ranger is." She took her full attention to Matt.

"I told you, Ray. I can't find that he's injured. No cuts, pulse strong."

She twisted herself over him and placed her head on his sideways chest.

"I told you, Ray, it's strong."

"Shhh," she said.

"Don't shush me."

"Shhhhhh." But her shush came with a hand motion as if she were directing music; there was love in her hand- and mouth-shushing. She lifted her head and remained squatted.

"I see," she said.

"You see what?"

"No, not see. I understand."

"Care to fill me in?"

"Not right now," she replied.

"Oh, for chrissakes, Ray."

She closed her eyes and changed from squatting to a full-sit on her rear.

I huffed and puffed over to Ranger. "You too?" he was in full bubble-producing slumber. "Am I the only one with my eyes open?" I turned to tree medic, but he'd finished triage and left to attend other tragedies.

Someone had to keep checking Matt was breathing, and that someone was me.

"Do you think he's in a coma?" I asked the meditating Ray.

"Okay," said Ray, opening her eyes. "Half an hour southwest of here. One of us goes, two of us stay with Matt."

"Two of us? How can one of us go, if two of us are staying?" Then I looked over at Ranger. "Oh, right. Well he's dependent on you for food, so by default I'll be going."

"It makes the most sense," said Ray. "I'm not trying to punish you. I'm trying to make the most sense. Ranger has to eat, I have to nurse him, so I'd be carrying him through to the landing site."

"And if you didn't find it you'd both be lost. Better me."

"That's not how I see it."

"Well I've been lost once before, so I have the experience."

"Dakota, I'm being practical. No one is going to be lost again. Brandi and Carl will eventually come this way, and Jake will land and not see us so do more searching. What we're wanting to accomplish here is the fastest way to get Jake to help us help Matt."

"No, you're putting me in the blue Chevy without a car seat."

"You were too young to store that memory."

"I was too young to see out the window and too young not to be protected."

"We are arguing overtop of a human who needs help as soon as possible."

"Oh Ray, we all need help as soon as possible. No, we are beyond help. We lost that chance when we fell off the earth."

"I thought you were clever, Dakota. We didn't lose that chance, we gained that opportunity."

"Ray, I am so sick of—"

"Koda-bear, close your eyes. Please. Close your eyes."

I shut my eyes. I shut my mouth. I shut down.

"Breathe," she said. "In. Two. Three. Four. Out. Two—with your mouth open for the out breath. Three. Four."

Anger would not leave. I opened my eyes. "Ray, don't you think Ranger's a little vulnerable in a lump over there? A bird of prey could swoop down faster than we could—"

She was like a poppin-hoppy from an old game where plastic characters are set on springs on rubber suction cups. Ranger was snuggled into Matt's curve before I could finish my concern.

"You are so smart, Koda. So smart."

"You're not offended by me saying a big bird could capture Ranger?"

"Why would I be upset by you wanting to prevent harm to him? If you'd wanted to injure me you'd have not said anything and left him to the talons of an eagle."

"But I meant it to—"

"Hurt me?"

Matt snorted.

She stared at Matt. I stared at Matt.

"Do you think he can hear everything we say?" I asked.

"If he did, he'll know we're both under a little bit of stress," Ray said.

"Stuck between a mountain and a hard place." I changed the cliché.

"You can still be angry with me. It's okay," she said.

That made my blood boil even more. I wanted her to fight. I wanted something to propel me to scrap with her right there on the ground and roll over pulling each other's hair and screeching at each other like cats in a territorial fight. If she could only cross the line and call me a bitch then I could let go of all this tension. I thought we'd healed. Now her selfishness in staying back in comfort had set me off.

"I can't operate that digital-direction machine Matt has in his pocket. It's not exactly low-tech," I said.

"You don't have to. Just use his boyhood compass. It's already set where you need to go."

We sat either side of Matt's and Ranger's sleep and passed water back and forth.

"What did he whisper to you before he, you know, checked out?"

"You have to do this," said Ray.

"No, what did he whisper. I know what I've got to do."

"We have to do this," said Ray.

"I know. I'll walk out, you stay here with the two rangers. Keep your little secret message then."

She stared at the crumpled cardboard, picked a fishbone out of the dirt, then dug into Matt's pack and retrieved a lip balm. She leaned over and mushed it over his lips and his nose and forehead.

"Oh my god. Did he tell you he loved you?"

Ray sorted through his pack, zipped it and swung it over the sleepers. It landed in the space between my crossed legs. "There's food, water, and a foil blanket. Don't forget the compass."

"That's your goodbye?" I said.

"Onikanapihiew," she said.

"Not only do I not know what that means, I have no idea why you needed to say it. I only asked you what he said. Like did he know he was going to, whatever… almost die," I said.

"I hope he can't hear you," said Ray.

"Fine, I'm outta here." I stood and hoisted the pack on my back, found the boyhood treasure from where Ranger had been, and faced the direction it told me to.

"I have no idea what comes next." My back was to her.

"We are all assigned our tasks," said Ray.

"I'm not turning around because I have to focus on this fricking S and W," I said.

"You don't have to turn around to see me," said Ray.

"I liked it better when you were Elton." My feet began to root into the ground.

"Half an hour if you stop yapping," said Ray.

Why was it up to me? Why didn't she start a fire for Jake? Why couldn't we all stay together and wait to be rescued? Why couldn't I suggest that we build a big ass fire and then Brandi and Carl and Jake would find us and fix Matt… and Ray and me? Or why couldn't we just stay and Brandi and Carl and Jake would all know we were missing and they would trace the route and look for us? Why did I have to do something?

One set of roots tore out of the ground and my right foot led. I marched forward, determined she not see me limp.

Her singing began as I imagined she watched me disappear over the first mound.

I'd buy a big house
where, we both could live...
And you can tell everybody
that this is your song... your song... your song...

"Fuck you, Ray," I said to the echoes. And I meant it. I could be lost forever, she would be found, and when I was dead, Matt would magically wake. Ranger would replace me. What kind of a rescuer was Matt, anyway? Why couldn't we have stayed inside the trailer and be hoisted up in one private move? "Fuck it all, and I'm not sorry, Green Jean." I threw the compass into some brush to the side and immediately recoiled as it came to life but not really came to life—it scared a grey bird out of its ground nest.

The nest was empty but for the compass. I pressed the back of my hand into the warmth from the bird's body. I wished I could shrink into a tiny me and live in that nest. The softness that went through my hand, moved through my arm and melted the anger in my veins. When the warmth of life and the texture of feathers reached my heart I moved away from the grey bird's home and whispered for it to return to its twiggy-grassy house. I had received the message I needed. I had to return to my own home.

The compass cleaned up nicely from the lining of my t-shirt. I now held it with reverence for its creation. My fingers traced an engraving in its wooden back. Generations had smoothed these impressions with their fingers too. I held it flat in my palm, waited for it to point north, then rotated it so the arrow was on the SW. Onward explorer. If I made the explorer Simpson proud, that would be a bonus; the main thing was to align with the compass inside me. The first thing it did was turn me from pity toward self-love and for that, no matter I was in the middle of a logistical crisis with a demand for the rescuer becoming the rescuer, I needed to release.

When the tears were in full flow, they cleansed all the sticky bits inside me. "Oh not fuck you Ray, not fuck you. I'm sorry Green Jean, I promised no fucks. I'm sorry August Starr that you will not know your twin. I'm sorry for your loss too, Ranger. I'm sorry. I'm sorry. I'm sorry for resentment, for judgement, for smugness, I'm sorry."

And then I was sitting, and the skin around my eyes was dry and I washed the saltiness off with water from my water bottle, and discovered the lip balm Ray had put back in the bag—for me, I believed. And I filled its waxy balm-ness into my starving-for-love pores. And I closed my eyes. Breathed through my nose two, three, four, five, six. Held, two, three, four. Blew out through my mouth two, three, four, five, six, seven, eight—keep going deflate completely, nine, ten. Hold. Rest. Sag. Naturally wait with patience until the body knows it's the right time.

Ray was putting her trust in me. I needed to trust Ray. I saw myself as the always-doer because I couldn't trust someone else. Now it was time to learn to trust myself because I could, not because I had to.

Ray didn't know what I'd do with a dead man if Matt died. She didn't know I'd spent time with a dead baby. She didn't know I'd danced in a dress made for a girl who was dead. She wasn't there right after Green Jean was killed. She probably didn't know my adoptive-mother-to-be was holding August in heaven. She only knew what she knew. I only knew what I knew.

If Matt was to die, Ray had pushed me to be with life. She wanted me to be among life.

When she said "we have to do this" did she mean that's what Matt had whispered, that Ray and I had to finish our own rescues? We each had to plant the seeds for the next season of our life.

I got up and picked up the pace.

"Where's Eagle when I need her most?" I said.

"She's there when you need her," said Midnight the horse. "But who said you needed her right now?"

Ahead, in the middle of a clearing was Midnight—a stick pushed into the ground with a mane of orange vinyl tape streaming in the breeze.

Fifty

F aith kept me company when the sun set. Jake had missed his timeslot. I had not missed the landing pad. I sat a distance from the imprint of the big skis that are underneath the body of a helicopter.

Before it went dark, I ate an energy bar then took the silver foil blanket and tucked it around me. Once in a while, when I opened my eyes, the moon highlighted the florescent tape on the marker stick.

"This is it?" Ray asked.

"This is it," Matt answered.

The sun warmed the wrapped little earth me. I knew it had risen, but I was still in dream mode, my ear to the ground listening to a different drum way below where it had swallowed up the essence of me in the night and was ready to grow a fresh Dakota plant.

"Leave her be," said Ray.

She and Matt sat close enough for me to see and hear them.

"I didn't invite you to my dream," I said. "But I'm glad you're here. You're okay Matt? You woke up?"

They ignored me, rested and chatted. Ray even told Matt she liked to write songs.

"Doesn't surprise me," said Matt. "I can tell you're artistic by the picture."

"Just lyrics." She qualified her talent honestly and giggled a little. "I don't read music or play an instrument."

"Got this friend in town, Keith, who plays guitar. Bet he'd put chords to some of your words. Play a few at the Vat—this little club in town."

I pictured some guy singing, "There were two chicks from Four Peaks And A Dog, they made a bench from some sticks and some logs," in front of a crowd of locals.

I continued to eavesdrop and clung to the foil, but the wind was taking it away. No, it wasn't the wind, it was Ray. "Rise and shine, baby." Her smile was wide.

I stood and we hugged each other at the same moment. Ranger's squirming body squished between us.

"But, what about Matt?"

"Nice job," he said. "I already told your mom that. Both of you. Great work."

"He woke just before sunrise," said Ray. "We took it easy, just in case he collapsed again."

"Think I've been overworking," he said. "Or too much Stupid Tea." He laughed.

"But you're gonna get it checked out, right?" Ray didn't laugh.

We lifted our heads at the same time, even Ranger squirmed. The blades chopped through the sky and announced Jake's arrival.

When it landed, Matt directed us to stand back. He leaned into the machine and shouted to the pilot. Then he put on a headset and spoke through it, maybe to someone else. After he returned the headphones to the pilot, he guided us under the spinning blades and introduced us to another bald man using only first names.

"Come be my co-pilot." Jake was as casual as the others, as if this kind of thing happened every day. He patted the seat at the same time Matt boosted me in. Ray, Ranger, and Matt sat behind us and we all wore earphones to block out the noise, yet we could hear each other through them. It was like an imagined ride at a fairground without the scariness or jolts, a smooth upward swirl and then everything getting smaller, but not so small you couldn't tell what things were. Jake tossed me a bottle of orange liquid. "Electrolytes anyone? Matty, you need rehydratin' too?"

Matt spoke into his headset. "Raylene, you okay? Look at the current this machine creates, look at the treetops how they sway, how resilient. Raylene, you are the wind and the trees."

"I am not broken," she replied.

The aerial view took my breath away. I kept swallowing sweet and salty orange stuff to prevent crying. Our little homestead was beyond outstanding. Though the highway and a logging road became visible, it was so high from where we'd landed, and there was no real knowing where we'd fallen through. Four Peaks looked different from above. Dog wasn't a dog from the sky.

Jake and Matt were respectful of the silence Ray and I created. It was an emotional time stretching out almost forever as Jake maneuvered close enough to the trailer that Brandi and Carl had to cover their heads. The cardboard backing from the survival book that was still clipped to the tree flapped around. For a second, I wanted to open the door and jump back down into the middle of it all. I had to restrain my heart from pushing me out.

"Seen worse." Jake gave a thumbs up.

"Jake thinks he'll be able to get it all," said Matt. I turned and reviewed how close to Ray he was sitting. "In a cargo net."

"Except the trailer, Mattie. Everything 'cept the trailer." Jake corrected him and Matt formed a "no kidding" with his whole face. "And I'll be usin' The Bear."

"Jake has animal names for all the helicopters." Matt explained. "The Bear is too big to land at the trailer, but Bambi wouldn't help—she'd land fine, but not be able to take out too much at a time. She can't even handle four people. That's why we thought it best for you to hike out, so we could get yers all out faster and at the same time."

"Is this The Bear?" I asked.

"Grrr-owl." Jake bared his teeth at me. It was strange to see his face and mouth make the shape, yet hear his sound through the headphones. I giggled; might as well have been tickled. "Negative," he said. "This is yer basic Chinook." He wriggled as if a salmon.

"You should see him do Bambi," said Matt.

Ray seemed relatively clueless to Matt's attention, and he was not getting that his attraction to her was front and centre. "But it's not officially our stuff," she said innocently.

"I think it's your stuff. Yours and Koda's," he said, patting my left shoulder from behind.

He buoyed us with continuous warmth. I knew his affection would be the consistent kind.

Fifty-One

F ieldstone Ridge." Jake pointed with his head.

We'd had too many crazy moments, me and Ray. I surveyed it all below through glazed eyes.

When we landed on a concrete pad, Jake growled at me again. He took off as soon as he deemed we were safely away from his powerful machine.

"Jakey will get the rest of your stuff." Matt rubbed his shaved head and looked at the setting sun. "Prob-lee tomorrow," he said, mostly to Ray.

Ray's smile of thanks was interrupted by her gasp. A huge black lab, with the largest paws I'd ever seen, charged us. The dog head-butted Matt's hips, throwing him off balance.

"Whoa Pauley, what's gotten into you?" He glanced at Ray, then me. "Short for Pauline," he said. He squatted and placed his hands each side of the dog's head, bringing his face close to hers, repeating her name over and over in baby talk. He looked up only once, as if to make sure we were still there, then continued fussing with the dog as if there was nothing unusual about a soft, and high pitched who-luvs-ya-pauley-smally-baby.

Matt rocked Pauley back and forth until he had head-wrestled her to the ground. Satisfied with this greeting, she rose, quick-sniffed Ray, then took a run at me.

Matt stretched himself up and ordered the dog to return, but his command fell on deaf ears. I braced myself, and then fell in happy-love with the dog while she licked every exposed piece of skin on my body.

Exhausted from the current excitement, and fearful of the future, we trailed after Matt into an A-frame office, me tripping over Pauley every two steps.

"Auntie Rose, thanks for coming. These are the ladies I told you about. Miss Raylene Harrison, her daughter Koda, and a bundle of newborn with the coolest name ever: Ranger."

I could tell, from his chest sort of puffing out with huge love, that the silver-haired mountain woman in front of us was important to him.

"Hi." Ray gently extended her hand.

Rosemary accepted it, then stroked Ranger's fuzzy head.

"Welcome, Dakota," she said.

A shiver ran down my spine. Matt had only introduced me as Koda.

"Call me Rosemary," she said. "You can add Auntie if you like. Most do."

I willed my arm to lift, trying to make my lips curve into a pleasant form, while attempting to stop the tremors inside. It was like I'd forgotten how to communicate.

She enclosed my trembling hand in a warm clamshell of smooth fingers that took away the jitters. "It's shock, my dear." Her hands closed tighter, filling me with a familiar energy. She looked deep into my eyes.

My heart skipped a beat and my legs began to give way. She shrugged off her fisherman-knit cardigan and draped it around the back of me. As she drew my arms through the sleeves and brought it up over my shoulders, I watched her long braid settle itself mid-back on her denim shirt. As if what she did wasn't grandmotherly enough, she fastened the leather-covered buttons to further insulate me.

If you ever fall out of your boat, pray to God, but swim to shore. Some shared wisdom from Green Jean trailed through my tangled imaginings. My insides had capsized, fighting to stay real. I wanted to fold up and be held by this woman who was a stranger but did not feel like a stranger. At the same time, I wanted to move independently.

"Let's get you settled and then get the local doc to come check you out. Rosemary parted Matt from Ray long enough to envelope Ray in a hug, then smiled approvingly toward Matt.

She put her pale-blue-denim-shirted arm around my shoulder. "We have the perfect place for you." For a second, I didn't know if she meant Ray and me, or Ray and Matt. She squeezed my shoulders with her entire arm and reeled me in, helping me walk straight. "Why don't we talk about it after a shower and some decent food."

Our pile of stuff was in the corner of the office—Ray's picture, still wrapped, her walking stick, my knapsack, the dreamcatcher and Coat. I knew I'd see it all later, but still experienced separation anxiety. Then, because her arm stayed tightly 'round me, I tried not to step on Rosemary's cowboy boots all the way up a narrow path between the trees. A visual check behind confirmed Ray and Matt were moving up the hill behind us. I suspected Ray might fall for our rescuer like the war-injured fall for nurses, or victims become infatuated with cops, but that Matt had already taken that plunge. "Oh boy," I said, mistakenly out loud.

Incredibly intuitive, Rosemary raised her brows and did a head throw in Matt's direction, then winked at me. We already had a secret.

By the time I caught sight of the giant log beams that framed her home, my heart had pretty much figured I'd go anywhere with this woman.

Rosemary explained that she lived with her husband, Charlie, who was out flying. We walked uphill from the landing pad and flight office toward a log home that overlooked the town. Lesser-used paths and overgrown vehicle tracks branched from various spots along the inclined driveway.

"Welcome again." The front door opened onto a gleaming hardwood-floored foyer. I inhaled daisies, wool, books, and cinnamon. Deep-cushioned willow and log furniture was grouped for conversation in a great-room that lay beyond. A loom took up the far corner. Pauley's claws clicked on the hardwood and her tail brushed a pottery lamp on the entry table as she circled us all and kept her eyes on me.

"This was Mathew's home when he was a boy. Still is, until he finishes building his own place," said Rosemary. She led us to the kitchen, then gave us each a bundle of towels and clothes and directed us to separate bathrooms.

Though the warm water, soap, and thick washcloths were clean, plush, soft, and everything I'd never had, I wanted to be with my mom. I tried to guess who would be finished first, and wondered how I'd find my way back through the house.

Pauley was lying outside the bathroom door. I folded up the legs of the jeans, rolled the cuffs on the shirt, then let her lead me to the kitchen. Matt was sitting on a tall chair at a huge granite island. He hopped down and pulled one back for me as Ray brought Ranger into the room.

"Whoa," Matt exclaimed as Ray plodded. She was wearing too-big-for-her-clothes as well.

"Sorry, they're a little large," said Rosemary, turning from her place at the stove.

"It's okay," said Ray. "They're soft and they're clean."

"I think they look real good," Matt said.

While Rosemary and Matt took turns telling us about Fieldstone Ridge, barley soup was ladled into bowls, and thick slices of buttered bread appeared. Pauley lay under my stool, shifting her bulk from side to side in anticipation of dropped crumbs.

"Remember," said Matt—all the time looking at Ray. "Hare and turtle." He smiled a totally goofy smile at her.

"Matt tells me you made something." Rosemary directed her comments to Ray. "Said that you're real creative. What else do you like to do?"

"I like to write songs," said Ray.

"She invented some tea." I contributed something more believable.

"And what do you do, Dakota-girl?"

"She's smart at everything. An amazing reader." Ray began to list a swath of things I never knew she knew about me. By the time she had to take a breath, I was already exhausted from thinking about how I'd be able to live up to it all.

"You're proud of her, I can see that," said Rosemary. They held each other's eyes, a mother-bond of sorts; they both cared about me.

"I am so proud." Ray looked at me, then her bracelet. I pushed too much fresh bread into my mouth and willed her to take her eyes back to Rosemary.

We ate while Matt shared a bit about his childhood. He'd come to Fieldstone when he was nine and lived with Rosemary from age ten, except for four years at Simon Fraser University in his twenties, and a long spell, later on, at another university out east somewhere for his masters, and then a doctorate.

"It's good to have him back. He's a specialist, a consultant."

"And an old man." He laughed.

"Wow," said Ray. "I thought you were about twenty-five."

He and Rosemary laughed ever-so-quickly, turning the laughter into a smile, not wanting to insult Ray.

"Well that's quite a compliment. I'm thirty-eight."

What I knew for sure was that he liked the fact she didn't care about his level of education. I was pleased Ray was taken in by his genuine goodness. I held my lips tightly together so as not to say, *Holy crap, he's in love, and you're oblivious, Mom.*

"It's this mountain air," Rosemary explained. "Keeps us all young. It hands us tasks then rebirths us all."

Matt explained he lived in the huge loft, where he'd always had a room, and he was building his own cabin on a property higher up the mountain. He never said what happened before he lived with Charlie and Rosemary, and we didn't ask, being experts in pasts unspoken.

The conversation went all over the place: my replies to questions about school and interests; general inquiries about our health and how much weight we might have lost. Matt's gentle talking and Rosemary's attentiveness were healing.

"This is good." Rosemary affirmed to the entire kitchen island. "Real good."

She began to parcel food into a cardboard box, not too subtle a hint that we should be leaving. "I'm sure you want to be on your way."

My spirits plunged—she was kicking us out? My emotions began to free fall. Where would we go?

Fifty-Two

"Oh, my. I didn't explain, did I?" Her words stopped me from hitting the ground. "Let me show you." She bundled Matt with food she'd packed and led us to the door.

Along the driveway, the distance of half a block, was a set of tracks wide enough for a car but somewhat overgrown. As we walked, Pauley tracked around our heels, rushed ahead, then returned. Matt carried the food, Rosemary carried Ranger in the hoodie.

The same distance again—about half a block—was an A-Frame cabin.

"There are others." Rosemary pointed to a few roof peaks.

Ray nodded.

"It's a place for you to stay and get some real rest. It will give you time to adjust while you decide what to do. Pretty small, but a roof, nonetheless. And real private. My cousin, June, lives in one. Has done for years. Got a beautiful garden going, she has. Loves it here," said Rosemary.

"I can see why," I said, taking in the surroundings, noting the efforts of a garden from some previous tenant.

"Yes, I believe you can, Dakota."

I decided I needed to take over. There were things to be worked out.

"Mrs... er..."

"Rosemary's fine."

I substituted her name with okay. "Okay, except for my emergency twenty in my knapsack, we have no money for rent or a damage deposit."

Rosemary directed her voice to Ray. "Miss Harrison, you girls will be doing us a favour. These cabins need the upkeep being lived in provides."

"We can't—" I began. Pauley was sitting at my heels and would have looked like a well-trained pet had she not been licking the webbing between my fingers.

Rosemary stayed focused on Ray. "Take some time and decide what you want. You never know, you might like to get a job in town. Between that and your art you'll probably make enough to move to something fancier almost right away. And if you want to stay here, which is more than fine with me, we can work out something so you feel you're contributing. I know that's important. But first things first. You need to settle. And there's no time limit on settling."

Not one glance my way. By concentrating on Ray, Rosemary had told us both who we were. She unlocked the door, then handed the worn key to Ray. Pauley forced her way through before Rosemary had let go of the key.

"When Jake and Charlie bring your stuff from—" Rosemary began.

"Four Peaks And A Dog," Matt said.

She smiled. "When you have your things, you'll probably feel more settled."

Rosemary took some time to look at the ground. It was a thoughtful break, like she wanted to help us but did not want to control us. Like she knew she must carefully direct two people before they fell again.

The door had stayed open after Pauley's entrance. Ray did a quick check; her smile said she loved it. Her heart followed a braceletted wrist inside, her fingers tracing the logs and chinking, embracing it all —but her feet stayed outside.

The big, black velvet face of the dog peered mischievously over the back of a small brown couch. "Looks like she's home," said Rosemary. I wasn't sure if she meant Ray or the dog.

Matt put the food on the ground, moved to Rosemary, and put his arm around her solid shoulders. Except for the shower, it was the farthest he'd been away from Ray all day. He stood there, silently begging us to accept it all.

"We are much obliged," said Ray. "Is there a school nearby, for Koda?"

I just about fell over.

"There is," Rosemary answered, beaming at Ray's correct mother-question.

Ray kept her feet outside the cabin.

Don't screw this up, I thought.

"You're too kind," said Ray.

Be the child, I told myself. Be the child.

I feared we were all nosediving into one of those boy-meets-girl-and-they-live-happily-ever-after romance novels Ray had read at Four Peaks. But Ray's feet weren't moving, she remained firmly planted on the outside of the doorframe.

For a second we all caught the sparkle of sunlight on one facet of her bracelet. She lifted her right foot. Her weight shifted forward, slowly, then her left foot came off the ground. And then she entered.

"Thank you," she said. "Are you sure you're okay to wait a few days until I can make the proper arrangements?"

Rosemary nodded, Ray moved in farther, Matt swooped behind

me and folded me over his arm like a guest towel on a bathroom rack. Pauley became caught up in the celebration, barking from her position on the couch.

Matt dumped me on the sofa. Pauley narrowly escaped, leaping over the back of the two-seater. The combined action exploded dust in a cloud that filled the whole room. As the dust began to settle, Ray began to laugh.

And then it was suddenly silent, everyone savouring the lull after the spontaneous fun Matt had created.

A flock of birds flew by, breaking up the party with their chirps.

Rosemary waved the dust away. "Maybe you should be stayin' at the house." She looked around, measuring the air quality, assessing the difference between the contents and quality of this home and hers.

"No, really. We'll air it out," Ray insisted.

"It's beautiful," I said. "We'll be fine, Rosemary. Thank you."

"This is a wonderful place for us to restart our lives. To do my art, and a perfect place to write songs, I mean as well as some paid work."

"That it is," said Rosemary. "That it is."

"Do you write love songs?" Matt realized what he'd said out loud and blushed a little. Rosemary couldn't contain a small giggle from escaping. Ray took him seriously.

"Sometimes," she said. "But mostly heartache and pain."

"Mattie, why don't you go down to the office and use the truck to haul what's in the office. It'll be good to re-establish a track through this bush." Her order was direct and sweet.

"I'm going to leave you girls alone. There's enough food here for a little while. I'll come see you tomorrow. Marlene, the doctor, she's an old friend, will come by later. She'll set you up with an appointment at the clinic so the three of you can be checked. For now, though, you need privacy."

"Privacy," I whispered. No matter how great these people were, I was already missing being alone.

"And you?" Rosemary ruffled her freckled hand over Pauley's head. "You stay here and take care of these amazing gals. And don't lick the baby." She pulled out the top drawer of a dresser, set it on the table, and placed Ranger in it. The dog barked and raced to one of the adjoining rooms, and I followed. She had jumped up and sat on the bed, my bed, her paw raising and lowering, inviting me up onto the mattress.

Epilogue

"Pick a day." Ray makes the request from Plaid Chair, her feet propped by Pauley the Footstool—a dog with a job. We both wear crocheted slippers. Our wet hikers sit by the door, the light dusting of late spring snow melting on the mat. "One special un-invented day to commemorate our life here."

I close my eyes. For almost a year, Ray and Ranger and I have lived in this cabin, one of six that used to be residences for railroad employees.

Ray pays the rent. Never misses.

Nights here are amazing. Gentle breezes of night air, different from day air, drift through the cabin and make me think that if I captured the night air in a plastic bag, and took it to a lit room, it would still be dark inside the bag. Like orange goldfish stay orange in a bag of water. Night sky, night breeze, nighttime, would stay dark if sealed by Ziploc or twist tie. I know this can't be true, but I like imagining it. I always think that if I did? Try it? And it worked? I would be credited with discovering something noteworthy and scientific. This only comes when it's still night and almost officially early morning.

When the room is still dark enough to allow a night air fantasy and I am suspended between wake and sleep.

I've spent a lot of time trying to figure out what made it all turn around for Ray. When we were out there, I was sarcastic, labeling her as having a head injury of sorts that she sustained when we fell. I didn't know her then. I didn't know me then. I know it has been the nurturing people around Ray who have empowered her to stretch. Just like Green Jean and Martha did for me. It might even be that Ranger has provided her the opportunity for a total do-over, but if that's true, it must have started during the pregnancy because she hit her stride the second she climbed out of the roof, repurposed the survival book, and created a home. And that's when I start thinking about stuff Matt has alluded to. I mean, I'm not saying she's not somehow related to Elton John, but she is connected to an Indigenous history.

And that means I am too.

I'm a believer of complete connection. A small world. A tiny planet. A common mother. Can we be connected to England and North America before it was North America? I think this because, when I dance, I feel that complete connection.

When Matt got the results of a CT-scan, and it said nothing was wrong with his brain, Ray said that his passing out had to be an intervention. That his task was to stop, for a little bit, being in our story so that we could save ourselves before our happily ever after. I remain on the fence as to how he could lose consciousness then regain it hours later with no medical explanation. But then again, Ray and I fell off the earth, and a budgie barked, and I sometimes still see Green Jean, baby August, and Brenda.

I try to accept all the above, being our whole lives, like I would a combo meal at a drive through.

Ray is unrecognizable. She likes lists, and she makes them often. She eats healthily, and walks regularly.

Our first official day, and those that followed, each qualify for Ray's pick-a-day. That first email I sent to Martha with the absolute truth of our departure and adventure. She replied with, "Dance out your life."

Rosemary's husband, Charlie, all silver-grey and denim to match her, driving down the road-track with Jake, Plaid Chair riding happily and proudly in the back of the truck box.

Charlie taking his girls—Rosemary and I—out for dinner, while Ray helped Matt on his massive cabin, or was busy collecting ingredients for her tea, or working as a companion-housekeeper for Jake's elderly mother who was managing well in what she called her cancer survivorship—all of this with Ranger in tow.

While Rosemary had begun teaching me about the loom, Charlie had insisted I learn some mechanical stuff. And so I'd done both. Sometimes in the workshop, when he wasn't flying, or when I was beside him in his float plane, he'd muse about life. One time he said, "She always wanted a child. And then along came Matt. Her cousin brought him from the city. She never looked at it as fostering." Every one of those times with each of them were worthy of Ray's pick-a-day.

Another day I heard Charlie say to the sky, after he'd turned the controls of the plane over to me, "And now she has a granddaughter."

The week we arrived, Ray hiked to gather the ingredients for a new and improved Stupid Tea. When she'd perfected her recipe, she designed the labels and printed them in the aviation office. Those first packages were the start of our business. Charlie delivered Stupid Tea to gift shops in nearby tourist towns where they sold—and still sell—quickly, and at a ridiculous price. At first Ray chose the name, Lyrics of the Mountains but within seconds we both blurted out at the same time, "Listen for Water."

She created another blend from Dandelions too. There weren't any dandelions at Four Peaks; none that I could remember, but then

I'd missed all the plant gifts the mountains offer—I know that because Carl has since shown me in pictures.

What about the day I couldn't remember as much. What day would that have been. After a month or so, I had trouble remembering the lay of the land. I recalled bits at a time, like going to war with only one photo in a locket and forgetting what your special someone looks like, so you have to keep looking at the image—but it's only a headshot and what's below the neck becomes a blur in the mind. And, if it's in a locket, the edges get bent from it not being cut the right size, and from opening and closing the locket too often when the war first started, and it was an old photograph anyway, so, eventually, there's only a nose and a mouth in a bit of a jagged, wrinkled face.

I could not pick one day.

Ray is in Matt's locket, but she doesn't know it. He tries to tell her all the time, but she is busy catching up with her own love.

There's no dust on Ray's notebooks. Her lyrics sit on the table, her signature little blocked letters on a piece of paper torn from a coil scribbler. Keith has written chords above some of the words. There's a coffee-ring in the corner, and someone, probably Matt, has drawn a bald-headed happy face in the margin.

Keith and another guy, Christopher, brought their guitars and girlfriends over, as a favour to Matt. Once they were in our cabin, they became our friends too. The next thing we knew, Christopher was strumming his guitar and singing Ray's words.

We met reclusive June—Rosemary's sister—a retired world wanderer content with sporadic contact. She gifted Ray seeds for a garden.

Aunt Janet and Ray have spoken on the phone and, next month when Matt goes to Vancouver to give a lecture, we will go with him, and the four of us will hop on the ferry to Victoria to see her. Ranger will be a handful—he's almost walking.

There is too much happening. And yet it is all okay.

Ray will be with Matt forever. He is that kind of guy and Ray is becoming that kind of woman. They are made for each other, their future set out for them to live here. Ranger adores Matt; beams when he hears his voice. Matt's home will be finished soon. He calls it ours, which is nice, but what he means is "theirs." Ray doesn't appear to interpret it the same way I do. And that's okay. At some point she won't want to be with me in the same way she won't want to be with Rosemary or Charlie. It is not an insult, it is life. She will want to be with Matt the way Matt already sees them. On her own time.

I am more independent. At first, I took the school bus, but now I drive a little pickup that used to be Rosemary's sister's. That way I can tutor after school. No one seems to be concerned that I have no license.

There is too much noise in some places.

When I get to school, and join the students banging into each other in school hallways, I want to be wrapped in a huge roll of cotton wool to protect me from breaking. When everything around me is spinning and people are saying things like, "See the one with the cane? Did you hear what happened to her? She's the one who survived. Did you know she's 'gifted', like really smart?" They don't know that I am the holder of a secret, and that I'm often anticipating another fall.

There is so much to learn. And I celebrate each day I am open to it.

The trust my almost-adoptive father had established, which I assumed might be a plaque on a park bench to honour his wife and his almost family, turned out to be much more than that. Rosemary contacted the law firm when I gave her the name from the Lifebook —I had to, because she was talking about my future. They confirmed that I'd be set for full university, and that my almost dad—a partner at that law firm—had remarried, had four children, and wanted to meet me if I was okay with that. But I don't know if I am. It's not that the Lifebook is a problem—I'm grateful for it, and I'm grateful for the foster parents and the helpers, and I'm not mad at Ray—I just can't remember any of it, and its still a painful lump inside me: the Little People Daycare, the plastic car, the Cheerios, puppy, kitty, mama, hi.

"You'll be covered for the convent," Ray had teased. "Maybe Sister Gabriella will be your instructor."

All those years navigating the dark because we didn't have light-bulbs, and now there is apparently nothing to fear and yet I am more scared now than any of those times.

"A day, Koda. Not Christmas or any celebrated now. A day that we could celebrate. And give it a name."

"Impossible," I said.

"Are you crying?" Ray's slippered feet dropping had brought her body forward and closer to mine.

"Dust," I said.

"Want some tea?"

The need to look at the back of what I believe is Four Peaks And A Dog has become compulsive. I look from it, then to the reproduced fish bone picture hanging over the fireplace, and back again. A major part of our life, our growing up time, was on the other side of that mountain.

At Four Peaks, Ray had her staff of life. When we moved into the cabin it took its place in a large pot at our front door, with lots of other hiking sticks she collected. Due to the leg thing mucking up something inside me, it was my turn for a silly stick... but it's weird, I don't need it all the time, and it doesn't stop me from dancing.

There are days when the word survivor is so far away from me that I don't even remember how to spell it. Then there are times when the fragility of my existence is present all day and well into the night. On those nights I dream I have transparent wings that are somehow attached to my back and seem way too small to lift me off the ground, yet I flit from peak to peak of every cabin on this mountain, except our own, placing my fears, like stars on the tops of Christmas trees, so that when I am awake my walk is on the gentler side of sanity.

Eagle was right, there is no unwanted drumbeat in my life. If I do have the dream, I don't remember that I have it. It is dreamed, then left in the place that dreams need to rest. And no one except the Eagle and me know about August Starr. I fixed one grief already—my own fetal grief. I will live with the other.

Rosemary said to me, "Never forget. This will always be your someplace to come back to. Your forever and ever home, Dakota. Like it is for Matty."

And most days, along with a silly stick and some Stupid Tea, that's all I hold onto.

Listen for Water Song

Verse 1

There are mountains, too far for climbing,
they sit on the horizon, waiting for me.
There are ranges, too wide to wander,
they swallow us under, deliver us free.
Chorus
But when you've fallen, you can only start over,
write on fresh pages, that's what I know for sure.
And the blue sky, it holds all the answers,
and stars heal all the pain.
Verse 2
There are rivers, too fast for wading,
they flow down the rocks' sides, and cut through the earth.
Take my hand now, drink in the clear flow,
breathe in and dive low,
to feel the rebirth.
Repeat chorus

R. S. Harrison

Book Club Bonus

We recommend taking *Listen for Water* to your book club. Get your tailored list of book club discussion questions here: https://ingeniumbooks.com/LFW-bookclub

Acknowledgments

AN UNCONVENTIONAL CHAPTER OF GRATITUDE

A lengthy acknowledgement does not necessarily have to be in proportion to the length of a book—the more pages the book, the longer the list, the more important the writer. That is not the purpose of acknowledgements—gratitude cannot be restricted.

I could not have conceived this story, or gestated the collective represented by Ray and Koda—yet alone birthed it—if it were not for the living stories of others, including every reader.

Is it strange to ask each a reader to insert their name into a first line of a love letter? Or find themselves in the lines of poetry (we do it when we listen to song, don't we)? Too quirky? Too ridiculous? Too intimate? No (say I), because someone has to hand the baton of eccentric and all-encompassing love, and someone needs to receive it.

Of course, I could fill this space with dozens of synonyms for thank you, and thousands of names—and every descriptive would be heartfelt and every name treasured—but I'd rather you find yourself in these words. Please know, every one of you is here. I hope you can see yourself.

To write a love letter to you… is to create a passionate piece of correspondence to the whole earth: the ground, the roots beneath, the night sky—everything in between the core and an altitude beyond which we cannot take the breath to speak the word love.

For you are the roots, the soil, the plants, the meandering pathways that promise adventure and journey for everyone you touch to visit the places they are meant to go. You certainly embraced me on your travels.

You are the mountains and the silver threads of glaciers. You are perseverance woven into peace-infused patience, spreading a blanket on the ground at sunset, reclining at twilight, watching the stars appear in a night sky, ticking them off as they go out, then witnessing the sunrise as a ginger cat plays with a strand of orange wool on the eastern horizon.

My deepest thanks for including me.

Beyond the love letter, your energy is in these works of gratitude which have been fueled by the spirit of Raylene and Dakota.

Listen For Water is a journey of almost fifteen years.

From those in writing groups, workshops, book clubs, and classrooms to the young man in Red Deer, Alberta, many years ago, who generously allowed me on the U-Haul rental lot and, at my request, sealed me in a trailer—oh! how I wish I had kept his name.

From the one and only Colleen Biondi, who said, "Would you like to try your hand at...?" and thus jumpstarted my entire writing career, to new people who feel as if they've been in my life forever.

From the Nicks, Marcys, and Coras of the publishing world who validated my lines, praised the paragraphs, and pushed me to be more, to the tireless listeners of ideas and original beta readers of the earliest drafts—the Joans, Kathleens, Jennifers, Carols, Wandas.

From those who teach me officially to the lesson-givers in daily life: the Kates, Donitas, Audreys, Lauras, Loris, Patricks, Cheryls, Anitas, Kathys, and Cathys.

From passionate clients who bring incredible ideas and true lasting friendship to my desk and into my heart, to brilliant contributors who advocate for human rights through peaceful means.

And…

the soulmate

RICHARD
I was told
you were the most honourable and noble man they knew…
They were right.
You're my wall and sounding board,
truly the love child of Spock and Mother Teresa
your logic and love
never cease to amaze me

the children

MICHAEL
my first real, live Lifebook
my forever son
and my forever sun
nikawi (mother)
nikosis (my son)
the book of love

JENNIFER AMY
following the moving truck
"mom, if we lost everything in there, we'd still have all we
    need"
the phenomenon
the river of love   ·

SCOTT
on the way to hockey
"mom, you're a great writer,
and you're going to finish this book and others, I just
    know it"
the voice of love

THE INCREDIBLE BONUS CHILDREN

CANDICE
always my Red Deer baby
and grown-up friend

RACHELLE
a personal messenger from nature
with valuable messages about motherhood

KORI LEIGH
my true atlas of darkness
and guide to the light

JENNIFER DAWN
metaphorically and literally global,
my north star

ADRIENNE
ambassador of patience
and welcomer extraordinaire

TIM
optimism guru
and, sometimes, my brill IT guy

SIMON
the soul for whom the path of potential was created

THE SISTERS

JACQUELINE AND CHRISTINE
…I mean, who knew we were destined for this renewed love?
I guess each of us did, for here we are, the wiser, the better, the greater for the whole.

THE SISTER WHO CHOSE ME

KATHLEEN
Your faith in me blows my mind and your gentle ways calm me. Please never stop quoting Winnie the Pooh to me.

THE DREAM TEAM

BONI
your brilliance shines at the intersection of professionalism and wisdom. Your values endlessly echo kindness and goodness.
JOHN
intelligent and skilled, your dedication is a gift to all in your sphere.

The Ingenium Books' team
designers, proofreaders, beta readers: you are make-dreams-come-truers. I love working with you.

SOMEWHAT LESS CONVENTIONALLY

my mother and our Romani ancestors

When the water in the river disappears
And people haul away the exposed rock to make houses,
    pasture walls, firepits, rabbit traps, diamond rings, and
    doorstops
And the mud becomes an intricate pattern of cracks and
    molded dust
The mosaic surface waits for the bare feet of children to dance
    a road to nowhere

When the peonies are tired
And its roots hold next year's children
But its flowers still cling to stem
They are easily snipped, then gently shaken overhead
Confetti caught in the hair, on the shoulders
Scattered pinky-white mottling the grass
Like walking on velvet over moss

When my mother made magic
From powdered bone from the abattoir, and the earth's meat
    from the Cornish clay pits—bone china clay
And kneaded it with olive oil
And formed flower after flower
Placed in rows too delicate to touch
And she never stopped

And called it piece work
But I thought it meant peace work
I learned our sugar sandwiches and my gingham dress were
    measured by quantity
A dozen roses and twenty daisies

I can smell her hands
And the table's top
And the drying ceramics
Her fingerprints visible on the underside of each petal
I never knew they contained the bones of animals
I would have cried
I would have wanted to forget the forget-me-knots
I could have never loved the daffodils
I could never have twirled a stem between my fingers
Or watched a rose formed from the rolled centre, petal-by-
    handcrafted-finger-pinched-petal
And now I cannot stop loving them because I tasted them in
    the innocence of childhood

I loved every flower as if it had been grown from seed planted
    by my own tiny hands
I loved all the flower-makers too much
I loved her too much
To have the clay's components sour me now

When sleep will not come
And awareness overlaps abstract
The mattress over a box spring
That rests on the floor
In a room at the top of the stairs
That is over the kitchen

Where coins are carefully manufactured from black and white
    patterned tobacco tin lids
to make tokens to insert in a metal box on the wall that turns
    on the electricity
I will be happy for creativity and sad for the actions that
    gifted the space for escape

Somehow she'll find the money to replace those fake coins
When the meter man comes and empties the hungry
    contraption
In the kitchen over the foundation
Beneath which the city's sewer pipes interlock to aching
    systems
Above which two thousand gigantic bottle ovens exhale into a
    grey sky, six days and six nights out of seven

Near black churches of beige sandstone thought to be black-
    stone by children who grew up in a life coated with coal
    dust—with soot

Next to narrow yards behind terraced houses where laundry is
    hung on Mondays because the fires were relaxed and the
    ovens were emptied on Sundays

Beside factories where girls sat on chairs either side of long
    tables making flowers to be glazed, fired, painted, fired
    again, then placed in pots and sent away to be displayed
    on windowsills

Not one of them knew they were artisans
They were earning a living, handing over their pay-packet to
    their mothers

Receiving a fraction back for stockings, cigarettes, a movie
    admission, or dance ticket

The master crafters
Of clay as industry
Of clay as art
Of clay as soul

Oh past, rain down on me
Render me mud
Take me to my roots
Under the peonies
Under the table
Beside my mother's legs
A four-year-old gathering scraps and making my own flowers
An age ago, to the riverbed
When my great-grandmother's caravan followed future
When my bare feet carried me over the dried crust of a gone
    river
As fast as I could
With two younger girls
Whose determination appeared as strong as mine
And predetermination made them my sisters

We shall curse and thank all the people for all the days they've
    gifted us

But then we were innocent, and breathless
Running by all the people collecting exposed rocks
And tripping over depressions made by a donkey's hooves that
    pulled a home
Chasing the yellows, reds, and blues of a caravan

Breathless because we must not lose sight of ourselves
Because our mother who is not yet born will make clay
    flowers when she is fifteen
As will her twin and her niece
And the younger will become a legacy builder to honour the
    craft

Cannot lose sight of the caravan
So that our mother can save my life when I am one day old
Protecting me in her arms when she falls down a steep flight
    of stairs
Pull one sister from a fire when she is five
Turn another upside down in Woodward's deli to dislodge a
    chicken bone

MY FATHER AND HIS ENTREPRENEURIAL SPIRIT

Once upon a lifetime
In a land where bluebells turned fields into sapphires
And roads were only wide enough for two motorbike-and-
    sidecars
And Robin Reliants were often spotted lame and tipped
Where red phone boxes reeked of iron and piss
And the best public houses had contrasting nouns:
The Moon Under Water
The Bull and Spectacles

You came home with a map
And two new words
Immigration and Canada

There had been so many daytimes

When we didn't see you in person
But we still saw you
In the fantastically engineered, heavy duty Play-Doh machine
    you created for us
The bunkbeds you made
In a dark green tin of three-penny bits in the hall closet that
    you saved for our holiday spending money
And in a doll's carriage you painted but I didn't know you
    painted until I was an adult
In a red Michelin diary where you accounted for us all and
    planned our transition
That is
When you were not working on cars
Which was all the time
Plying your trade.

About that map…
Did you have a vision?
How did you know to go?
Did an angel visit you?
Had you glimpsed our future?

Once upon a year later
After a pin had been pinched and waved around, then stuck
    in the city of Calgary
There were plane rides:
Five of them; the last one from Toronto to Calgary—the final
    flight tossed around by lightning and all of us in a crash
    position
Weren't we anyway?
In crash position?

Four suitcases, four people
And the pouring rain

Once upon the future that is now the past
After paper curtains
A donated wringer washer
And a new culture
There was a Canadian baby
All wondrous in her Jacqueline-ness.

And we were all
Daddy take us swimming.

We frequently chanted the A&W advertisement
But we all thought root beer tasted like toothpaste.
Dandelion and burdock memories prevented new flavours
Yet we loved it when the tray was placed on our wound-down
    window
Balancing a meal of momma and poppa and baby burgers

And we loved it more at Bar-X
Where we pushed our trays down the silver-piped runway
Of a cafeteria counter
And ordered steak
That would come impaled with a plastic cow whose colour
    matched its doneness
And on your tray
A long stick with a number—like a flagpole and flag
To which we smiled when it was called
Our order-flag waving
To direct the tray-laden server to deliver the prize
Like food bingo.

A jacket potato, a steak
Was there a salad or veg?
Wobbling cubes of orange or green jelly in a thick glass goblet
    for dessert

And there we all were
With an electronic secretary in the basement
A house on 45th Street
And the whole world at our feet

Creativity was your means
Entrepreneurship in your veins

We sometimes thrived
We sometimes endured
We sometimes held in our sadness so as not to upset each
    other
And other times we exhausted our patience in little camps of
    against-ness
Yet we knew
That once upon a lifetime
Is never once upon a lifetime
But always forever under an eternity
Of unconditional love

That only once up on a future
Brings day after day

Daddy, the Dairy Queen
Please stop
Which sundae?
We don't know

Hot fudge?
Can I have caramel?
I love cherry
I changed my mind
And…
Always blackcurrant for mom
A Buster Bar for you

ALL THE WRITERS, MENTORS, AND ENCOURAGERS

When I was older than yesterday, but not yet today old,
I was suspended in the hallelujah between two heartbeats.
I was the rock-a-bye baby praying for motion,
but not too much that the bough might break.
And Time spoke to me and said she was my real mother,
And I said, I thought nature was,
And Time said, nature is my daughter,
And I asked whom I should revere,
And Time said, here is a pen.
The ink tasted like terror.
I prayed for the moment to end,
So that I did not have to hold it,
Or print one letter,
Because I knew if I did,
Print one letter,
I would never let go.
Because when I was older than yesterday, but not yet
    today old,
I didn't know,
I was the prayer.

All the land, city, and mountains in the setting chosen for *Listen For Water* was once under the stewardship of Canada's Indigenous Peoples. With every breath I take, every wildflower I step around, and every river I hear, I hold my hand to my heart and acknowledge that I am a visitor and, as part of a larger group of non-Indigenous, I am accountable for the actions of the communities before me, and make an effort to be part of a meaningful reconciliation.

The events in *Listen For Water* are strictly a product of my imagination. But the four girls who board the bus in chapter two wore orange hoodies for a reason: orange is the colour selected to recognize the mental and physical trauma experienced by First Nations, Metis, and Inuit in the time of residential schools. Orange was chosen because it was the colour of a shirt that was taken away from Phyllis Jack Webstad—along with all her other possessions—on her first day of residential school.

Marie Beswick Arthur

About the Author

Marie Beswick Arthur is an award-winning writer of poetry and fiction who has worked with countless authors as a ghostwriter, editor, mentor, and coach. She co-authored, with Tricia Jacobson, the 2021 multiple-award-winning book Nova: The Courage To Rise. She writes to change the world and tell the stories of neglected, yet resilient, children.

A recipient of the Brendon Donnelly Award for Children's Literature and the Calgary Writers Association Short Fiction prize, Marie is a member of the Canadian Authors Association, and former juried member of the Professional Writers Association of Canada. Listen for Water is her first solo published novel (and it won't be her last). Marie spends part of each year in Puerto Vallarta, Mexico, and part in Calgary, Canada.